M2551

NAIL DOWN THE STARS

Also by John Morressy

STARBRAT

JOHN MORRESSY

NAIL DOWN THE STARS

WALKER AND COMPANY
New York

First published in the United States of America in 1973
by the Walker Publishing Company, Inc.

Published simultaneously in Canada by Fitzhenry &
Whiteside, Limited, Toronto.

ISBN: 0-8027-5559-3

Library of Congress Catalog Card Number: 72-95788

Printed in the United States of America.

10 9 8 7 6 5 4 3 2 1

for
BARBARA
and
DICK POWER

NAIL
DOWN
THE STARS

I.
The Apprentice Skillman

JOLON KYN GALLAMOR spent his tenth birthday watching two old men decide his future. One of the men was his grandfather, Faxon Gallamor, a stocky man with close-cropped white hair, stubby-fingered hands scarred and seamed with black grease, and a worried expression that never left him, even when he tried to smile. Everyone called him "Fixer." He was the best driveship mechanic in their home system.

The other man was a stranger to Jolon, but not to Fixer, who spoke to him as to an old acquaintance. He wore a traveling cloak, which he repeatedly pulled close around himself as if he were cold, even though the back room of Fixer's little shop was stuffy and warm.

"Understand, Fixer, if the boy comes with me, you'll never see him again," the stranger said.

"I have no choice. I spread the word that he left with Jolonne. If he stays here, someone's bound to find out, and then we're all finished."

"I'm glad you started the rumor. Bad to have curious people making inquiries," the stranger said. "Tell me, did Kynon teach the boy anything?"

Fixer shook his head. "A few tricks. Nothing worthwhile. He wasn't very interested in his son."

Jolon opened his mouth to speak, but thought better of it. He knew his father had cared for him. Old Fixer had never understood. He went to the spaceport every

3

day and got dirty and greasy and always came home smelling of work and sweat. But Kynon Fax Gallamor had dressed and walked and talked like a king, as if the stars overhead were his personal property, on display for the delight of the poor scared little people all over the galaxy who could never hope to have stars of their own. He used to tell Jolon, "Son, in all this galaxy, there's just two kinds of property: ours and theirs. And whatever isn't nailed down is ours. You remember that." When the boy learned to repeat it, Kynon laughed and hugged him, and Dolo and Jixx, the two big men who always stayed close to Kynon, smiled proudly. But that was over now. They were all dead.

"I'm glad to hear that. The less he knows about his father's business, the better for all of us," said the cloaked man.

"Try to make him something better than his father was. I did my best with Kynon, but it went all wrong."

"If he works hard and learns what he must, he'll have a place for as long as he wants it." The stranger rose and turned to Jolon. "Do you hear that, boy? Do as you're told, work hard, and you can make something of yourself. You're joining the great merchant house of——." He paused, gathered his cloak, and looked around warily. "Perhaps I'd best withhold the name until we're safely spaceborne." To Fixer, he said, "I'll be here at this time tomorrow night. Tell no one. Have him ready to leave."

When the man in the cloak was gone, Jolon asked his grandfather, "Do I have to go with the man, Fixer?"

"Yes, you do. It's for your own good."

"I don't like him."

"He's a good man, Jolon," Fixer said impatiently. "You do as he tells you, and you'll be successful some day. You won't have to spend your life running and hiding, the way your father did."

4

"Kynon didn't run and hide," the boy said.

"Well, he should have. He'd be alive today, if he'd had the sense . . . . " Fixer fell silent. He beckoned the boy closer, and put his big hands on the frail shoulders. "Let's not quarrel now, Jolon. It's past your bedtime, and you're tired. Tomorrow we'll have a little farewell party. Your grandmother is baking a nice cake, just the kind you like. We want you to be happy. This is all for your own good."

"Why can't I go to my mother?"

"We don't know where she is, Jolon. Your father wouldn't tell anyone where he sent her."

"I don't want to go with that man, Fixer. Let me stay here, please," the boy pleaded.

"I can't do it. You wouldn't be safe. None of us would. Go to bed now, Jolon."

The boy went obediently to bed, but he did not sleep. He lay awake, troubled and frightened. He knew, from things he had overheard, that the people who had pursued his father were now after him, and he had to go away. He accepted this. He did not much enjoy staying with Fixer, anyway. But he disliked the man in the cloak. Jolon had no wish to be a merchant, even a successful one. Kynon had always laughed when someone spoke of merchants, as if they were people he could not take seriously, and the boy did not want to be part of any such group. For much of the night he fought off sleep, trying to determine what Kynon would have done in this situation, and just past midnight, he decided. He slipped out of his room, carrying the few possessions his father had left him, and made his way to the spaceport.

Six ships stood in the landing ring area: a small sharp-nosed scout; a massive Third Stage transport; three dirty, dented Second Stage tramp cruisers; and on the farthest ring, a chunky solo explorer. One of them had to be the ship belonging to the man in the cloak, and that one he must avoid. But how was he to know? He clenched his fists in frustration and looked wildly from ship to ship for some indication, but there was none. He had to trust to luck.

The transport was nearest him. Loading was nearly completed, so it was sure to be lifting off soon. The people around it were not at all like the cloaked man: they were colorfully dressed, and seemed to represent all the races of the galaxy. That decided Jolon. He straightened up and walked directly to the rampway, all the way remembering his father's advice: "Never act guilty, son. Always act as if you're entitled to it all." Once aboard, he slipped into the first empty compartment he found and curled up in the bottom of a closet. Within minutes he was in a deep exhausted sleep. He stirred and opened his eyes when the transport leapt into drivespeed, but the odd sensation of bodilessness passed in a split second, and he slept once again.

The man who found Jolon was not unduly rough in his treatment. He took a firm grip on the stowaway's arm and, with no exchange of words, marched him to the bridge.

He was taken before two men. One of them was in a kind of uniform. His head was completely bald, and a thick brown beard covered the lower part of his face and much of his tunic. Dark, heavy eyebrows gave him an angry expression, but his manner was almost friendly.

"So, we've got a surprise passenger, have we?" he said, stooping and placing big hands on his knees as he brought his eyes to the level of the boy's. "Well, at least you're a small one. What's your business, lad?"

"I came aboard when you were loading."

"I might have worked that out all by myself, but thank you for enlightening me," the man said, straightening

6

and taking a few paces backward, inspecting Jolon all the while. "Ran away to join the circus, is that it?"

"No, I just ran away."

At this, the bearded man laughed aloud and glanced at the older man seated near him. He was slender, and he, too, had a beard, but it was pure white and curly, like his long hair. His clothing was unlike any the boy had ever seen: a long black robe, so black it seemed to suck up light and devour it; at the wrists, and at top and bottom, were broad bands of some shiny substance; the entire robe was covered with strange symbols that flashed and shimmered against the blackness and moved as the old man moved. He had a soft voice, and the kind of gentle faraway expression that the boy had only seen on very old people.

"A point for you, Commander," he said, smiling at the bald man. "May I speak with our young stowaway for a bit?" His way of speaking was slow and very dignified.

"I'm no stowaway," the boy said.

"Indeed?" the older man said, still smiling his faint smile. "In that case, honored sir, I apologize, and welcome you aboard the *Triboulet*. This is Commander Vogler, and I am Porrex Prospero, part owner of this splendid vessel and sole proprietor of the Original Galactic Circus, a universe of wonders and delights certain to tease, tempt, tickle, and titillate the intellects, palates, and varied sensory apparatus of human and humanoid alike. And you?"

"Jolon, son of Kynon Gallamor," the boy announced.

The two men exchanged a glance, and Jolon suspected that it had been a mistake to reveal his name. Now he was in trouble. Vogler and Prospero seemed genuinely upset. The Commander looked sharply around the bridge at the men on duty, then said to Prospero in a low voice, "I don't think anyone heard. Get him to your quarters, just to be safe. I'll join you soon."

The older man rose and motioned the boy to follow. Seeing no alternative, he followed. Prospero did not look to be an evil or a cruel man, like the ones Fixer had spoken of after his father's accident. He looked kindly, and had a comforting manner. But still, Jolon knew that he must trust no one. His father had shown him evil men who looked even more kindly than Prospero. "You can't be sure about people, son," he had said. "You can only be careful."

They went only a short way before Prospero stopped, unlocked a door, and gestured to the boy to precede him inside. It was a pleasant compartment, much smaller than any of the rooms in Fixer's home, but very comfortable looking.

"Sit down, my boy," Prospero said. Jolon sat in a deep chair and his host settled in one facing him. "Now, first of all, tell me this: are you truly the son of Kynon Gallamor and Jolonne, once owners of the Pleiades Palace?"

The boy hesitated, then nodded.

"Good. Did you tell your name to anyone else on board?"

"No."

"Not to anyone? Not even to the crewman who brought you to me?"

"Not to anyone."

"Then you may be safe. I don't believe anyone on the bridge heard you. Vogler is checking that now. I know what happened to your father, and I can imagine what you've been going through. Orcull's men are relentless."

"Are they the men who are after me?"

"Indeed they are. Most people don't escape them."

"Is the man in the cloak one of them?"

Prospero looked puzzled. "I don't know, Jolon. Can you tell me more about him?"

The boy decided to trust Prospero just a bit. He wanted to be sure he had not slipped aboard the

8

merchant ship—it seemed unlikely, but he wanted to know—and so he told of the secret meeting in Fixer's shop. Commander Vogler entered while he was speaking. He took a seat at a sign from Prospero and Jolon continued his account uninterrupted.

When the story was told, Prospero said, "I imagine the cloaked gentleman was aboard the cruiser that was loading on the adjoining ring."

"The Triandal merchant ship. It blew up early this morning," Vogler said to the boy.

Jolon looked wide-eyed from one to the other. Prospero nodded and said, "Yes. Completely destroyed just as they finished loading. No survivors. I'm surprised the explosion didn't awaken you."

Vogler said, "At least now Orcull believes the kid's dead."

"Let us hope he does." Prospero was silent for a time, then he sighed and said, "I knew your father, Jolon. He joined us on Meriton, a long time ago. Before the *Triboulet*."

"Before Porrex Prospero, too," Vogler added, grinning.

"A man is entitled to upgrade his name to match his fortunes, Vogler. The public expects no less," Prospero said mildly. He turned to Jolon. "Remember that, my boy. One must be prepared to change one's name to suit one's circumstances. In view of this, we ought to decide on a name for you at once. We certainly can't go on calling you Jolon Gallamor."

"Why not? It's my name."

"Precisely why we must change it. Orcull probably believes that you died in the explosion, and for your safety and ours, we must see to it that he continues to believe this. If your name should be overheard, and Orcull learned of it, he'd be after you again."

"Why?"

"Because that's the way he is. Let's not discuss it further. It makes me uneasy. The important thing is to get you a new name."

"Kynon and Jolonne always called me Son."

"I would have expected something a bit more imaginative of them," Prospero said drily. "Suppose we call you Lon? Do you like that name?"

The boy thought about it for a moment, then said, "Yes."

Prospero looked pleased, and said, "We'll even give you a family name. Have you any suggestions, Vogler?"

The commander grinned at the old man. "How about Trimmer? That fits the family."

"A bit too obvious, I think, although I like the sound of it. Let's make it Rimmer. Lon Rimmer. What do you think of that name, my boy?"

"It's a good name."

"Then use it from now on, for your safety and ours. Will you promise to do that?"

"If you want me to."

"I do. I want to help you. Your father was almost a son to me, years ago. He helped me to acquire this magnificent driveship. I taught him a great deal, and he——"

"He taught you a few things, too, if I'm not mistaken," the commander said.

"Exactly what I was about to say, Vogler. Now, what's our story? Why is Lon Rimmer aboard the ship?"

"He ran away to join the circus," Vogler said. "Kids do it all the time."

"I've been in this profession all my life, Vogler, and I've never met one child who ran away to join the circus. Not one, in all those years."

"What about Kynon?"

Prospero chuckled and shook his head. "Kynon was no child, Vogler, and he didn't ask to join us, I invited

10

him in." Turning to the boy, he asked, "Tell me, Lon, did your father teach you anything?"

"He showed me some tricks with cashcubes and cards. But he said my hands were still too small for the cards."

"I believe I have cards in various sizes. We might find a deck just right for you, and you'll have a few weeks to practice before we land. Suppose we allow you to work off your passage by joining the Original Galactic Circus?"

"Won't you pay me?"

Vogler laughed aloud. Prospero turned away and was silent for a moment before saying, "After our first stop we'll talk of payment. Agreed?"

"Agreed."

"Very well, then. You're Lon Rimmer, runaway, soon to be known throughout the inhabited galaxy as the Amazing Saltimbanco, Wonder of the Nine Sectors, the Precocious Prestidigitator of . . ." Prospero snapped his fingers impatiently and finally said, "You pick a planet, Lon."

"Skyx!"

"Magnificent!" Prospero cried, clapping his hands. "A master stroke!"

"Suppose someone asks how he got to Skyx?" Vogler asked. "It's a quarantined planet."

"Remember Gburrux? Ghastly Gburrux from Gfor?" Prospero rose and extended his hands. His voice dropped to a hollow, ominous intonation as he recited, " 'Once in a millenium the lost wisdom of the shrieking spirits who ride the wind that blows eternally between the worlds is permitted to find a resting place in the mind of a mortal . . . .' And so forth. It worked for Gburrux."

"He *looked* ghastly."

"Well, we can take the opposite approach with Lon. Look at that fresh, open, innocent face."

11

Vogler shrugged. "You run the show, Prospero. I just run the ship."

The newly-christened Lon Rimmer broke in with a question. "After our first stop, will you be able to take me to my mother?"

"It all depends, Lon. Where is she?"

"She's . . . safe. My father sent her to a safe place."

"Don't you know?" Prospero asked.

"She's home. She went home, with my little sister."

"Home, for Jolonne, could be anywhere in the galaxy, Lon, and the galaxy is a big place. But you be patient, and we'll try to find your mother and take you to her. You'll be safe with us, meanwhile. If I know Kynon, he told you not to trust anyone, so you probably don't trust the commander and me. Very well, I won't ask for your trust. I'll wait until you're ready to give it freely. But you must do as I say. Don't ever mention your father's name or your mother's to anyone, and never tell anyone your real name. Work at your tricks every day until you think you're perfect, then work twice as hard."

"I'll do all those things," the boy said.

"Then we'll get along and you'll be safe. We work a standard galactic day on the *Triboulet*, practice sessions morning and afternoon for the skillmen, rest at night for everyone who isn't on duty. It's the only way to stay in condition. You'll get used to it in no time. Everyone will help you as much as he can. You'll like the others in the circus, Lon. Have you ever seen Quiplid tumblers, or a Quespodon weightlifter?"

"I had an uncle who was a Quespodon. He was very strong."

"Was his name Jixx, by any chance?" Prospero asked.

"Yes! Did you know my uncle Jixx?"

"I knew him quite well. He and your father met on this very ship and decided to team up. Perhaps 'decided' isn't quite the word to use when speaking of Jixx," Pros-

12

pero said reflectively. "He was not a man given to deliberation. But he was very strong."

"Did you know Brita? The Qreddn woman who used to tell me stories?"

Prospero's eyebrows rose. "Did you actually have a Qreddn reciter of your very own?" At the boy's affirmative answer, he said, "Kynon once boasted that his children would want for nothing, but I never imagined. . . . The Qreddn reciters work for kings and emperors, not . . . not people in Kynon's line of business. He must have done very well indeed."

"Kynon was rich," the boy said simply.

"He certainly gave you a good start. With a Qreddn woman's stories in your memory, you've got another skill to fall back on. We'll make a master skillman of you, Lon Rimmer. We start tomorrow."

In a short time, Lon Rimmer had met everyone aboard the *Triboulet*. The crew admired his resourcefulness and courage, and the members of Prospero's Original Galactic Circus were impressed by his skill. He was a lively, attractive little boy who knew when to speak and when to listen, when to be clever, and most important of all, when to praise. Kynon had taught his son well.

Lon's popularity and ready acceptance were not traceable solely to his personal qualities, nor to an inherent affability on the part of those around him. Actually, they were a solitary lot, and they appreciated Lon more as a symbol than as a person. The crew and performers saw in him, newly-minted and still clean and bright, something they had all possessed at one time, and they liked him for the bit of themselves that he gave back in idealized reflection. In their eyes, Lon was not a runaway but a misfit, a reacher, a seeker, the kind of lad who left the farm for the city, the land for the sea, the planets for the stars. So, to some degree, was everyone else aboard the *Triboulet*, and nearly all the people in space. For space had turned out to be something quite different from mankind's expectations. The first exodus from Old Earth had been a mass flight from a dying planet, and it had proven to be quite enough for the pioneers. They faced trials that the Academy of the Stars had not foreseen, and when the trim and disciplined academy officers panicked and lost their reason, a different breed of men took over; and even for them, space was a hard challenge. The great gulf between those lights in the black void was too vast, too overwhelming, too frightening for all but a very few: the misfits, the reachers, the seekers, the men like Kynon Fax Gallamor and Vogler and Prospero and all the rest aboard the *Triboulet*. And only when three generations of extraterrestrial settlement had healed the fearful memories of the first exodus did the new seekers begin to appear.

The circus folk were among the innocuous minority of starfarers. Most of the ships that threaded their private ways in silence and darkness between the scattered systems at velocities beyond imagining were bent on missions that had little to do with bringing entertainment to isolated settlements. They were filled with restless, hungry men and humanoids—pirates in search of plunder, slavers hunting for cargo, warriors seeking battle and glory. Among them, the legitimate trader, prospector, or traveler was the exception.

For the billions of planetbound souls who would never again dream of removing both feet from solid ground at the same time, safety lay in obscurity and the mathematical comfort of long odds against chance discovery. For the handful of innocent starfarers, the only security lay in armed guards and speed, and the latter was the true haven. Vogler's crew all wore sidearms and were ready to use them when necessary, but everyone aboard knew that the call to repel boarders meant that the end was near. The best defense was flight, and here the *Triboulet* was secure.

The ship was a product of the last great age of drive-ship design. She could sustain multiple lightspeeds on a cross-galactic run without overheating her drive coils, and herein lay her safety margin, for a ship was impervious to detection and attack only as long as it remained in the lightspeed range; below lightspeed, it was visible and vulnerable. All of the First Stage driveships and most Second Stage models required periodic rest of their drive coils; this involved an interval of drifting at a speed below light, and consequent exposure to danger. But the *Triboulet* could travel from system to system in one uninterrupted rush, and hence remain safe.

The ship was a little world, made to accomodate crew, company, and cargo with the maximum of economy and yet without undue sacrifice of comfort and convenience on long intersystem runs. She carried a crew of twenty-seven, a troupe of sixty-one, and a small but valuable menagerie, plus ample storage space for the provisions and spacious training areas. It took Lon some time to learn his way around the *Triboulet*, but he worked at it conscientiously, utilizing his small allotment of free time to explore and question.

As a novice, he was kept busy throughout the day and spent his nights sleeping soundly, exhausted from long rounds of training and exercise and his ship's duties—most of them arduous and nasty, as befitting the newest and youngest member of the company, still to prove himself as a skillman. But he worked hard, practiced dutifully, watched and listened with rapt attention to every lesson, and at his very first appearance The Amazing Saltimbanco, The Precocious Prestidigitator of Skyx, performed with a cool assurance that impressed even the old hands. On the first night back in space, in accordance with the customs of the *Triboulet*, Lon was feted by the company and received as a full-fledged apprentice skillman. He was now truly a part of the Original Galactic Circus, not just a runaway boy working off his passage. The nasty chores still had to be done, of course, but now they were done in a different spirit. They became, if not pleasant, at least endurable.

Lon grew to know the others better from this time on, and he sought to deepen casual acquaintanceships into friendships. He was not often successful. His first acquaintance had been among the Quiplids, the group of nimble little double-jointed soft-pelted humanoids who comprised the company's acrobatic team. It soon became clear to both Lon and the diminutive tumblers that the only bond between them was that of stature—the biggest of the Quiplids, their leader Numple, reached barely to Lon's waist—and they drifted apart without ill-will on either side.

Lon next tried to befriend Jespoxx, the strongman, an independent-minded Quespodon who reminded him somewhat of his father's friend and protector Jixx. Jespoxx was unusually strong, even for a Quespodon. His mottled skin bulged taut over great knots of muscle. Under a certified 1.00 standard gravity, he could lift twice his own weight in each hand. But Jespoxx was not possessed of an intellect in any way proportionate to his strength. Impressive to watch, he was painfully uninteresting to speak with. Lon still sought a friend.

He found a friend, and much more than a friend, in Poldo-Simbassi, a slender, sharp-featured Thresk whose juggling was one of the highlights of the circus. She had the quickest, most agile hands Lon had ever seen. For sheer dexterity, she surpassed even Kynon, and that alone sufficed to fill the boy with awe. Until this time, he had believed that women existed only to be beautiful, like his mother, or pleasantly useful, like Brita. It

16

impressed him deeply to see a woman who was both beautiful and useful, and could also do something no man could hope to match. He became a worshipper of Poldo-Simbassi the first time he saw her perform.

Lon did not realize at once that she enjoyed a peculiar advantage over the other skillmen. Like all female Threskillia of the arboreal races, Poldo-Simbassi had a pair of slim blue-green tentacles sprouting from each shoulder, and the combined dexterity of her hands and her tentacles enabled her to perform feats of skill that left audience after audience dumb with amazement. The boy saw only that she was great.

The juggler was a kindly woman, nearing the middle years of her lifespan and very lonely on a ship that contained no one else from her people. She enjoyed the boy's adulation and became his advisor and confidante in all matters pertaining to the circus. Noticing Lon's native ability, she offered to teach him some skills that few non-Threskillians had ever been shown. He accepted her instruction eagerly and showed his gratitude by mastering three difficult feats before their next planetfall. At her suggestion, he practiced in secret and kept his new accomplishments to himself for the time being.

Not everyone on board the *Triboulet* was approachable, nor were they all as kindly disposed toward an inquisitive child. Some of the company were aloof, some unfriendly, and a few were openly hostile, not only to Lon but to everyone, including Prospero and Vogler.

Most aloof of all, a total isolate even in the crowded dining hall, was the Lixian known to everyone as Longshank. At his own request, he was quartered alone in a small cabin near the storage area, far from crew and company. He ate alone, in silence, sitting cross-legged on the floor in a corner of the hall. The only words he was ever heard to speak were concerned with circus matters of immediate importance; he greeted no one, never chatted with the other skillmen, never praised or censured a performance. He practiced alone, when the others were asleep, and spent most of his time in his cabin, deep in meditation.

Lon was fascinated by him. Like all Lixians, Longshank had a massive chest and shoulders, long slim arms and legs nearly as strong as a Quespodon's in spite of their seeming fragility, and a small wedge-shaped head. He was a full three meters tall, and consequently he walked through the *Triboulet* in a perpetual half-crouch. When he performed, rising to his full height and whirling those long arms to fill the air with flashing finger knives in a dazzling display of skill, Longshank was majestic. But as soon as his act was over, he seemed almost to slump and dwindle even as he hurried to return to the solitude of his quarters. Lon ached to know him better, but he dared not speak to him first, unbidden. The icy wall of reserve that Longshank had thrown up between himself and the rest of the universe was too forbidding.

Lon endured his curiosity in silence for a considerable time until one evening when he and Poldo-Simbassi were practicing together. She happened to observe that the tricks would be more easily mastered if only Lon's arms were a bit longer, and the boy seized upon this opening.

"Like Longshank's, you mean?" he asked.

"Not quite *that* long," she said, amused. "You'd look very strange."

"He always acts so sad. Are all Lixians like that, Poldo?"

"Many of them are. The Lixians live by a harsh code. They aren't a very happy people, Lon."

"Why do they live that way, then?"

"They always have. They're not the only ones in the galaxy to do it. Even the Threskillia . . . ."

When she did not go on, Lon asked, "Aren't your people a happy people, Poldo?"

Her composure was shaken for a moment, but then she smiled and drew the boy to her, smoothing his hair gently with one tentacle while her hands clasped his. "Thresk is a beautiful world, Lon, and I would never have left it of my own will. But my people have strong traditions. When my family violated one of the traditions, there was no longer a place for us on Thresk. We were sentenced to dispersion. I think something like that may have happened to Longshank."

"Do you think he did something bad?"

"I didn't say that, Lon," she said severely. "I didn't say anything like that at all."

"Could we ask him?" the boy pressed.

"That would be very cruel. We can wait, and perhaps some day he'll choose to tell us. Perhaps he won't. The choice is his, not ours, Lon."

"But maybe we could help him."

"Not unless he asks us."

The boy shook his head. "I already have helped Longshank, and he didn't ask. He dropped a belt of finger knives in the companionway, coming from practice, and I helped him to pick them up. He thanked me. I told him we'd always be glad to help him——"

"We?" Poldo asked.

"I didn't think you'd mind."

"I don't mind, Lon, but I wish you'd . . . I don't want Longshank to think we're prying. We don't do things like that on the *Triboulet*. That's why we get along. Do you understand?"

"He didn't seem angry. Do you think he'll tell us about himself now, Poldo?"

Poldo did not think it likely that Longshank would suddenly blossom into sociability, and she told Lon as much. For the remainder of the voyage, her estimate proved to be the correct one, but when the *Triboulet* was spaceborne after its next engagement, the situation changed abruptly. One day as Lon was on his way to his duties in the mess, Longshank stopped him in the companionway.

"I have need of you. Do you still wish to help me?" the Lixian said in his deep, booming voice.

"Yes," Lon replied without hesitating.

"There must be a woman, too. Will the Threskillian come with you?"

"She will. I know she will."

"Come to my cabin as soon as you have eaten tonight," Longshank said, and moved off quickly before Lon could frame a single question.

After dinner that evening, Poldo and Lon made their way down the seldom-used passages leading to Longshank's quarters. He had not appeared that day in the dining hall, and Poldo was beginning to have second thoughts about intruding on him.

"Are you sure he wants both of us, Lon?" she asked once again as they drew near his cabin.

"Yes. He said there had to be a woman, too, and he asked me to bring you. Honest, Poldo."

"I can't imagine why all of a sudden——" She tightened her grip on Lon's hand and stopped, jerking him to a halt. "Do you suppose he saw someone at our last stop, and learned that things have changed?"

"How should I know?" Lon said, pulling his hand free and rubbing his shoulder.

"Maybe he's found a way to go back," Poldo said, her voice soft, thoughtful.

"Let's ask him when we get there," Lon said, moving on.

The Lixian was squatting cross-legged on the floor of his cabin. A short cape, richly decorated, covered his wide shoulders, and a small assortment of objects lay before him. He did not rise to greet his visitors, but gestured to them to seat themselves on the floor. After a short silence, he began to speak. His voice was muted and distant.

"The time has come when I must undertake my termination. Under the ageless law of Lixis, I can do this only in the presence of my family. Because the boy once offered me his friendship, and because the woman is skill-mother to the boy, and comes from a people who know the ways of honor, I ask them now to become my family, so I may be free. Do you accept?" he asked, raising his bowed head to look into their faces.

When they had both accepted, Longshank turned his attention to the objects on the floor. As he spoke, he picked them up in turn and placed them one by one in a soft pouch.

"In this vial is blood from my veins. One drop, at least, must be spilled on the soil of Lixis. On this disc my true name is written in the ancient script; it must be placed in the Tower of Acceptance on Lixis. This blade must be given to the weapons keeper of the reigning land warden of the White Valley," he said, and when he had done this, he sealed the pouch and set it aside. Two objects remained. "The neck ring I give to the woman who is all females of my family," he said, extending a necklace of glowing stones to Poldo. She accepted it and slipped it over her head. "The knife I give to the boy who is all males of my family." Lon took the beautifully worked short blade and thrust it in his belt. "Now we are joined."

Longshank then remained silent for a time. The others sat motionless, waiting for him to continue with the ritual. They were mystified by the proceedings, slightly

apprehensive at the thought of what might be the out-
come of these preliminaries, but unable to withdraw.
They had given their word. Curiosity had drawn them
here; honor forced them to remain until the end.

The Lixian abruptly began to speak. "I am an exile,
dishonored and disgraced. My broodname and deed-
names all are forfeit and I answer to the mocking title
of Longshank because I deserve no better.

"On Lixis, I served in succession two Land Wardens,
two kings, and an Emperor. I served them well and
gained such honor that the Supreme Ruler chose me for
a royal mission of the greatest importance.

"Three blades were required. For the pride of my
family, I selected two close broodmates. When we
reached our objective, the betrayal came. One of my
broodmates slew the other and fled."

Here he paused for a longer time. Lon was almost
beside himself with excitement and curiosity, but he
dared not move now. Poldo-Simbassi sat as if
immobilized. The Lixian at last proceeded, "Wounded
by a treacherous blow, I could not complete the mission
with my single blade. By law and tradition I was bound
to avenge my slain broodmate, but the same law and
tradition obliged me to protect his slayer. I was disgraced and utterly helpless to act. I chose exile.

"Now I have learned that the slayer is dead. My honor
will be redeemed if I undergo self-termination in the
presence of my family. You are here." He paused, his
head lowered. "Soon it will begin," he said, then was
silent.

After a time, he tried to speak again. His voice was
strained and thin, as if the words came only with great
effort. "It begins," he said. He began to tremble. His
crossed legs were rigid, but his torso was many times
shaken by convulsions so severe that bones could be
heard to crack. After the last and most violent of these

seizures the Lixian sighed loudly and long, as if he were expelling the air from every crevice of his body; he seemed to shrink and draw himself together; he became very still.

Through the night he sat unmoving, and his two witnesses sat by him. Just as the first bells rang to rouse the company, he gave one final shudder and his head sank forward.

Poldo rose stiffly and probed both sides of the Lixian's neck with a tentacle. "He's dead, Lon," she said.

"What should we do?" the boy asked. He felt all at once the physical toll of his night's vigil, and his courage was fading at the thought of the consequences.

"We'll tell Vogler and Prospero. No one else." Poldo stooped for the pouch that lay beside the Lixian. "We have to see to it that these things get to Lixis some day."

"Will we go there?"

"One of us must. We're his family, and we owe it to him."

Lon began to wish that he had not been so curious about Longshank. After this, he sought new friends aboard the *Triboulet* less actively.

Toward the end of his second year with the circus, Lon began to spend increasing amounts of time with Prospero. This came about somewhat indirectly. From the very outset, the old man had shown a lively interest in the boy's progress as a skillman and praised him lavishly and frequently. It took some time for Lon to realize that praise was all that Prospero seemed willing to give. The promised payment never materialized.

When, after a serious conference with Poldo-Simbassi (who counseled patience) and an extended session of solitary brooding (which only confused him), Lon asked outright for his overdue wages, Prospero reacted with pained astonishment. He cited his unstinting generosity.

He quoted from a long list of crippling expenditures on Lon's behalf, and hinted darkly at the cruel persistence of unscrupulous creditors. He spoke of ingratitude, and his voice cracked even as he uttered the word. And then, in place of such crass and vulgar payment as cashcubes, Prospero offered to teach the boy the game of chess. It would, he promised, prove far more valuable in the long run than a paltry handful of cashcubes; chess would help to quicken the wits, improve the memory, refine the judgment, and hone the logical powers to a fine cutting edge. Besides, Prospero had no cash on hand.

Lon was still dissatisfied, but he remembered a saying of his father's: "Take what you're offered. If it's not enough, you can always come back when no one's looking and take the rest." He accepted Prospero's offer.

He learned the game quickly, and enjoyed it greatly. As a consequence, his days became extremely crowded. To his regular work and training sessions he had already added special practice times in which he concentrated on Poldo's techniques; now he found himself putting in time on chess problems and visiting Prospero's cabin in the evening to play with the old man.

Lon made his sole enemy among the company as a result of his increased contact with Prospero. One evening, as he sat at dinner excitedly discussing his latest discovery in endgame strategy, a topic which bored Poldo to yawning endurance, a husky, hard-eyed man paused beside their table. He folded his arms, studied Lon for a moment, then addressed Poldo.

"Be proud of your adopted beggar boy, juggler. He's quite friendly with our lord and master," the man said.

"Lon does as he pleases, Kedrak," she replied coolly. "It's no crime to be a friend to Prospero, is it?"

Ignoring her, Kedrak went on, "What I can't understand is why Prospero is so taken with him. The old man's too greedy to be thinking of an heir." He looked Lon over contemptuously and said, "Tell us, you, what do you do in the old swindler's cabin every night? What's he teaching you?"

"We play chess," Lon replied. He had heard talk of Kedrak, and what he recalled was disquieting.

"Chess?" Kedrak laughed scornfully and looked about at the group in the dining hall. "Come down and visit with my little friends some night, around feeding time. We'll teach you a game you can pass on to the old man."

He swaggered off, still laughing in a most unpleasant way, and Lon was glad to see him go. "What was he talking about, Poldo?" he asked when Kedrak was out of earshot.

"Ignore him," she said. "He always talks like that."

"He's a starbrat, and you know what that means," Jespoxx stated. He looked around from his place at the next table and nodded his small head sagely.

"What does it mean?" Lon asked.

Jespoxx stared at him, befuddled, and looked about desperately for assistance. Thig, Thog, and Thid, Quiplid brothers who had ducked under the table at Kedrak's approach, bounded to the table top and perched on the edge. Thid, their spokesman, said, "Any child born in space is cross and mean, and usually violent. That's what they say about starbrats. Right?"

"Right!" echoed Thig and Thog.

"Always going around making accusations and calling names. Insulting people for being little."

"Hitting them, too, sometimes," Thig and Thog added, rubbing remembered bruises.

Jespoxx glowered. "If he hits you, you just tell me."

The Quiplids, cheered by the promise of a champion, began to stage a vigorous mock battle on the tabletop. Amid the activity, Poldo made a half-hearted and utterly unconvincing attempt to excuse Kedrak's behavior.

25

"We mustn't forget that he's a beast-trainer. He's been working with *snargraxes* all his life."

"Hope they eat him!" a Quiplid voice cried.

Jespoxx gave a knowing wink. "You know what they say about men who work around beasts."

"I know what I say about them," came another voice from the rolling tangle of Quiplids.

"He's spent his entire life working with the deadliest predators in the galaxy," Poldo said, persisting in her appeal. "You can't expect him to be sweet-tempered and gentle."

"We're not *snargraxes*, we're people," Thig said boldly, and Jespoxx and the other Quiplids seconded the assertion.

In the days that followed, Lon pondered long over Kedrak's remarks, and he felt them more troubling as he thought more deeply on them. If others were finding Prospero's interest in him a matter of concern, someone might become curious enough to ask about his origin, and question his ready acceptance by the masters of the *Triboulet*. Lon knew that he could not explain Prospero's solicitude without revealing more about his origins than seemed safe. The solution he hit upon was to remain as close to Prospero as he could without actually getting under foot. If he could not be safe with the master of the circus, then there was no safety to be found anywhere, he reasoned, and he might as well save himself a lot of anxiety by going below and jumping into the *snargrax* cage right now.

As time passed, Lon assumed the role of Prospero's regular chess partner. It lessened the amount of time he spent among the other skillmen, but he found that what he had initiated in the interests of self-preservation had become enjoyable in itself. He grew to know the circus master well, and to perceive certain aspects of his character that he had not noticed before. Unnoticed by either of them, the boy was growing up.

Over the chessboard one evening, Lon idly asked the old man, "What was your name before you changed it to Prospero, Prospero?"

Prospero frowned across the board sternly and said, "I've forgotten, as every man who changes his name should do."

"Don't be angry with me."

"I'm not angry, I'm annoyed by your lack of caution. We're secure here, but nevertheless it's injudicious for you, of all people, to bring up the subject of former names."

"I only wanted to know why you picked *Prospero*," the boy said; then, advancing a piece, "Queen to Knight three."

The elder studied the board, evaluating Lon's unexpected move, smiled, and said, "I won't let you get my Rook quite that easily."

"If I capture it, will you tell me why you picked Prospero, Prospero?" Lon asked quickly.

"I'll tell you now, if it will get your mind back on the game," Prospero sighed and leaned back in his chair, looking impatient but resigned. "Actually, there's very little to tell. Prospero is the name of a great wizard and magician in a book by Lord William Shakespeare, the famous poet and dramatist of Old Earth. I came across the book, the name seemed an appropriate one for me, so I took it. That's the whole story. Now, may we continue?"

"Do you have any real books, Prospero?"

"As a matter of fact, I do. I have a rather impressive collection, if I say so myself. Four authentic books, all on paper. Two of them were actually printed on Old Earth, the last one only eleven years before the exodus

27

began. It's one of the last Old Earth books ever printed, I'm sure."

"Can I see them?"

"Some other time, Lon. Right now we're playing chess. Queen takes pawn."

"Rook to Queen one," Lon countered almost at once, then went on, "When can I see them?"

"See what?" Prospero said testily, studying the results of the move. "You've pinned my Queen, you little prestidigitator," he mumbled.

"I'm going to mate in three moves. When can I see the books, Prospero?"

"Tomorrow, if you stop tormenting me. Haven't you ever seen a book?"

"No. We didn't have any."

"Can you read, Lon?"

"No. My father was against reading. He said it distracted the wits and ruined the memory."

Prospero nodded thoughtfully. "That would be right in character. I recall a certain distaste on your father's part when I first mentioned reading. He was never venturesome in the intellectual sphere. Odd, to think of him as cautious in any way, but there it is." The old man leaned over the board and studied the pieces with growing dissatisfaction.

"Does it?" Lon asked, breaking the brief silence.

"Does what?"

"Does reading distract the wits and ruin the memory?"

"Not half so much as . . . ." Prospero choked off his reply and glowered at the boy for an uncomfortable length of time, then said in a taut, controlled voice, "We will proceed with our game. Not a word will be said by either of us until the game is over. Then, perhaps, we will discuss the advantages and disadvantages of literacy. Until then, not one word, Lon. Not so much as a syllable!" he said, raising a monitory forefinger as the boy's jaw dropped.

Three slow, deliberate, well-thought-out moves by Prospero, each followed quickly by a decisive move on Lon's part, and the game was over, Prospero's king mated. Immediately after his final move, the boy slipped from his chair and went to Prospero's side. Tugging at the old man's sleeve, he said, "Come on, Prospero, show me the books."

"But you can't read, Lon."

"I'll learn. Come on, you promised."

"I promised you'd see them tomorrow, *if* you stopped tormenting me."

"Tomorrow I train all through first shift and have mess duty on second. I won't have time. Show me now," the boy insisted.

"And just how will you learn to read?"

"I'll learn. Show me the books."

"Tomorrow, Lon. You can leave practicing early and come here. I may have a surprise for you."

"Are you going to pay me?"

Prospero made a wry face. "Don't be greedy, Lon. You'll be paid when the time comes. You don't need money now."

"What's the surprise, then?"

"Come here tomorrow and you'll see."

Lon returned to his quarters satisfied, looking forward to a pleasant day: time off from practice, the chance to see genuine books, and a surprise. Prospero's surprises were always good ones. And on top of everything else, he had beaten Prospero at chess for the ninth night running.

The next morning seemed interminable. Lon wolfed down his breakfast and hurried to the practice room. Under the sharp demanding eye of the training master, he and the other young skillmen went through preliminary exercises and then did the full regimen of finger manipulations. This completed, each one performed his specialty before the highly critical jury of his fellow skillmen, all of them alert for the smallest lapse from perfection. Lon was the last to perform on this morning, and when he had finished he and the rest of the group sat down to their mugs of hot *scoof* for a brief rest.

The training master, a wizened Karrapad named Hotor-tor-Mitibi-i-Doandep-dep Eloevorr and known to all aboard the ship as Tib, was seated by himself, tuning the nineteen-stringed linlovar to be used in the next training session. Lon joined him.

"I know what you're going to ask me. You want to leave off this morning's training early," the Karrapad said as Lon sat on the bench beside him.

"How did you know?"

"I saw Prospero."

"Can I go, Tib? I'll make up the practice time tonight."

"You can leave when you've done your turn on the linlovar. I'll let you play first this time."

"What are we doing today?" Lon asked.

Tib laid aside the linlovar and picked up his mug. It disappeared in the grip of his seven-fingered hand. *"The Dragon Song*. Hard chords for the left hand in this one," he said after taking a sip of the hot sweet *scoof*.

"I didn't like that one about Old Earth. It was sad."

"I don't like it much myself, but I don't pick these pieces for fun. I'm not training you just to sing, I'm developing your hands. You've only got four fingers and one thumb, Lon. You have to develop them to their peak. Nothing like the linlovar for keeping fingers supple. My people play it all the time." He emptied the mug and set it down. Snatching up the linlovar, he struck a harsh arresting chord and called out, "Time to get back to work, you stub-thumbed greasy-fingered fumblers. You have a lot of work ahead of you before you're good enough to wear the wristlet. Gather around me, now. I'll go through the song once, then I'll do it once more without the words. Watch my left hand closely."

The skillmen formed a half-circle around the training master. He sat cross-legged on the floor, nestled the sound box in the crook of one knee, and began to play. His voice was high and clear, blending easily with the high notes and contrasting vividly with the loud jangled chords that ended each section of his song.

"Curled like a miser's curse around
A musty mound of ancient gold
Deep-buried in a lofty cave,
The dragon slumbered, day by day by day.
    And further down the mountainside,
    The village people lived and died
With fear an old familiar friend.
They knew that all depended on
The sleep of a restless dragon.

Years passed,
And the dragon was a fact, like rain, or cold.
Centuries passed . . . .

And to those who had not seen his scales
(Platter-sized, still darkly sea-glowing,
Alive beneath their crust of living moss)
Nor felt nor smelt the hot stink of his breath,
Nor heard the slither and thump of his crested tail
As it tumbled treasure in his fitful sleep,
The dragon grew to legend.

31

A quaint tale . . .
A joke from the past upon the past . . .
And no concern of the living.

> Then in the village on the mountainside
> The people smiled, and put their fears aside,
And prospered.
The curious came to sniff the smoke,
And drink a glass of wine
In the town that laughed in the shadow of the
    dragon.
And the dragon slumbered, year by year by year.

The town still draws the curious.
They come now to sift the ashes,
Break off a souvenir of blackened wood,
And peep cautiously into an empty cave.
When they go home, they watch the sky
And listen for the flap of leathery wings."

The skillmen devoted a few moments to a discussion of *The Dragon Song*, and Lon was unenthusiastic in his comments. He compared the piece unfavorably to a story Brita had once told him, an old Skeggjatt legend of a great golden hero, strong and fierce as a bear, who did battle with a tarn-monster and fell at last as an aging king, fighting to save his people from a firedrake. Telling the tale, Brita herself had become the bold hero, the hissing enemy, the roaring firebreather. The boy felt the cold chill of the deep tarn, smelt the choking sulphurous breath of the dragon. Despite Tib's great skill, *The Dragon Song* was not as effective as Brita's tale.

"Why don't you write us a better one?" Tib asked.

"Someday I will. I'll learn to make great songs," Lon replied defiantly.

Tib was unimpressed. He had heard the boasts of too

many young skillmen in his time. "Good for you, Lon. Right now, learn to play."

Lon performed *The Dragon Song* without an error, and Tib let him go. He hurried to Prospero's quarters. At his knock, Prospero's voice bade him enter.

Lon stepped in, closed the door behind him, and then he stopped short at the sight of the man with Prospero. It was not the fact of the man's presence that startled Lon—Prospero was often engaged in business when he entered—it was the fellow's appearance. Except for Longshank, he was the tallest person Lon had yet seen on the *Triboulet*, and he was as slim as a bone. His skin was pale and dry-looking, his hair long and black, his eyes bright in deep caverns under heavy brows.

"Come in, Lon. You're not intruding," Prospero said warmly, gesturing to a seat.

"The books . . . ," Lon began uncertainly.

"You'll see them. Meanwhile, I have a surprise for you. This is Drufe. He joined us during our stay on Velodon, and he hopes to stay with us for a while. When I mentioned your interest in books to him this morning, he volunteered to teach you how to read."

The gaunt man did not give the impression of having done anything of the kind. He looked blankly down at Lon as Prospero introduced him, then turned his attention elsewhere as the old man went on.

"Drufe has some interest in books too, Lon. That's why he joined us," Prospero said.

"I have 'pondered, weak and weary, over many a quaint and curious volume of forgotten lore,' " Drufe said in a deep monotone, still gazing off somewhere beyond the cabin walls.

"Drufe was once an explicator among the Poeites," Prospero explained. "A most respected one."

"But my name is accursed among them, and rightly so. 'Men usually grow base by degrees. From me, in

33

an instant, all virtue dropped bodily as a mantle,' "
Drufe intoned. " 'Oh, outcast of all outcasts most abandoned!' "

"Drufe is no longer a Poeite, Lon, but he retains his
interest in the texts. For that reason, I thought he'd be
. . . an effective teacher." Prospero trailed off uncertainly, studying the entranced figure beside him; to
whom at length he said, "Perhaps you ought to rest for
a while. Lon will report to your cabin tonight for tutoring."

The tall man bowed his head respectfully to Prospero,
and then, to Lon's surprise, repeated the gesture to him.
He left at once, without a word to either of them.

"Drufe has his idiosyncrasies, but you can learn a lot
from him, Lon. I particularly want you to learn to read
and write."

"I will, if you want me to."

"Do it, for both our sakes," Prospero said, placing a
fatherly hand on the boy's shoulder. "Perhaps you feel
I'm pressing you too hard, but I have plans for you. Ever
since you joined us, I'm increasingly aware of how much
I looked upon your father as a kind of son to me, and
now you . . . . I don't have more than eight or ten galactic years of this kind of life left in me, and when I retire
. . . Work hard, Lon, and learn all you can."

"But what about now, Prospero? Why don't you ever
pay me? You pay the others."

"The others are all business associates. You're more
like my family. There's no need to talk of pay and salary
between us, my boy."

"Then give me some, and I'll stop talking about it."

"Soon, soon," Prospero said in a calming voice, raising
a hand to silence Lon.

"Will you at least show me the books?"

"Of course. I'd forgotten that's why you came here in
the first place. It's the years, Lon. My memory . . ."

Shaking his head sadly, Prospero went to the far wall, touched it gently, and a section swung aside to reveal three shelves containing an assortment of trophies. On the topmost shelf stood four unfamiliar objects. Prospero removed them with great care and carried them to his table, where he laid them down. The objects were all the same shape, a kind of rectangular box, but they differed in size, thickness, and color. All had markings on their lids, but the markings on each one were different.

"These are books, Lon," Prospero said reverently, lifting one and opening it, holding it safely out of Lon's reach, turning it so the boy could see the dense thicket of marks on the pages. "Back on Old Earth, even in the Bloody Centuries, it was not uncommon for people to have this many books in their homes. Some people had enough to fill a whole shelf," Prospero said, his voice hushed with wonder. "Anyone who had that many was called a *librarian*."

"What did they do with them?"

"They used to read them."

"No, I mean what did they *do* with all those books? What became of them?"

Prospero shrugged and spread his hands in a gesture of helplessness. "No one is really certain. I suppose most of them are rotting back on Old Earth. A few pioneers brought books along when they left, but they were the exceptions. Most people were content with the sound tapes and visual prisms, and didn't see any need for books. There appears to have been a revival of printing on some planets late in the first century of colonization, but it died out in a very short time. No one makes books any more."

"Then why should I learn to read? Why should any-one?"

"Power." The boy looked up sharply, taken aback by this response, and Prospero repeated, "Power, Lon. It's more than five centuries since the great exodus from Old Earth, and humans have spread themselves pretty thinly around the galaxy and intermixed with alien races and cultures. A lot of the Old Earth knowledge has been lost, slipped away bit by bit until now it's almost all forgotten. But it still exists, Lon," Prospero said, lifting one of the books, "I'm sure of it, and if the old knowledge is ever to be rediscovered, it will be by reading these old books. That's where our forefathers stored everything they knew. Can you imagine the power a man could acquire if he possessed such knowledge?"

Lon looked dubious. "Drufe can read. Why isn't *he* powerful?"

"Being able to read is only the beginning. You have to find the right books, and then you have to decipher their true meaning and know how to use it properly."

"Are these the right books?"

"I don't know, Lon," Prospero confessed. "I can read quite well, but I haven't yet penetrated to any real meaning. I think if I *could*, though, these books would reveal important things. Some of them would, anyway. This one, for instance," he said, picking up a book bound in deep green and holding it out for Lon's inspection. "Drufe thinks it may be a book of prophecies, like the writings of Poe."

"Does it have a name?"

"It's called *Finnegans Wake*."

"How do you know that?"

Prospero pointed to the cover. "This is the name. Every book has a name, just like people."

"Do you think it's a book of prophecies, Prospero?"

"I can't imagine what it is, Lon. It could as easily be a book of prophecies as anything else. It's beyond me," Prospero said, throwing up his hands.

"Are the others all prophecies, too?"

"We can't be positive. I think Vaslov's *History of Planetary Expeditions* is, but Drufe disagrees. This black one is supposed to be the life story of Moran, the twenty-first century dictator, and I suspect it's just that, and nothing more."

Lon pointed to the lengthy title impressed in gold on the black cover. "It has a bigger name than *Finnegans Wake*," he observed. "Does that mean anything?"

"*Born To Conquer: The Life And Destiny Of Bordon Moran, Ruler Of The Civilized World And Liberator Of All Men*," Prospero read. "I think it means only that Moran was very vain."

"What about the big one? That has a long name, too," Lon said, pointing to a thick book bound in red.

"Ah, yes," Prospero said affectionately, as if speaking of an old friend. "*The Complete Plays Of Lord William Shakespeare*. A real treasure, Lon. This was actually printed on Old Earth, where Lord Shakespeare was born. It's a very rare book. The only edition of his works that I've ever heard of, in fact."

"Are they prophecies?"

"Our tentative opinion is that they're partly prophecy and partly stories, although I must say there are people who disagree. They take stories like this—plays, they're called—and they pretend to be the people in them. They call themselves actors, and they live out a story, over and over, in front of other people. That's how they make their livelihood," Prospero said, an edge of disapproval in his voice. "To hear them talk, you'd think they were skillmen, but they're not on our level."

"Is this the book where you got your name, Prospero?" Lon asked.

"Indeed it is. It's in a story named *The Tempest*, about a wizard who can cause storms and make himself invisible."

"How can he do those things?"

"He learned from books," Prospero said. "His books were more valuable to him than a dukedom."

"Is a dukedom valuable?" Lon asked. "I never saw one."

"It's something like being a king. Very valuable."

Lon weighed this information. Finally he said, "I'll learn to read, Prospero. If it's that good, I want to know it."

After dinner, Lon reported to Drufe's cabin for his first lesson. His eagerness to learn was somewhat tempered by his uneasy memory of Drufe's appearance and manner, and he was relieved and surprised to find his tutor looking both more robust and less forbidding. When Drufe greeted his pupil, even his manner of speaking was different.

"Come in, Lon, come enter my dreary cell and settle your bones for an hour's hard and apparently pointless work. We'll begin with the alphabet. Do you know the alphabet?" he said, all in a rush.

"I know a few letters. L-O-N is my name, and——"

"Forget everything you think you know. We'll begin at the beginning and learn the blasted thing in proper order, once and for all. I'll recite the alphabet through once, then I'll do it letter by letter with you repeating each letter after me. You'll have it by heart before you leave this evening. Ready? E-A-O-I-D-H-N-R-S-T-U-Y-C-F-G-L-M-W-B-K-P-Q-X-Z-J-V, just as it appears in *The Book of The Gold Bug*, slightly altered to include certain forms he omitted for reasons which do not concern us at the moment. Now, repeat after me, Lon: E."

And thus, without tedious preliminaries, came Lon's abrupt introduction to literacy. His memory training at Tib's hands had been so effective that he mastered the alphabet before his lesson time was half over, and could in fact recite it backward and forward from any starting point.

Drufe was impressed. "You learn fast, Lon, and learn well. Tomorrow I'll teach you to write the letters. By the end of the week, you'll be reading."

"How soon can I read *The Tempest*?"

"In time, Lon. Don't expect to learn everything in a few lessons."

"But I want to, Drufe. Prospero said the books can teach me . . . ." The boy paused, suddenly cautious. If the books truly held power, why tell others of it? Drufe might know already, but if he did not, it would be wiser to keep him in the dark, or he might not be so willing a teacher.

"Go on. What can they teach you?" Drufe asked.

"New tricks. Better ones."

"Perhaps." Drufe laughed. "From what I hear, you know more than enough tricks already, and you're only . . . how many years, Galactic Calendar, Lon?"

"About fourteen, I think."

"And how many of those with the circus?"

"Four."

Drufe pursed his lips thoughtfully. He studied Lon for a moment, then asked, "What do you believe in?"

It took Lon some time to reply, "The ship, and my skills."

"And beyond that?"

"What is there beyond that?"

"A whole universe, filled with billions of people, Lon! Stars and planets, whole systems, and unimaginable gulfs of space surrounding it all. Why are they here? Where are they going?" He thrust a lean finger almost into the boy's face. "Where are *you* going—do you know?"

"To Nereus. We arrive in twelve days."

Drufe laughed once again, that same laugh, drained

of all humor and seeming weary and pained. "Of course. To Nereus. When you've learned to read and write, Lon, I'll give you some passages from the master to copy out. I have them in my memory. We'll discuss them. Until then . . . we proceed to Nereus."

"You don't like doing this, do you?" Lon asked, making his question a statement of obvious fact.

"Teaching you, you mean?"

"Yes. You don't like it. I could tell this morning, in Prospero's cabin."

Drufe's expression darkened. "That was different. I was not myself then. You may see me sometimes when I am not myself. Pay no attention."

"If you say so."

"I say so most emphatically. Now, let's hear the alphabet once more, right through from E to V, and then backwards, and then I'll let you go."

Lon worked hard and learned fast. The stop at Nereus ended all lessons for thirty-three planetary days—nearly fifty-one days, galactic reckoning—but once the circus had boarded the *Triboulet* and resumed normal spaceside routine Lon was back at his studies, his appetite for learning undiminished by interruption. Indeed, the long layoff seemed rather to fix his early lessons all the more firmly in his memory and increase the speed of his progress. He soon could copy a page of slow dictation from Drufe without a single error, and by the time of his fifteenth birthday he was at work transcribing the entire works of Poe in his own hand as Drufe recited them from memory. He could also read aloud accurately from printed passages of unfamiliar material.

A sense of his accomplishments began to turn Lon's head. He appeared less frequently at training sessions, and when he did condescend to participate he remained markedly aloof from the other skillmen, whom he no

40

longer considered his equals. At first, they accepted his new pose good-naturedly; as time wore on, they took to ignoring him; but eventually their patience wore thin at his frequent references to their illiteracy and general inferiority. It was not considered necessary, or even advisable, for a skillman to know how to read and write. But Lon's remarks suggested that he alone, of all the skillmen aboard, was serious about his trade.

A further complication was given to the situation by the fact that Lon, no longer the youngest member of the company, was now acutely aware of the opposite sex. There were no young ladies of his age in the company, and very few single women of any age; the competition for the favor of the unattached females was understandably keen. Lon's candidacy was not welcomed by the other men, particularly since Prospero had already shown him so much favor that it was generally assumed among the company that Lon would one day be the old man's successor. Still, most of the company chose to ignore the brash young man. Of the rest, some were jealous of Lon; some feared him; some merely disliked him. Had Kedrak made his earlier remarks at this point, he might have found himself the spokesman for a number of the skillmen. Thus events, plus Lon's immaturity, begot resentment, which turned to ostracism, which threatened to lead to bad feelings within the company.

Above all things—nearly all things—Prospero wanted to keep peace aboard the *Triboulet*. Six days out from Farr's System, with a long trip ahead, he sensed a crisis and acted swiftly to avert it. He assembled the company and informed them of his plans for a few immediate shifts in personnel.

Certain announcements were expected, and these were received with little reaction. Tib had stayed behind on Farr III; another Karrapad, possessor of an equally

41

baroque name and therefore known as Max, was named to replace Tib as chief trainer of skillmen. Two new Quiplid tumblers had joined the company, replacing old Numple, whose pelt was white with age and whose joints were losing their suppleness; they were introduced to the company. Then followed the news that Lon Rimmer, known as The Amazing Saltimbanco, was to withdraw from public performance and be made Prospero's own special assistant.

Lon tried to see Prospero at once, but the old man slipped away. That night, when the boy arrived at Drufe's cabin for his regular lesson, still without having seen Prospero, he received two surprises in quick succession. The first surprise was the sight of *The Complete Plays of Lord William Shakespeare* on Drufe's worktable. The book was one of Prospero's treasures, and Lon had never known him to allow anyone to touch it, much less remove it from his cabin. Yet here it was, and it had not been stolen, for Drufe would never have dared to do such a thing.

The second and far greater surprise came when Drufe, after greeting his pupil, pointed to the book and said, "Prospero wants you to take this book. You're to concentrate on it from now on."

"Is he giving it to me?" Lon asked, astonished.

"For the time being."

"I see," Lon said, deflated at once. "He's not giving it to me."

"What difference does it make whether he gives it to you now or later, Lon? Everyone knows that when Prospero decides to retire, the *Triboulet* and the circus will be yours," Drufe said somewhat crossly.

"I've heard that rumor, but I never heard those words from Prospero. He hints, but he never promises."

Drufe frowned and turned away. "You have no right

to talk that way. The old man treats you like his own flesh and blood. You ought to be more grateful."

"Grateful? I've been with the company for six or seven years, maybe more, working hard, and he's never offered to pay me. He talks of the future, but here and now he gives me nothing," Lon said bitterly.

"I've never seen you without a good stack of cashcubes."

"Winnings. Not pay."

Drufe studied him for a moment. "Winnings? All of it? Your luck must be unusually good. And very consistent."

Lon shrugged, but made no reply. He saw no reason to tell Drufe how he used his skill to keep the odds in his favor. Kynon had once taught him an Old Earth saying: "A fool and his money should be parted at the earliest possible moment," and explained that this was an unwritten law of the galaxy. Lon was only obeying the law.

"Be careful, Lon," Drufe advised. "Most people lose once in a while."

"I have to win. It's the only pay I get."

"You've been well paid in other ways," Drufe countered. "You've learned to read and write, and those are priceless skills."

"So you keep telling me. I'm sick of them."

"You never complained before. You always liked reading and writing. What made you change so suddenly?"

"They've put nothing in my pocket, for all my efforts."

"They will, Lon. Even if they don't, you're a good skillman, an expert on the linlovar, a master——"

"All I know is tricks, Drufe," the boy broke in. "If I want to leave the circus, where can I go? Everyone speaks as though Prospero is doing great things for me, when all he's doing is making me a prisoner."

"You're being very ungrateful."

"No, I'm not. You heard what he said today. I'm to be his special assistant. He won't even let me work by myself any more. When I tried to see him, and talk to him, and ask him why . . ." Lon stopped himself. He was revealing too much. He suppressed his feelings, then went on to speak more calmly. "It's as though he announced to the whole company that I'm a failure, not good enough to work alone. All the other skillmen will think that, and I'm ten times better than the best of them, and I can read, too, and write. It's Prospero who's been unfair, Drufe."

"Do you know why he made you his special assistant?"

"I only know what the others will think."

Drufe waved off the statement with a scornful gesture. "Why should you care? You *are* ten times better than they are, Lon, and Prospero knows it. Would he trust any of them to touch one of his books?"

The boy could not contest that point. Drufe looked at him smugly, pointed to a chair, and when Lon was seated, went on to explain, "You're beginning the hardest part of your education now, Lon, and the old man doesn't want you dividing your efforts. You'll do maintenance training only, just to keep supple. The rest of the time will be spent on this book. We'll go through Shakespeare line by line, word by word, until you know how to decipher like a master. This is why you were taught to read."

"What am I supposed to look for?" Lon asked.

Drufe laughed and shook his head. "If I told you, there'd be no point in looking. Look for everything."

"But *why*?"

"Because that's what books are for," Drufe said, a bit impatiently. He tapped the cover of the thick red-bound volume. "This book contains thirty-nine of Shakespeare's plays, plus eight more attributed to him. Many of the plays are no more than they appear to be, but some of the pieces in here are actually cryptic histories, or philosophical or scientific systems, disguised as plays."

"I still don't understand. Why are they disguised as something else?"

"Shakespeare was a genius, Lon. Like all geniuses, he didn't want to make his knowledge available to ordinary people, so he concealed it in what appear to be ordinary stories."

"But suppose nobody ever uncovered it, Drufe. Then all that knowledge would be lost."

Drufe smiled condescendingly and shook his head. "An explicator can find anything, Lon. A good one can find things that even the author himself is unaware of having said. No, nothing gets by us."

"And you want to teach me how to explicate."

"Exactly. When you can handle Shakespeare . . . well, Prospero will tell you what comes next," Drufe said. "Let's get to work. We're going to start with a revenge tragedy. Do you remember the saying 'Nemo me impune lacessit'?"

"Yes. It's from Poe."

"Where in Poe? What does it mean?"

"It means 'no one injures me without being punished,' in the Caesaro-Etruscan dialect of Old Earth."

"And where does Poe use it?" Drufe pressed.

"In *The Book of The Cask of Amontillado*. What has all this got to do with Shakespeare and revenge tragedies, Drufe?"

"*The Book of The Cask of Amontillado* is the most significant expression of many Poeite doctrines, including revenge. Since we are about to begin the close study of a revenge tragedy, it seems obvious that we should refresh our memories regarding the basic principles involved."

Lon looked puzzled. "But isn't that story about the Creator Montresor punishing his fallen creatures?"

"Yes, it is, Lon, but it's *told* in the form of a revenge tale. There are certain affinities of form between Shakespeare's work and the Poe tale."

"Shakespeare wasn't a Poeite. He couldn't have been," Lon objected.

"Not in the strict sense. But one need not be a Poeite to enunciate the principles of the Master."

Lon frowned critically. "I've heard the Lovecrafters——"

"Lovecraft! A blasphemer, and no true disciple!" Drufe exploded. "Ignore his works and his followers. The truth can all be found in Poe. Come, now, let's get to work."

During the preceding months of training, as Lon's interest had quickened and his competence increased, his daily lessons had been expanded in duration. Now, under Drufe's prodding, he managed to wring from the four words of the unwritten epigraph sufficient matter to occupy his full session without proceeding to a single line of the play. But though he rattled on glibly, his thoughts were on other things. He did not show it, but he was deeply troubled. For the first time, he doubted the wisdom of his mentor. The thought occurred to him—an unwelcome and fleeting thought which he did his best to bury, unacknowledged, under the accumulated trust of years—that Drufe was dead wrong. Lon did not know the intricate details of the numerous Poeite controversies well enough to perceive the convenient elisions in Drufe's explanations; nevertheless, he felt now what he had never felt before: that Drufe was quashing a question because he had no answer to it and wanted none.

When the lesson was over, Drufe shut the book and pushed it to his pupil. "Take it, Lon," he said. "Read

The Tragedy of Othello, Moor of Venice through, and we'll start working on it tomorrow." As he spoke, he reached for the jar that rested, securely stoppered, on the corner of his table.

"That's a lot to read in one day."

"You'll have time, now. You're Prospero's special assistant, remember? This is what he wants you to do, not training or ship's duties. You're finished with all that."

"Nothing but studying from now on?" The sudden prospect took Lon by complete surprise.

"You've got a lot to learn before we arrive at Basraan. Well, go ahead. The lesson's over."

"I want you to tell me something, Drufe."

Drufe had by now slid the jar to a position in front of him and opened it, and he was dreamily inhaling the sweet heavy odor that arose from the open top. The jar contained his *zaff* leaves, steeping in a solution of brine and herbs to release their full potency. It was his custom to indulge himself in the leaves every evening after Lon's lesson, and he allowed nothing to interfere with his routine in this respect. Lon, ignored, repeated himself twice, with growing impatience, as Drufe prepared a leaf. At last he gripped his teacher's slim forearm firmly. Lon was a strong boy, and Drufe could not ignore the pressure.

"The lesson is over, Lon. Leave me."

"Tell me what I want to know," Lon said, releasing him.

"Tomorrow," Drufe said, shaking the last moisture from a leaf the size of his hand, folding it into a small wad, and placing it in his mouth.

"Tell me now. Why was I suddenly made Prospero's special assistant and given this book?"

Drufe bit down slowly with his back teeth, crushing juice from the wadded leaf. He savored it, swallowed slowly, and then said, "Prospero does not explain his decisions to me."

"Why are you stepping up my lessons? You can answer *that*, can't you?"

"Prospero's instructions. He wants you to be ready when we land on Basraan."

"Ready for what?"

Drufe did not answer at once. When he spoke, his voice was a deep distant monotone. "The books . . . power and pride."

"What?"

" 'I spoke to her of power and pride/——But mystically, in such guise/ That she might deem it nought beside/ The moment's converse . . . ,' " Drufe went on haltingly. "The books of mystery in simple guise . . . are soon to come . . . ."

The comas came on Drufe faster now, and lasted longer. His eyes closed contentedly and a faint smile spread over his gaunt face as he relaxed and slumped deeper into his chair. Lon knew the signs well by now. One day Drufe would enter his last coma, the one that never ended, and he would waste away and die, still smiling blissfully. That was the way it ended. Lon took his book and left.

The next day he confronted Prospero with the questions Drufe had answered so unsatisfactorily. The old man was no more cooperative at first, but Lon persisted, growing bolder and more outspoken and pressing him harder as the evasions continued. At last Prospero yielded and admitted that he had learned of a vast stock of books—as many as ten, perhaps even more—to be found on Basraan, their next stop. According to the source of this information, the books had been found in the wreckage of a First Stage driveship. They had been printed on Old Earth to be taken to the stars. Prospero's eyes grew bright as he spoke of them.

48

"They're what I've been after all these years, Lon, I'm sure of it. They'll reveal everything!"

"What can they reveal, Prospero?"

The old man glanced around the cabin cautiously. He went to the door, looked out, then closed it and secured it firmly. Drawing Lon to a far corner, he spoke to him in a lowered voice. "They can reveal something that will make the *Triboulet* feared throughout the galaxy, and make me, and you after me, the most powerful man alive. I'll tell you more, Lon, but first you must swear to tell this to no one else."

"Not even Drufe?"

"Above all, not to Drufe. Do you swear?"

"I swear I'll tell no one, Prospero."

"Swear it on the memory of your parents. Put your hand on your heart and swear," the old man instructed. When Lon had done so, Prospero cast one final furtive glance around and proceeded. "The race of Old Earth had weapons that could destroy a city ten times the size of the domed cities on Barbary. They could blow a fleet of driveships out of the sky in the time it takes you to blink. I know this must sound fantastic to you, but it's true. It's all there in Moran's book. Now, Lon, you've seen the *Triboulet* from one end to the other. What weapons do we carry?"

"The crew have pistols and swords. The company carry daggers, mostly, and a few pistols. Skaalder keeps a big axe in his cabin." Lon paused and furrowed his brow in deep concentration. "That's all I know of."

"That's everything. What's the most powerful weapon on board?"

"The pistols, I guess."

"You're right. They're the most powerful weapons on any driveship. Now, suppose I could learn to make one of those Old Earth weapons, Lon. Who could oppose me? Who would dare to, with swords and pistols?"

"No one," the boy said softly, awed by this revelation of the old man's dream.

"And I would rule the galaxy." Prospero paused, savoring his own words, then turned to Lon and said, "That's why I must get those books, and why you must help me to pluck the hidden knowledge from them. I know it's there. It has to be there."

"Wouldn't it be better to try to find one of the old weapons?"

Prospero frowned on him. "Do you think that hasn't occurred to me? Of course it would. But in all the centuries since the exodus, no one has ever found a trace of them. There aren't even rumors of them. For some reason, the first travelers didn't bring their weapons along."

"Maybe they were too big," Lon said, trying to be helpful.

"Maybe. Although some of the references in Moran . . . I want you to read that book before we land, and tell me how you interpret it. Whatever the reason, the weapons were not taken out—which means that the plans *must* have been," Prospero said. "Somehow, those plans were lost, and they've remained lost all these centuries—lost or completely overlooked, because people don't understand how to read them. There's no other answer. Why else would men with weapons capable of destroying a world fight with swords and pistols?"

"I can't imagine, Prospero. You must be right."

"I am, Lon. I'm sure of that." The old man was silent for a moment, then he said, "Now you know what I've had in mind all these years. My plans are close to fruition, and with your help, I can't fail. This is what I've trained you for, and I'm depending on you. No more Saltimbanco. You'll be my Ariel."

"What's that?"

"Prospero's invaluable helper. Read *The Tempest*,

Lon, and you'll find Ariel. And remember, you're to tell no one what we've discussed. You've given your word."

Now that his studies had a clearly-defined objective, Lon applied himself more conscientiously than ever. He spent entire days in reading, and memorized long passages from all the plays. Every night he went to Drufe's cabin and endeavored to spin from the lines of Shakespeare a satisfactory commentary on the prophetic wisdom of the master, Poe of Old Earth.

The more he did so, the stronger his doubts became.

He could not determine, when he thought back on these times, at what precise point it first occurred to him that Drufe was intent on finding certain meanings in the lines of Shakespeare regardless of whether or not such meanings were in fact there to be found. All he knew was that one evening, quite abruptly and without warning, in the midst of a labored explication, it was unmistakably and undeniably clear to him that Drufe was leading him to uncover deep significances that existed not in the mind of Lord William Shakespeare, but in the convictions of Drufe. And he knew at once that the same might be said of the writings of Poe.

To credit this revelation would force upon him certain consequences which Lon was not pleased to accept; and yet he could not reject what his own observations and judgment daily confirmed. He mentioned the problem to no one. Throughout the trip to Basraan he continued his daily lessons, memorized, read deeply, probing the lines to their hearts, and performed every evening for Drufe. Behind the impassive exterior he had developed during recent times aboard the *Triboulet*, he fought a constant battle.

Drufe had impressed him once, years before, with his wisdom and skill. No one else aboard the ship could do the things that Drufe did so effortlessly. He could actu-

51

ally decipher those ranked scratches on the page and reproduce them quickly and accurately on a writing plate. Such talents had appeared to Lon as bordering on wizardry. Only Prospero approached such skill, and he was the first to proclaim Drufe's superiority.

But now Lon himself could do these things as well as Drufe, and sometimes better and faster. He saw that Drufe was not a wizard after all. He was a *zaff*-rotted failure, a Poeite explicator cast out by his fellow believers for some unspecified transgression and now reduced to peddling his gifts for a bare existence and a daily supply of the leaves that were slowly killing him.

As his picture of Drufe changed, Lon revised his estimate of Prospero. True, the old man had sheltered him all these years; but The Amazing Saltimbanco had drawn crowds at all their stops, and the promised payment never came, only excuses and even more generous promises. Lon became convinced that he was being used. Prospero wanted a clear young mind to focus on the old books and pry loose the secrets of Old Earth power, and Drufe was molding a young mind for him. Lon was a tool. And perhaps all the dreams of power were no more than a delusion, a fantasy spun by an old man, nurtured by a castoff broken-down explicator looking for a place to hide. Perhaps Lon's whole life was to be wasted seeking imaginary revelations in centuries-old books.

Once he was convinced of this, Lon surrendered to the full bitterness of disillusionment and began to nurse a growing anger for the trusted men who had treated him so. He brooded on their betrayal and his anger deepened to hate. He could not satisfy himself as to which of the two bore the greater share of guilt, so he hated both equally and laid plans for revenge.

It was a long way to Basraan, and by the time the *Triboulet* touched down, Lon's mood had changed. In one respect, he had softened. He pitied the deluded old man and the desperate wreck of an explicator, and foreswore all revenge on them. They caused suffering enough for themselves. But in another way, he had become inflexible. He was through with the ship, the circus, and his mentors, and he was determined to escape from them.

II.

Actor and Language-Maker

LON MADE HIS MOVE during their fourth night on Basraan. Drufe, as was his custom, had headed directly for a *zaff* house, there to spend his planetary stay. Basraan, though not a pleasure planet, was well provided with such establishments, and Drufe, after stops on three successive anti-*zaff* planets, was eager for a long immersion in the forgetfulness the leaves offered. Lon planned a rude interruption of his dreams.

Prospero intended a more active stay. No sooner had the *Triboulet* touched down than he put Max in charge of the unloading, charged Lon with the responsibility for all forms and clearances, and then vanished into the streets of the city. The members of the company speculated on the reason for his disappearance and the visibly growing anxiety of their leader over the latter part of the trip, but only Lon knew that Prospero was in search of the Old Earth books that rumor had placed here on Basraan. Lon, meanwhile, was not idle. He spent his evenings in his own pursuits, found what he was seeking, and laid his plans.

For three days, Prospero searched the city, leaving the circus quarters early in the day and returning late at night. The Basraan day was long, nearly thirty-four hours galactic standard, and Prospero returned exhausted and haggard. But he persisted. Late on the fourth day he burst unannounced into Lon's quarters and said in a hoarse voice, "I've found them!"

"The books?"

"Yes. Six of them. That's all there ever were," Prospero said, seating himself on Lon's pallet. He sighed deeply, yawned, and fell back heavily. "I'm worn out. Been searching the city since the day we landed. But I've found them."

"Did you see them? What titles?"

Prospero spoke haltingly. "*Psychology of Isolated Groups*, by Jermolovich . . . *Alien Terrain Survival Handbook* . . . Two history books . . ."

"Anything about weapons?"

"Can't tell. Maybe in the *Survival* book, or one of the histories." He propped himself on one elbow and said, "I'm afraid, Lon. What if there's nothing? What if they're just books?"

Lon shrugged. "Then you'll have to keep looking. When will you get them?"

"Tonight. You come, too. Look them over carefully."

Lon nodded absently. He was thinking of the enormous amount Prospero would have to pay for six genuine Old Earth books, objects which were literally priceless, and wondering where it would come from. Would he dare spend the payroll of the entire crew and company? He could not sell the *Triboulet*. How could he raise the sum?

With a shock that nearly sickened him, Lon realized that he himself was an excellent source of ready money—young and strong, with a good long life expectancy; a trained skillman who could also read and write; someone who would not be missed by family and friends, or even by Prospero, who would still have Drufe to explicate for him. Daltrescan slavers would pay well for such a property, and their agents were sure to be found in a spaceport as busy as this one. An old man could easily and safely lead him into their hands. Lon remembered his father's instruction—"Trust no one" —and realized its soundness. He had been too trusting for too long.

"What's the matter? You look awful," Prospero said.

"Nothing. I . . . it's my stomach. This water."

"Get something to fix you up. I want you with me tonight, after the show."

"That's late, Prospero."

"It's when they do business. Not my idea."

"Who else is coming?"

"No one. This is to be kept secret." The old man looked suspiciously at his assistant. "Why all the questions, Lon?"

"No reason. Just curious. Why don't you rest there, Prospero, while I get something for my stomach?"

"Good idea," the old man said, sprawling back once more. "Don't wake me when you come back."

Lon grinned at the recumbent figure. "I won't." He picked up the little sack that held his belongings and slipped out silently.

Darkness had fallen before Lon reached the shabby building just off the main marketplace. It was a spacious structure that looked to be on the verge of collapse and smelled like the animal pens on the last days of a long voyage. Outside, flanking the entrance, were lurid posters. Written under them, for the few who could read, was the message, "Final performance tonight." Three youths studied one poster eagerly, while an older couple examined the other with evident disapproval.

Lon took a seat on one of the long benches near the rear and watched the two men on the low stage. They were involved in a loud, rather one-sided dispute, but Lon did not have a chance to catch their meaning.

He sensed someone near him, turned, and saw the aging admittance man looking down on him suspiciously.

"You again? You're early tonight," he said.

"I want to see Vallandis. He's usually busy afterwards."

"That he is," the admittance man agreed, cackling softly and libidinously to himself.

"May I speak with him now? It's a business matter of some importance," Lon said.

"Go ahead. He probably wants to be interrupted, anyway. He can't stand that new fellow, and he knows it's a waste of time trying to teach him anything. Go on, go right up to him. But if you're still here when the show starts, you have to pay."

"I know, I know," Lon said. He walked unobtrusively down the side aisle and took a place on the foremost bench, at the end. Here he could distinguish the subject of the argument between Vallandis, the actor-manager of the little company, and the young actor. It was easy to judge who would be victor.

Vallandis was tall and broad of frame, with a head that seemed disproportionately large for his body and a voice disproportionately large for any mere human being. He moved smoothly and gracefully, like a dancer, in spite of his great bulk. He had the power and resonance of a Lixian in his voice, but his range and expressiveness were unique. His skin was a brown so deep as to be almost black, his hair and short beard a whitish-gold so fine in texture that they seemed almost to form an aureole around his large head, gathering light from all sides and wreathing it into a visual backdrop for that magnificent voice.

The young actor who stood before him was a pallid, whispering wraith in comparison. He winced at Vallandis' words, shrank from his expansive gestures, and could do no more than blink at each new burst of censure.

"An actor does not observe his role calmly, from a safe distance, my friend. He enters it. Do you grasp that simple fact? He assumes his role, becomes a different person, acts and speaks and even thinks as that person because while he is on stage, he *is* that person. But not you. Oh, no. You practice your craft with a difference, you do. You're a multiple murderer in this play," Vallandis said, as if he found the words absurd but was forced to speak them nevertheless. Toting up on his fingers, he went on, "You've stabbed your wife's family in Act I. That's three people. In the next act, you throw your wife from the battlements and strangle your infant daughter. Five, so far. In the last act, you poison your mother and brother, and as you enter your father's chamber to smother him, this is how you sound." Vallandis shrank his voice to a boyish piping, hunched himself to half his size, stiffened into immobility, and gaped out toward the benches, reciting awkwardly and mechanically,

" 'The old man sleeps. 'Tis well the deed is done,
His sleep made rest, that all the rest might sleep.
Soon rest in me the powers of state that now,
Arrested, stand. . . .' "

He turned upon the novice abruptly. "You make those lines a sick spew of childish prattle. If I had anyone to take your place, I'd throw you out with my own hands!" he roared.

Lon rose and came forward. "Try me."

"You? Who are you?" the young actor asked, shocked into speech.

Lon ignored him, directing his remarks to Vallandis.

58

"I've seen the last two performances. It was obvious that you'd need a new Ricardo if you were to do this play properly, so I came here to try out for the part."

"What's your experience?"

"Does it matter, if I can do the part?"

Vallandis laughed, a deep internal rumbling that burst into a flash of teeth before subsiding. "Maybe not. Do the speech I just did."

Lon drew up one shoulder and cocked his head to the side. As he walked, he dragged one foot slightly. His eyes were bright with amusement and cheerful self-satisfaction, his voice almost merry, as he slipped into the role of the murdering usurper Ricardo.

> " 'The old man sleeps. Now let the deed be done,
> His sleep made rest, while all the rest court sleep.
> Him gone, the sleeping powers of the state
> That now, arrested, rest in feeble hands,
> Ricardo, restless else, wrests to himself. . . .' "

When Lon ended, he and Vallandis stood alone on the stage. The third performer, mindful of the actor-manager's threat, had chosen to exit under his own power.

"You did well," Vallandis said, "but you didn't speak the lines as I did. You changed things."

"There were things that needed changing. The word-play must be clear to all."

"You speak as one familiar with the play."

"I am. This is a clumsy piece of work," Lon said coolly, "but it is not without points of interest. It deserves care."

"Do you know many plays?" Vallandis made no effort to hide his interest in this stranger.

"A few, but none of them are very good. That's why

I'm here. I can not only act in the plays you have, I can make new ones for you, better than any you've ever seen. What would that be worth?"

Lon had given this matter much thought in the days since his disenchantment with Prospero and Drufe. He could not stay with the Original Galactic Circus any longer: besides growing restlessness and newly-hatched personal antipathy, unhappy rumors were spreading about his extraordinary good luck at gambling. It seemed wise to move on. But his skills were not readily marketable. Jugglers and manipulators, even outstanding ones, were not in great demand around the galaxy. A presentable young man who could perform well before a crowd might join a company of actors; even so, there were always more presentable young men than there were opportunities. Lon wanted to be free, but he had no wish to starve. He pondered his predicament and decided that his ability to read and write—and if necessary, to explicate—would be his strong point.

When he dropped in on a performance of *Ricardo, The Usurper of London* being presented by the Twelve Systems Repertory Company, he found the solution to his problems. The play was quite bad, but it was reportedly the best of the four plays in this company's repertoire, and Vallandis' company was by common consent the best in the sector. It struck Lon at once that a company that did so well with mediocre material might approach greatness once provided with plays of the first order. And he had just such plays.

Lord William Shakespeare was a thousand years dead, but his words still stirred the human heart; Lon knew as much from his own experience. Five hundred years before, when the first driveships had left for the stars, Shakespeare's words had gone with them. The implications of that fact were staggering: men who had not brought weapons had nevertheless taken with them the works of this author. It was as if a great albino *snargrax* had exchanged his claws and fangs for the ability to sing.

Somehow or other, in those intervening centuries, the plays had been lost; or corrupted, through wilful piracy and human fallibility, into clumsy travesties of the originals, degraded almost beyond recognition. Even their creator's name was lost. But not to Lon. He had a treasure locked in his memory.

"New plays?" Vallandis said thoughtfully. "You can actually create new plays?"

"Completely new. Made just for the Twelve Systems Repertory Company."

"There hasn't been a new play—a good new play— since . . . since before . . ."

"Since the exodus, I suppose," Lon completed the thought. "And now people speak of it as a lost art. But I've rediscovered it."

"Can you deliver one right now?"

"I'm working on one."

"How many could you make?"

Lon shrugged. "One, two . . . ten . . . I can't say. Take me into the company and give me a chance. You need a new Ricardo for tonight, anyway."

"Morbin can do the role, if necessary. It will mean some switching around, but if we must . . ." Vallandis trailed off, frowning thoughtfully over the offer, reluctant to commit himself.

Lon was not ready to let him slip out of the situation so easily. "Tell me, what's your next stop?" he asked.

"Godric III. We leave after tonight's show."

"Arriving when?"

"Twenty-two days, galactic time."

"Well, how about this: Take me along as a member of the company, and I'll give you a new play by landfall."

Vallandis pondered that. "Can't you do it sooner? We'll need rehearsal time."

"How much?"

"Five days, minimum."

"I'll promise you three. Are we agreed?"

"Don't be hasty," Vallandis said. "If the play fails, you may end up on Godric III looking for a job. It's not much of a planet."

"I'll take my chances. Agreed?"

Vallandis thrust out a big hand. "Agreed."

"Good. Now, where's my changing room? I have to get ready for tonight's show."

"I'll take you there and introduce you to the others," said Vallandis. "What's your name, anyway?"

It was not Lon Rimmer, not any longer. That was Prospero's label for Prospero's tool, a name for a life now behind him, as meaningless as the silly "Ariel" that the old man had taken to using once the purpose of the tutoring sessions had been made clear. The new name came to his lips at once. "Call me Will," he said.

"A good short name. I like it." Vallandis nodded his approval. "Tell me, Will, what's your experience? You seem to know how to stand up and deliver a line."

"I've been with old Prospero's circus for some time. Until recently, I was The Amazing Saltimbanco, The Precocious Prestidigitator of Skyx."

The actor-manager raised an eyebrow. "You? The little juggler? You look a good size for a boy wonder."

"Indeed, I found myself forced to stoop somewhat in recent times. It's one of the reasons I left."

"And the other is that Prospero never paid you. I know his reputation, Will, and I can tell you this: we're not as big as Prospero's operation, nor as successful, but what we have, we share. I think you'll like being one of us."

Will soon learned that Vallandis' words were not a boast. The Twelve Systems Repertory Company was small and closely-knit, but nonetheless receptive to the newcomer. Prospero had not spoken fairly when he dismissed actors as would-be skillmen seeking undeserved recognition for minor talents. These were dedicated people who took pride in their own skills, and they respected skill and the urge to perfection in others. They gave Will the chance to prove himself.

He began winning them over with his very first performance—the audience demanded three repetitions of the long soliloquy preceding Ricardo's murder of his father, and he delivered them passionately—and by the time they touched down on Godric III he was accepted as a full-fledged member of the troupe. What clinched his position was not his performances, but his play.

He set it down in odd hours during the harrowing twenty-nine day trip—it was, he learned, Vallandis' custom to underestimate travel time by about a third—working from memory sketchily assisted by scenes transcribed into his notebooks as texts for explication. This was his first effort, and it was more difficult than he had anticipated. Simply copying down lines from memory was not possible; the lines were not always there. For one dreadful stretch he thought that his father's judgment on the perils of literacy might be true, and his memory had indeed been ruined. But then the lines came back to him. So copiously did they return, in fact, that he was overcome by their abundance and decided to make a single new play out of two remembered ones. Borrowing heavily from one about an unfortunate Moor and another about a Scottish regicide, he put together *The Downfall of Moran*, which he announced to the company as a historical tragedy.

They grew radiant as he read the script to them. It was not a setting he would have chosen as one in which an audience could devote its full attention to a reader: they were adrift, resting the feeble old drive coils for the fourth time since departing Basraan; their ship, *The Empress of Space*, was too old to have a scanner system, and so they could hope for no warning in case of attack; their entire armory consisted of four pistols, twenty-three rounds of ancient ammunition, and seven daggers. Under the circumstances, their only choice was between cowering in terror of imminent destruction or enjoying themselves as best they could, and they chose enjoyment. As part after challenging part was brought forth, they took to applauding every speech wildly and calling for repetitions. Will could scarcely croak by the time he reached the closing scene, but he was as jubilant as they. An exciting story, fine speeches, and a good part for everyone—Lord William Shakespeare himself, Will thought contentedly, could have done no better.

He had written *The Downfall of Moran* to suit this company. For the three ladies he had created the driving, ambitious Lady Moran; the murdered innocent Desdemona and her sharp-tongued and devoted servant Emilia; and as an ensemble, three clairvoyant crones who lure Moran ever onward with treacherous promises of victory. The ladies were delighted at such an opportunity to display their versatility.

The men of the company were equally pleased. The senior member of the company, gruff-voiced scowling Morbin, was a perfect Bordon Moran; Vallandis played Othello, the black general who turned the tide against Moran, saved the world from his tyranny, and then in a fit of madness strangled his own wife. For the other members of the company, Will created lesser roles, but even these afforded a small scene, or a few lines, in which the actor could be the center of attraction. For himself, he reserved minor parts—messenger, porter, attendant, doctor, an old man. Such self-effacement endeared him permanently to his fellow actors. Now he was truly one of them.

64

The Downfall of Moran played twelve successive nights on Godric III, and each night's crowd was larger than that of the night preceding. No one wanted to see *Ricardo, The Usurper of London* or *The Murderous Wife*, the company's old standards. The crowds wanted Moran, and they were given Moran at every performance.

Vallandis was awed by his good fortune, but not so awed that he overlooked the value of his newly-found playwright. On the company's next stop, the audience was treated to *The Downfall of Moran*, Parts I and II, played on two consecutive nights, and to crowds larger than those on Godric.

Will worked harder than he had worked since his earliest days with the circus, and he found himself, to his surprise, extremely happy. Besides his daily stint at composition (he had quickly come to think of the plays as *his* plays, and instead of the cool efficiency of the copier he cultivated the anxieties of the creator), he followed a heavy schedule of study and exercise. He attended to all his duties most conscientiously, and still found spare moments for pleasure.

The itinerant acting companies of the period had little to aid them but their own skills, and over the generations, they had developed these skills to a point of near perfection. Without properties, with only the simplest costumes and no makeup at all, performing in whatever playing area was available to them, they created their illusions with voice and gesture, and their training started in early childhood. The discipline of his circus years now stood Will in good stead. He had to undertake a concentrated regimen of muscular control exercises that would have been impossible for anyone not already trained to a high degree. In time, he learned to bring about subtle alterations in his facial muscles that could give him the appearance of a man three times his age, and to increase or decrease his stature by as much as a hand's breadth. The strain was great, and the pain at first was excruciating; but he persisted, and the time came when he could sustain the physical characteristics of a blustering giant or a withered ancient throughout an entire performance. Voice training accompanied his physical efforts. As a bully, he rumbled and roared, assaulting his audience with a bombardment of sound; as an old man, he spoke in a piping voice of cracks and catches. So convincing did he become that after one performance he overheard several irate senior members of the audience condemn Vallandis for his cruelty in subjecting a sick old man to the rigors of space travel and repertory acting. He savored his accomplishment, and left the critics to their illusion. They seemed so happy to be outraged.

During engagements he had no time to write, but a small nook was found for him in *The Empress of Space* and there he spent the first part of each traveling day. On a long voyage, he could complete an entire play; on shorter trips he worked on scenes and did revision. He learned to husband his stock; it occurred to him that there was no telling how long his memory would hold up, and to be too prolific would only raise troublesome expectations. His source was, after all, limited, and he felt that original creation was as yet beyond his powers. In his first year with the Twelve Systems Repertory Company he delivered five plays; in the second year, three. From that time on, he planned to do no more than two annually.

He found that his most successful efforts were those that dwelt on murder, violence, and revenge. The more widely he voyaged, the more this fact puzzled him. If his experience of the galaxy had been confined to warrior planets; if his acquaintance had been restricted to Lixians, Skeggjatts, and starbrats, he might have been convinced that violence and revenge were the normal concerns of the humanoid races. But he went to planets where no one wore a weapon, where the words for acts of violence did not exist, and to raise a hand in anger against another was unthinkable. And yet these peaceable audiences were as receptive to his blood-drenched tragedies as were the beweaponed brawlers of the warrior planets.

He could not understand this at all. The galaxy was still in a state of relative pacification. Occasional skirmishes with a mysterious race known only as the Rinn had not yet shown signs of expanding into full-scale war; the pirates, renegades, and slavers, though horrendously cruel, were few in number; the destructive weaponry of Old Earth seemed forever lost; and still human and humanoid alike, with rare exceptions, took pleasure and satisfaction from watching the slaughter of their own kind enacted.

Will found the paradox interesting, and puzzled over it for a time without reaching any philosophical conclusions. He did, however, make some revisions in *Ricardo, The Usurper of London*, and found that additional deaths brought new life to the old standby: doubling the number of murders greatly increased the size of the audiences.

When he was not training, acting, writing, or sleeping, Will was most often in the company of a Malellan girl named Thenea, the youngest of the ladies in the company and to him, the most beautiful and desirable woman in the Twelve Systems. During his last years on the *Triboulet*, he had always looked upon space time as the time of loneliness and anticipated the next planetfall; here was the time for pleasure. Will was a trim, handsome young man. Planetbound girls were always interested in a widely-traveled young skillman, and Will assiduously accumulated a stock of pleasant memories to sustain him through the starfaring days of hard study and the long evenings of chess. But now, thanks to Thenea, the ship was home. Once aboard, the two were seldom out of one another's company.

The troupe members were firm believers in minding one's own business and experienced enough to know that where love is concerned, no encouragement is needed and no discouragement is sought. Will was on his own. After years of being made to feel like a child, he was being noticed by an attractive woman, encouraged, flattered, made to feel important, and the experience blinded him to things he should have observed. It was some time before his idyll came to an abrupt and shattering end.

They were leaving a warrior planet where *The Downfall of Moran*, Parts I and II, had been tumultously received. The climactic death duel between Moran and Othello had been called back for five encores on the last night, and Thenea's portrayal of Lady Moran had won her nine bids of marriage from warriors of rank. Will himself, as the author, had been generously rewarded by the First Ranger.

Once aloft, he exchanged congratulations with the others and went in search of Thenea. She was nowhere to be found. Just as *The Empress of Space* lurched into the highdrive range, every plate of her old superstructure groaning its protest, Morbin stepped up to him and without a word of explanation thrust a packet into his hand. The packet contained a small motion painting Will had given to Thenea when they had first agreed to stay together. No note accompanied it—she could not write—but none was needed. The message was clear.

On the long lonely voyage to their next planetfall, Will kept to himself as much as was possible in the cramped confines of *The Empress of Space*. When forced to endure the presence of others, he remained moody and silent. He had no desire for companions. He wanted solitude in which to search his memory for a play about false love and betrayal. For the first time, he visualized himself in the leading role: the faithful trusting lover mocked and destroyed by a deceitful woman seeking only her own gratification, using her lovers remorselessly and discarding them at whim. But the woman to play opposite him was gone, mated with some scarred and musclebound brute of a warrior. May he beat her morning and night, Will prayed through clenched teeth, and immediately relented and qualified his plea—but not too hard.

He moped and mourned his way from waking to sleeping again and again until, saturated in self-pity, he began to set down the words to suit his feelings. They came from a play he had never liked before or expected to use, and now, as he savored the bitterness of each line, he wondered at his past obtuseness. He gave the piece to Vallandis, and heard no more of it for two full work days. When the customary praise was not forthcoming on the third day, he sought the manager out.

Vallandis was blunt with him. "We can't use your new play, Will. It's too bitter. You've been through a bad experience, and you've probably learned a lot. Putting it down like this may have helped you, but an audience doesn't care about your problems. They come to us to be entertained."

"Then they're stupid!" Will snapped, hurt and enraged by this reception. "It's time we taught them what life is all about."

"Do *you* know?" Vallandis looked amused by the notion.

"I know more than *they* do," Will retorted.

"Maybe, maybe not. But we're not teachers, we're entertainers. And in any event, we're not going to Bellaterra to work, we're heading there to take a long rest.

69

It's a beautiful planet, and the people are different from any race I've ever seen."

"I've seen a lot of races, Val," Will said ill-humoredly.

"I'm twice your age, and I've traveled ten times as far, and I'm telling you flatly that there's no group in this galaxy like the Bellaterrans. They're a beautiful, kind people. Each time I've been on that planet I've wanted to stay there for good."

"Why didn't you, if it's so wonderful?"

Will had spoken so to provoke an argument, but Vallandis was suddenly moved to mildness. He shrugged and shook his head helplessly. "I still don't know. Maybe I just need to keep moving. The thought of the same audience for the rest of my life . . . I don't know, Will. I only know that each time I left I felt as if I were tearing myself apart."

Unsatisfactory as this conversation was in some respects, it took Will's mind off his disappointment and aroused his curiosity. Since arrival was close, he kept his questions to himself, but once *The Empress of Space* had dropped below lightspeed and the cloud-mottled ball of blue-green expanded before them, he could hold back no longer. But by this time, everyone was too taken up with landing procedure to spare him a word, and he could only wait until they reached the planet.

Planetfall came in the final hours of darkness. At dawn, Will was seated against the trunk of a tree at the crest of a long, gently sloping hill. Behind him, forgotten, *The Empress of Space* was cradled in the planet's single landing ring. Before him, the sun rose over Bellaterra, and he watched the slow spread of pink and gold with the sensations of a man who awakens after troubled dreams to find himself in Paradise.

From space, Bellaterra had looked inviting; seen from its own surface, it was breathtaking. Will's position

70

afforded him an uninterrupted prospect in three directions. Here at the crest of the hill he had the sensation of being at once a participant in and a spectator of a sweeping pageant of color and sound and scent. He had traveled far in his short life; but travel in the featureless gray dimensions of lightspeed was an experience more likely to stunt the mind than to enlarge it, and the worlds he had seen were too often as grim and uninviting as space itself. The very concept of seasons was meaningless to him. Born and raised in a domed city, he had never walked across a green meadow or a field of flowers. He had never swum in open water, never seen a snowfall or a blazing autumn forest, never felt the cool of the deep woods in summer. He had seldom breathed fresh air. But now he was on Bellaterra, and all was different.

The crisp, clear air seemed to lend definition to the most distant objects. Will felt that he could number the leaves on the farthest tree and count each feather on the gaudy birds that floated lazily overhead, their underbellies gilded by the rising sun. Beyond them, over all, stretched a pale blue sky dotted with soft clouds whose edges swirled and tumbled in upon themselves as they raced toward the horizon. At his feet unrolled a landscape in innumerable shades of green, and beyond, on a deep blue lake palisaded by giant trees, gold medallions flashed and quivered under the ascending sun. A feeling of immensity swept over him. This small planet, this dust mote in infinity, seemed vaster than the gulf of interstellar space. It was alive and moving and aglow with color.

He breathed in deeply the cool sweet air, and rose to his feet. Speechless with emotion, he reached his hands up to the sky. He wanted words to describe this beauty that caught at his being, words of his own, not stolen but truly felt and wrought out of his own experience, but the words were not in him. And the beauty was so great that his failing brought him no anger, but rather tranquility, a calm certainty that one day the words would come. He had only to stay, and seek them here.

He was not immediately aware of Vallandis' big hand resting on his shoulder. "How do you like Bellaterra, Will?"

It was Will's turn to search for words. He could think of only one sight of comparable splendor: the wall-sized motion painting that had once been his father's most prized possession. Even that, the life's work of four master artists, seemed no more than a child's scrawl beside the reality of Bellaterra. "I've never . . . of all the planets . . . ," Will groped, and lamely settled for, "It's beautiful."

"It is. And the Bellaterrans deserve a planet like this. You'll meet them soon. Their settlement is over there," Val said, pointing toward the lake.

"The planet seems nearly empty," Will observed as they made their way to the settlement. "Why aren't there more people on a planet this lovely?"

"It's not on the charts. Never will be, if I have my way."

"Why not?"

Val's voice was a deep, angry rumble. "Can you imagine what this place would become if a gang of renegades made a landing? Or the Kepler mining interests started ripping holes in it? Or the Watsonians decided to put buildings full of machinery on every open piece of ground? The galaxy is full of ugly chunks of rock for their kind to defile. I like to know that there's something men haven't ruined yet. Maybe I've heard too many tales of what happened to Old Earth, but I don't care. Bellaterra's safe as long as no one knows where it is, and I'm not telling anyone."

"How did you find it, Val?"

The big man did not answer, and when the first of the Bellaterrans raced up the forest path to greet the arrivals, Will understood. Three men arrived, followed closely by four women, and as they neared the settlement others joined them, singly or in small groups. They were a handsome people. All had the same fine hair, gold or gold-streaked, and the same luminous large eyes. The adults ranged in height from Vallandis' two meters to just below Will's shoulder, and in color from a deeper brown than the actor, through a spectrum of tan and copper and gold, to a light cream. They spoke everyone, haltingly, in the common tongue of space, but only Vallandis was able to converse with them in their own language. He was home, among his own people; and from his expression and his gestures and the laughter that burst from him at the least provocation, Will judged that he would be in no hurry to leave. To his own surprise, the thought pleased him.

They feasted at nightfall on a wide variety of fruits and drank cold water as clear as the air, and Will felt that he had never dined so richly, or with such joy. All through the meal, Vallandis acted as interpreter, but the Bellaterrans themselves did their best to be helpful. The women were beautiful, slender and graceful and eager to make their guests at ease. The younger ones were busiest of all, and one in particular was most solicitous toward Will. She singled him out, selected the most succulent fruit, peeled it for him, poured the water and lifted the cup to his lips, and for his comfort placed a soft cushion against the tree. When he leaned back to lick the last drops of sweet juice from his fingers, she laughed, threw her arms around his neck and began to lick the juice from his face, and then to kiss him. The Bellaterrans all around seemed pleased, and made no move to interfere. Will did not let their presence inhibit his response. Then he heard Vallandis' boisterous laughter, and the Bellaterran girl sprang to her feet, ran to Vallandis, and embraced him. Will rose and said, with more good humor than he actually felt, "Why don't you find your own girl, Val? We were just getting to know each other."

"This is my girl," Vallandis said, swinging her up in his arms and setting her down lightly at Will's side. Like a child, she took Will's hand at once in hers.

"I wouldn't have known."

"Well, she is." Val paused, then beamed proudly and announced, "She's the daughter of the daughter of my first son. Her name is Melimela. At least I think so. I lose track." He asked the girl a question. She replied at great length, with much laughter, and he nodded. "Yes, that's who she is."

"But how? She's at least . . . well, she's no child, and you can't be more than . . . no, it's impossible," Will said.

"I've spent a good part of my life at drivespeed travel, Will, and when you do that, funny things happen to time. I'll explain it some day. Right now, we've got something more important to talk about. How do you like Melimela?"

Will looked at the slim girl beside him, with hair bright as noon, soft skin the color of sunset, eyes as fresh and clear as dawn. "I like her very much. She's the most beautiful creature I've ever seen."

"Good. Take her hands in yours." Will complied, and Val went on, "Now, kiss the backs and then the palms. Let her do the same. Congratulations, both of you." He turned to the others, who had watched the brief ritual with obvious pleasure, and at his first words they broke into cries of jubilation. "They're congratulating you, too," he said to Will.

"Why?"

74

"You're married."

"Married?!"

"Yes. We Bellaterrans are an informal people, Will. We——"

Will was genuinely shocked by this offhand attitude. "Val, she's your own kinfolk! You know I can't stay here. Even if I could . . . how can you do this to your own family?"

"I know how things are, Will. So does Melimela. Nobody will force you to stay here. One of the oldest sayings of the Bellaterrans is 'Be happy while you may.' Do you understand that?"

"I can't even speak her language!"

Vallandis looked at his playwright, as if disappointed. "You're a healthy young man. A bit pale, but not bad looking. She's a beautiful young woman. Look at her. Are you really worried about not knowing her *language*?"

Will looked back sheepishly, then drew Melimela to him. "I guess I can learn," he said.

The feast became a festival, with dancing by everyone, declamations by the guests, song and chant by the hosts, and great merriment for all. Will did not hear it end. After embracing every Bellaterran in reach while Melimela, in turn, embraced the company, and after exchanging mutually unintelligible noises indicative of good will, he and Melimela slipped off to a shelter far removed from the celebration.

Will awoke once late in the night and heard her breathing softly beside him. All else was still; only her breathing, and no other sound in the universe. He turned to her and studied her moonlit features, so soft, so lovely. His, now, as he was hers. So this is how it happens, he thought. A day ago I was miserable and hated everyone, and now I'm here on this paradise with a beautiful bride by my side. He lay unmoving, musing, filled with wonder at his happiness. He had fled and struggled, worked and studied and traveled across the galaxy, learned to do a score of difficult and ultimately useless things, labored hard and been cheated of his just wages, and now a few moments had moved all the jagged fragments of his life into seamless conjunction; it was all worthwhile because Vallandis had taken him here and allowed him to make this golden woman his bride. She stirred and sighed and he took her in his arms. Everything was perfect.

At the beginning they needed no words beyond the simple phrases of the *lingua franca*. But soon they wanted to know things about one another that could not be expressed by embraces and laughter, and Will set himself to learn the language of the Bellaterrans. Melimela was a conscientious instructor, but he found the going difficult. Unlike most of the languages he had encountered, Bellaterran was not immediately recognizable as an Old Earth dialect. Here and there a familiar word turned up, but it always meant something entirely different from what Will expected. Bellaterran speech—they had no written forms—was rooted in a different kind of thinking. Will had no difficulty in learning the words, and his training enabled him to perfect his pronunciation rapidly, but he often grew confused, desperately so when Melimela clearly understood his words at times when he himself did not.

Will had never made a formal study of grammar, but his reading had made him aware of the existence of certain recurrent structural patterns in language. He looked for such patterns in Bellaterran and was disappointed. His failure to achieve real proficiency frustrated him all the more when he contrasted it with the apparent ease with which Melimela improved her grasp of the common language of spacefarers. Still, he was not displeased. Now, at least, they could converse more freely.

From time to time, as much to practice and display his old skills as to entertain his wife, an ever-appreciative audience of one, he would enact some of his best roles. Once, when he tired of solitary declamation, he recited one of the stories Brita had told him long ago. Melimela reacted excitedly.

"This is like the stories the old man tells!" she cried.

"What old man?"

"The reciter. The one who tells stories."

Will recalled a face he had not seen since the first night's festival. The broad forehead and the shape of the eyes had made him think of someone he once knew, but the memory remained misty until Melimela's words jolted it into clarity: Brita, his old storyteller, had had similar features. The man was a Qreddn reciter.

"When can we speak to him?" Will asked.

"Someday," she replied.

The imprecision annoyed him. Melimela had not yet mastered the concept of time sequence. A Bellaterran *someday* referred to all the future, from the very next instant to the end of time, without distinction. This was not much help, since Will wanted to speak to the Qreddn soon. He tried to clarify his wish. Melimela listened with close attention, wrinkled her brow, then nodded and said, "After the next sun rises, we go to the old man's home in the settlement."

Will was delighted. A Qreddn was sure to be a master linguist. He could clarify things that Will and Melimela, for all their earnestness, simply could not convey to one another. Vallandis might have done the same for him, but Will was reluctant to ask his help. They had seen little of one another since arrival, and Will enjoyed his feeling of independence from the troupe, seeing it as the cachet of manhood.

The next day Melimela and Will went to the settlement. They had not been there since their marriage, but much to Will's relief, no more notice was given to their arrival than had been given to their departure or their long absence. Curiosity was not a trait of the Bellaterran temperament. Melimela had picked a basket of small glossy-black berries, and when they came to the Qreddn's house she presented them to him. Will tried with no success to follow their conversation, but then the old man addressed him in the tongue he knew.

"My name is Qballan, of the house of Fourehx, son of reciters for six generations. I bid you welcome," he said.

"I am Will, of the Gallamors. I've come to ask your help in learning Bellaterran speech."

Qballan glanced at Melimela, then at Will, his expression kindly but amused. "You have the fairest teacher on the planet. An ugly old man will be far less inspiring."

"Melimela is beautiful and I love her very much, but in spite of all her efforts the learning is slow. With your help, I could learn faster," Will explained.

"Life is long. There is no need to hurry."

Will drew Melimela closer to him. "Sharing a language would bring us happiness. Why not enjoy the happiness as quickly as we can?"

Qballan pondered, then said, "That is sensible. I agree to help you. Best you stay here." At Will's sudden look of dismay, he added, "You will have privacy."

"It really isn't necessary . . . ," Will said weakly.

"What is necessary? It will be pleasant, and we will all enjoy your stay here. Evenings I recite tales to those who wish to listen. I tell them in the original tongue and in Bellaterran. It amuses the people and helps me to keep my memory fresh. Listen to the tales at night and we will discuss them the next day. You will soon speak as well as your lovely bride," Qballan said. He took them by the hand and led them to a spacious private chamber. "This is yours for as long as you stay with me."

"You're very kind, Qballan. What can I do in return?"

"For the present, learn well. We will speak of return when we know what I have given."

"That's fair. Qballan, I have a question: is it true that all Qreddn reciters are in contact, wherever they are in the galaxy?" Will asked.

"True in a way. I cannot explain it."

"A woman named Brita was my storyteller when I was a child. She was very good to me, but we were separated."

"Brita is of my house, the house of Fourehx. She is the best of all the reciters of our generation." Qballan studied Will closely for a moment, with new interest. "Were you a king's son, to have your own storyteller?"

"My father was a very rich and successful man, for a time. Can you tell me if Brita is well?"

"If she were not, I would have sensed it. As I have said, this is a difficult thing to explain, but it is so. Your old storyteller is well," Qballan said. He again fell silent, a thoughtful distant look in his eyes, and at last he smiled apologetically and said to Will, "I confess I am surprised. To think, a Qreddn reciter of the skill of Brita, working for a rich man, when emperors once begged for our services . . . ." He shook his head and sighed. "And I do not even do as Brita did. I sit by a fireside, telling tales to amuse myself and whoever chooses to listen. But still, I am happy. I know peace."

He looked off into the green distance beyond the doorway, and without turning, said, "A story is told of the last king of Toxxo, Pasilans Varam the All-capable. He dreamed of a splendid palace, and forced his people to build it for him. When he entered, he wept at the nakedness of the walls, and he ordered the finest painter on the planet to paint them with scenes recalling the great deeds of the Varam dynasty. The painter worked for a long time. On the day the last stroke was completed, Pasilans Varam gave the painter one hundred times the amount promised, then had the man's hands struck off so he could never duplicate his work. The nobles, enraged, rose against Pasilans Varam, slew him, and abolished the monarchy forever."

"What became of the painter?" Will asked.

"He lived comfortably for many years. He had never known wealth before, and he greatly enjoyed possessing it. On his deathbed, he honored the name of Pasilans Varam, saying he had given fair exchange."

That evening, after sunset, Qballan requested Will to light a small fire. He took up his place by the hearth and waited for the sky to darken and his little group of listeners to gather. Then, abruptly, he spoke. "This is a story I myself discovered as a young man. I tell it in one voice." He paused, and when he spoke again, this time in the common tongue, his voice was different. It was weary, drained, pale with time and many disappointments, the voice of a strong man at the end of his strength.

"No one now remembers when the wolves first came down from the far mountains. In the beginning they came singly, it is said, but soon they began to gather in packs that grew ever larger. By the time of our grandfathers, a single huge wolf pack numbering in the thousands ranged the countryside.

"The toll of sheep was fearsome. The great flocks owned by our people were decimated with each attack. Our sheep continued to breed at their prodigious rate, but even that was barely enough to keep pace with the ravages of the ever-growing wolf pack. When the attacks were at their worst, it was impossible to sleep for the piteous bleating of slaughtered animals. Our grandfathers were forced to plug their ears with wool in order to drown out the cries.

"Various measures were tried, without success. The wolves ignored the poisoned meat set out for them. They avoided the traps with unbelievable cunning and seemed immune to bullets. With great difficulty, and at great expense to the people, herds of deer were driven into the area to provide the wolves with a natural source of prey. The wolves fell upon them and devoured them all within a short time. When the last deer was gone, the wolves returned to the sheepfolds with keener appetites.

"Our people faced starvation. All defenses against the wolf pack had failed. Some spoke of migration as our last hope, but many believed that if we were to leave, the wolf pack would follow us to new lands and life would be the same. Apathy possessed our fathers. They lost all hope, and reconciled themselves to death.

"And then it was suggested that since their masters could not defend them, the sheep might be trained to defend themselves. In an earlier day this idea would have been greeted with derision, but our fathers had reached the point of desperation. They roused themselves for one final attempt at resistance.

"They began to breed sheep for size and strength. They took the biggest and strongest animals and fitted them with razor-sharp steel horns, steel spurs for their hoofs, and steel fangs. These sheep were then taught to reject their accustomed food and relish the taste of flesh. They were treated in ways calculated to arouse mistrust and ferocity. The sheep who could not change were left to the wolves.

"When they were fully transformed, the sheep were set loose upon the wolves. Within a brief period, the wolf pack was reduced to a handful of scarred and terrified fugitives, and soon after that no trace remained of the great pack that once roamed our land.

"But now the sheep refuse to give up their steel horns, and their spurs and fangs. They roam the countryside at will, and have taken to killing and eating our cattle. They ignore the poisoned meat set out for them. They avoid traps with almost human cunning, and seem immune to bullets. They breed at an incredible rate, and it has been reported that the young are now born with horns, spurs, and fangs."

When Qballan finished his tale, he drank a small bowl of water and then began his narrative over, this time in Bellaterran. Will listened carefully. He missed some subtleties, but he perceived a great deal more than he missed. The story seemed easier to understand than most Bellaterran conversation, and only in their next day's discussion did Will learn that Qballan had chosen this particular story because its single mode of action made it easier for a non-Bellaterran to follow. In succeeding days, the tales of Qballan became more complex, but Will listened carefully, asked many questions, and strained to fill his memory.

Will and Melimela stayed with the old storyteller for nearly forty planetary days, and when they were not with him they were alone together. From time to time a member of the troupe would visit Qballan to hear a story, and stay to talk with Will, but for the most part, the visitors honored the Bellaterran code of *laissez-faire*.

Will felt at home on this planet. He loved Melimela, he respected Qballan and enjoyed his stories, and he found each new day a joy. When at last they parted, he asked Qballan what he could do to pay him.

"Work hard at the language. Perhaps one day, if you stay, you will take my place," the reciter said.

"I couldn't," Will said, overcome by the suggestion. "I don't know the stories, and my Bellaterran . . . I'd like to do it, Qballan, but I don't see how."

"Your memory is good. You know many stories, and

can learn to make more. You have a strong and versatile voice, a clear way of speaking. All you need is the language. Will you work at it?"

Will nodded eagerly, and the reciter went on, "Visit me sometimes, and we will talk. When you seem ready, I will begin to teach the stories."

"I want to ask a favor, Qballan. If you don't object, I'd like to copy down the stories you've told, and use them in my studies."

The reciter looked at him in wonderment. "Can you set words down so that others may read them?"

"Yes. That's one of the things I did for Vallandis."

"Then you are surely the one to replace me. You can set down all the stories of Bellaterra before they are lost forever. Perhaps you can even devise a way for the speech of Bellaterra to be set down as your speech is."

"Maybe I could," Will said, awed by the role being thrust upon him, and surprised by his own unsuspected eagerness to accept it. More confidently, he said, "Yes, I can. I'll make a written language for Bellaterra and save all the stories. I'll do it, Qballan."

His mind was made up now, without a doubt. He was staying on this planet forever. He had told Melimela that he would remain, but she had seen him come with Vallandis and expected him to go again, despite his promise. He had mentioned to several of the company his desire to stay. They all smiled tolerantly at his words, and clearly gave them not one jot of belief. In solitary moments, he had even felt doubts himself. Bellaterra was a dazzlingly beautiful world, and each day brought delight. To make love under the stars, to swim in clear cool lakes and lie in one another's arms in a bowl of sunlight with sweet fruits at their fingertips, to sit silently on the crest of the hill overlooking the long lake and watch the sun go down: these were experiences of wonder to which he could return unsurfeited for a lifetime of days. But at times, when Melimela was not with him, he found no especial pleasure in lakes or sunsets or the antics of the small friendly animals that populated the plains and forests. In fact, he grew bored and wished for something to do. The Bellaterrans lived in a dreamy state of semi-wakefulness from which they seldom emerged. From time to time, one of them would look at a sunrise, a tree, a cloud, a bird, and shout with joy as if to announce a great discovery. At such times, they struck Will as being rather infantile. A Bellaterran could pass an entire day happily watching the capering of a fat, furry little *churrut* or a longtailed *grink*, but Will was not a Bellaterran.

Now his doubts were resolved. He had a task, something monumental and time-conquering, something he alone of all on the planet could accomplish. He would create his own immortality. Perhaps he would never truly create stories of his own, as he had pretended, and still hoped, to do; but except for the bards, no one had done such a thing for centuries. He could, and would, transcribe the stories of Qballan and the legends of Bellaterra, and he would bestow on the planet a written language of its own. When he told Melimela of his decision, he knew that she at last believed in his promise to remain with her.

The Twelve Systems Repertory Company left Bellaterra when the leaves were turning bright and the first faint chill came on the night air. Vallandis was the last to say goodbye.

Will found it hard to speak. "Goodbye, Val, and thanks for all you've done for me. It's been . . . I can never begin to repay . . ."

"You've paid me well," Vallandis said, raising a hand to silence him. "Nine good plays is more than any company in the galaxy can boast. I only wish you were coming along to act in them."

Will shook his head decisively. "I'm on Bellaterra for life, Val, thanks to you. You've led me to everything I ever wanted."

Vallandis waved off the words of gratitude. "Pure selfishness, my friend. I wanted someone to look after my planet and my family while I win fame among the stars. In truth, Will, much as I hoped for it, I didn't think you'd stay. I told Melimela so when she first saw you. But she didn't care. She wanted to be with you, even for a short time."

"Has she told you what I'm going to do?"

Vallandis smiled broadly. "She's told me what *she's* going to do in the spring. Congratulations."

"Isn't it wonderful, Val? Our child will be the first one brought up to read and write in the Bellaterran language."

"The Qreddn told me about your project. I suppose it's more important than being a wandering actor, but I doubt it will be as much fun. Good luck with it, Will. I'm glad I brought you to my planet."

"Don't look so sad, Val. You'll come back."

"I'll try. But if space doesn't get us, time will. You won't even know me next time. You'll be a lot older."

Will dismissed the notion with a casual gesture. "We'll both be older. A few years can't change us very much."

"No. Time is different out there. When you travel at drivespeed . . ." He paused, uncertain, then abruptly said, "You see how old Qballan is. When I last left Bellaterra, that old man looked younger than I do now, and Qreddn don't age quickly."

"That's impossible!"

"It's true. How old do you think I am, Will?"

"I don't know. Older than I am, but not *old*."

"You're married to the daughter of the daughter of my son. Think about that. The last time I checked the Galactic Standard Calendar, back on Stepmann VII, the year was 2604. That means I'm about eighty-six years old. But here, where it counts," he said, thumping his chest, "I'm not half that. I don't know exactly how old I am physically, and I don't much care, but I know I'm not closing in on ninety."

Will looked on, dumbfounded, and Val said, "Some people give a lot of importance to the GSC. They say it's the only thing that keeps the descendants of the Old Earth pioneers together and fosters a sense of continuity with the past. Maybe it does, but that doesn't mean I have to believe it. Don't look so shocked, Will."

The words came out faintly. "I was born in 2568. I'm nearly forty years old by the GSC. I'm twice as old as my wife."

Vallandis looked at him for a moment, then he burst into laughter. Will glared at him, stung by what he took to be callousness. "It's not funny, Val," he said angrily.

"It *is* funny! What do you believe, numbers spat out by a machine, or your own body? You're a young man, and Melimela is a young woman, and that's enough. You're not even twenty, whatever that foolish Galactic Standard Calendar tries to say."

Uncertainly but hopefully, Will said, "I never thought about it before. I would have said I'm about twenty."

"Then you are, and that's an end to it. Twenty is a state of mind, Will, and I wish by the blazing rings I could capture it again."

"I wish I could *understand* it."

"No one does, not even the people on Watson, and they claim to know everything. I've heard that they can give you figures and quote formulas, but they can't give reasons. And since nobody knows, why let it worry you?

"I won't, Val. But if it's true, then I won't see you for a long time. Maybe never again. Good luck out there."

"With your plays, we can't fail. Give my people a language, Will, and take care of my girl."

Vallandis embraced Melimela, and the two men clasped hands one last time. Each knew that it was their final parting. Space was too vast, time too long and erratic for friends to count on the future. But past and present were good enough.

Seasons passed quickly. In the last days of autumn, Will and Melimela returned to the settlement and once again shared the home of Qballan. Will marveled at his first sight of snow and rejoiced at the coming of spring, when all of Bellaterra returned to life and Melimela gave birth to a son. They named him Val. With his mother's golden skin and his father's brown hair, the child was the handsomest creature in the galaxy, as Will assured all who came to see him. He was a proud, happy father.

Bellaterran custom required mother and newborn child to spend the days among the women of the settlement until the child could walk. Will was not pleased with the enforced separation, but he respected the beliefs of his wife and the ways of his adopted planet. He busied himself in the mornings by listening to Qballan, and in the afternoons by transcription and study. His collection of tales grew, but his work on a written language slowed and finally came to a halt.

"I can't go any further, Qballan," he explained to his mentor. "There's too much I can't grasp. I just can't learn to think like a Bellaterran."

"I knew this would come, and it comes at a most opportune time," the reciter said calmly. "You must go to the ruins."

"What ruins? Where? I've never seen any ruins."

"They lie in the high country, twenty days' travel beyond the lake."

"Why should I travel twenty days to look at ruins? What good will that do me?" Will asked.

"The ruins contain stones with pictures on them. They can help you understand the Bellaterran mind and language."

"If they can help me, why didn't you tell me about them before this?"

Qballan shook his head solemnly. "Before this, the ruins could not have taught you. You were ignorant. Now you have learned enough to become confused. You perceive the need for guidance, and you know enough to choose what will guide you well, and avoid what will only mislead you. This is the time to study the ruins."

That evening Will discussed Qballan's advice with Melimela. By now, she was as interested as he was in his plans to create a written language for their descendants, and since her time was absorbed in the Bellaterran childhood rituals through which young Val was passing, she urged Will to journey to the ruins.

He left the settlement three days later. He traveled on a *haxopod*, a six-legged beast similar to animals he had seen on other planets. The Bellaterran *haxopods* were smaller in stature, and utilized only four legs. Their two foremost legs were atrophied into the cramped position of a suppliant's hands. They moved smoothly and quickly over all terrain, and Qballan assured Will that a *haxopod* could convey even an inexperienced rider to the ruins without discomfort or difficulty.

Will passed through forest and marshland, followed a river valley for some days, then ascended to the highlands. The air was cooler here, the terrain harsher and hardier. The soft colors and gentle outlines of the countryside around the settlement were replaced by sharp blacks and whites of light and shadow, and shapes that seemed etched against the sky. He came at last to a level expanse of stone and sand, a cold land buffeted by a moaning wind, a place unlike the temperate Bellaterran midlands he knew. Yet even this landscape had its beauty, like the sterile magnificence of space. He rode often by night, to enjoy the moonlight, and on his twentieth day of travel he came in sight of the ruins.

They jutted from the bare ground like crooked teeth in an old man's shrunken gums. As he rode closer, Will's heart sank at the sight of their abundance. A lifespan would be insufficient time to study the stones that straggled in fixed ranks halfway to the horizon.

It was with mixed feelings of disappointment and relief that he found many of the stones to be blank, and many more so badly eroded by time and wind that the marks on their faces were indecipherable. But the ones that remained were so astonishing that all other feelings vanished in the awe he felt when gazing on them. There, in flat linear engraving that seemed somehow to extend to great depths and sometimes to move before his very eyes, he saw things for which his mind had no analogue, his memory no words. At first he drew back, shaken by sights that seemed to clutch his consciousness in a tight, wringing grip; but his curiosity held him among the ruins. He returned to them, studied them, traced their lineation with his fingertips and copied it crudely in his own hand, and at night, alone under the fancied figures of the stars, he listened to the moaning wind and wondered at what he had seen.

New concepts formed in his mind. His thoughts moved in ways he could not explain. All was not yet clear, but certain confusions that had loomed like obstacles to his progress now vanished. The Bellaterran disregard of time appeared perfectly logical. The painstaking exactitude with which a speaker was required to indicate relative positions of persons and objects had once seemed absurdly, even maniacally, elaborate to Will; but now that he had seen and comprehended the message of the ruins, he understood the interlocking of place, time, and identity that lay at the core of Bellaterran thought. For the first time, he felt that he had glimpsed the ethos of the planetary diety, the creator and sustainer, the omnipresent giver-of-all. His mission now seemed possible of achievement.

On the last morning, riding away from the place of the stones, he stopped and turned for a final look, and on a sudden urge he shouted a single Bellaterran word into the silence to express his feelings. As he rode on, he tried to recast the expression into his own language, and found that he could come no closer than, "Now I know that I have always known what I always knew I did not know." So stated, it sounded foolish; yet it made perfect sense in Bellaterran.

He pressed the little *haxopod* hard all the way back to the settlement, eager to test his new knowledge by speaking to his friends and neighbors in their own language. On his way, he translated some of his songs and stories into Bellaterran. It came easily to him now, and he was pleased to see how greatly some pieces were improved in the process.

On the morning of the nineteenth day he stood on the far shore of the great lake, smiling in anticipation of his welcome. He could see the far thin smoke of the cooking fires. The homecoming feast was already being prepared. He circled the lake and entered the forest. At midday he emerged, about an hour's leisurely ride from the settlement, and he paused here for another look at the rising smoke. It seemed wrong. There were too many fires for the settlement, even in a time of festival. They were dense and thick now, and their color was wrong. He urged his mount on, and when he rode into a crosswind and smelled the smoke for the first time, he dug his heels into the weary animal's ribs in a seizure of fear.

He swung down from the *haxopod* in the center of the settlement, and the horror of the scene choked off the cry that rose instinctively from his throat. The festival place was crisscrossed with trails of blood. Hacked, mutilated bodies lay sprawled in the open, across the thresholds of their homes, and atop smoldering heaps of embers. He feared for a moment that some collective madness had seized them, but no weapons were to be found. This was the work of others. But who could have done such a thing to the Bellaterrans? Their oldest legends mentioned no enemies. The other Bellaterrans lived the same peaceful life as these people had, and dwelt as far away, in the opposite direction, as the ruins.

Shocked, horrified, sickened by the sight of blood and the stench of death, Will leaned against a wall, shuddering, until his strength returned. In the house of Qballan he found what he most dreaded. His wife and son had been butchered.

He sat numb and mute, cradling the bloody corpses in his arms, until he heard a low moaning. He laid Melimela's body down tenderly, placed young Vallandis by her side, and covered their faces. Then he went in search of the still living creature whose moans of pain were the only sounds to be heard.

He found Qballan hunched in a corner, doubled over, arms clutching his stomach. The old storyteller lay motionless, and only his spasmodic groans gave evidence of life. Will knelt beside him.

"Qballan, it's Will. I'm back," he said. "Poor old friend, what happened? Who did this to you?"

Qballan's once-powerful voice was weak and broken. His account of the massacre came in gasping phrases. A black ship landed. Thirty or forty men and humanoids emerged. The people of the settlement welcomed them. At the festival, the visitors suddenly turned on the Bellaterrans. Pursuit and slaughter had lasted through the next day.

"But why, Qballan?" Will begged. "Why did they do this?"

"They laughed . . . when I asked . . . . Slit my belly open. . . . I tried to survive . . . until you . . . ," the Qreddn forced out, then he said no more.

"You did, Qballan. You made it. I'm back now, and I'll help you," Will said.

Qballan died during the night. Will carried his body to where Melimela and Val lay, and sat over them silent, beyond weeping, until sleep overcame him.

The first grave was for his wife and child, the second for his friend and teacher. In the days that followed, he made a huge mass grave in the festival place and one by one placed the people of the settlement in it, keeping careful count. None had escaped. When the grave was covered, he leveled the village and put it to the torch.

III.

Trooper
of the
Sternverein

IN THE DESOLATE TIME that followed, Will often felt that
he would burst apart from the conflicts raging within
him. He wanted to remember every moment with
Melimela: the sweet scent of her hair, and the way it
caught the light of the setting sun; the smoothness of
her skin, the music of her voice, the taste of her kiss;
even the language they awkwardly shared, laughing so
often at his helpless confusion and always communicat-
ing, at last, through their love. But he wanted to forget
all these things, too, for they were a torment to him.
He wished that they had had a score of lifetimes
together, and then he wished as fervently that he had
remained a spacedrifter, never met her, never heard of
her world. At times he started from sleep in horror and
ran madly in the dark, sprawling headlong over roots and
stones, bruising and lacerating himself with branches
and briars. He felt none of this until he awoke deep in
the woods, aching and bloodied, naked, shivering with
the morning chill and the remembered dreams of dese-
crated corpses whose hollow voices wailed for vengeance. He forgot all he had learned from the ruins, took
to practicing his old skills, and performed sometimes
from light to dark and on into the black hours of the
night before his audience of the dead.

Once he tried to leave the settlement, to range Bellaterra in search of humankind. But the urge for companionship left him after a few days of travel, and he returned to the graves of his adopted people. At last he built himself a shelter on the hillside overlooking the burying ground, and here he remained. He told himself that he was waiting for Vallandis to return. In a sense, this was true, for he had nothing else to anticipate. There he stayed, waiting, indifferent to the days that lengthened into seasons and pursued their unchanging rounds. For time was an absurdity to him. If a man could at once be both twenty and forty, or forty and eighty, how could reasonable men speak of time? The Bellaterrans had been right to dismiss it from their language. And how much more meaningful was space, that great pitiless nothingness bringing forth random malevolence? Time and space and existence itself were all absurd and meaningless to him now. Nothing could be explained, and those who sought explanations were as foolish as those who offered them. Let the Poeites believe in their maelstrom, the Bellaterrans trust in their planetary diety, and the others place their faith where they chose; he would not hinder them or mock the contrivances that consoled them, but now he knew the futility of it all. Beliefs were walls of straw erected against a roaring wind that leveled forests. A man had to face the fact that he was nothing, his creations nothing, and the only purpose for existence was existence itself. Beyond that there was nothing, nothing at all, ever, anywhere in the universe.

Despair brought Will to contemplate death. He thought of starving himself, or plunging from a mountaintop, or opening his veins with the Lixian knife he still carried, but he had sunk into an emotional and mental topor. Nothing mattered. If he was to die, he would die; in his solitary state, a fall, a broken bone, an infection could bring his end. He did not care. He took no reckless chances, but neither did he take precautions.

Death was no better nor worse than life. To seek it out would be as foolish as to flee from it. So he lived on.

One day he built a fire in the ruined settlement and burned all the work he had done: Bellaterran legends and myths, the tales of Qballan, his own remembered stories. He decided to have them die here, with him, when his time came. The blind gropings of an extinguished race meant nothing to the universe. He stripped himself of everything but the memory of Melimela and the desire for vengeance.

In his isolation and despair, Drufe's Poeite epigraph had come back to him. "Nemo me impune lacessit" was a principle that could give meaning to continued life, a truism that excused survival in a purposeless universe. He would live for revenge. He bent all his thoughts to this end, creating plans and intricate designs, and after long brooding on this grim subject he realized that it, too, was futile. While he remained on Bellaterra he could do nothing but plot and hope and shake his fist at the anonymous and uncaring stars. If he left, he could do little more. He could not pursue the pirates alone, and no one would assist him. No one cared. The only law in the galaxy was force, and that was on the side of the marauders. To wreak vengeance he would have to adopt their ways, and that would make him one of them. His wife and son and all his friends would still be dead, and if there was awareness among the dead, they would look on his actions and be ashamed. Even revenge was pointless. The only thing left was to survive in the hope that a driveship would land. With the passing of time, he came to realize that he wanted to live, and to get away from Bellaterra. And thus he waited for two full planetary years.

One morning he was jarred into wakefulness by the shrill oscillating whine of a drivecoil. He sat upright, stunned, as the noise deepened to a ground-shaking hum and died abruptly on the clang of a driveship settling in the landing ring. He snatched up his ragged garments and ran to his lookout. Across the valley, on the high plateau, rose the upper portion of a white ship. Even from this distance, it loomed enormous. It was not *The Empress of Space*, nor could it be the raiders' vessel. Someone new had come to Bellaterra.

A clear trail led from the plateau to the settlement, and he was sure that whoever landed would eventually come that way. He hurried down the hillside to take up his position. If they came in friendship, he would ask for passage. If they were pirates or renegades, then he would die on Bellaterra and be reunited with his wife and son. One way or another, the waiting would be ended this day.

The newcomers were not long in appearing. Two of them entered the outer clearing, walking cautiously, circumspect, long-barreled pistols leveled and ready. They broke through the new growth, advancing alternately until both had circled the ruins of the settlement and returned to the burial mounds, then they conferred briefly. They were close to Will's hiding place, but their voices were too low for him to overhear. One of them stepped to an open spot in clear view of the hillside and gestured with his arms. The other remained by the mounds, alert.

Down the path and into the clearing came a dozen men. Like the two scouts, they were dressed in black from head to foot. All carried the same pistols, held in one raised hand with the barrel crossing the chest to rest on the opposite shoulder, ready for instant use. They marched as rhythmically as a machine, striding through the waist-high undergrowth as if it had been cleared for their passage. The clump of their boots on the packed ground was drumlike and regular, the swinging of their free arms in perfect unison. From his vantage point, Will looked on and felt a momentary thrill of admiration for such discipline. The admiration was tempered by a sensation of uneasiness akin to fear. They were too disciplined. Enemies or friends, the newcomers were formidable.

At a shouted command from their leader, the force slammed to a halt and stood rigid to receive a volley of orders. Will listened carefully. He could hear without difficulty this time, and while the constructions were awkward, the vocabulary was familiar. These black-clad men, far from being pirates, were lawmen in pursuit of a pirate force. It was all he had to hear. With his hands open and empty, arms low and out from his sides, he stepped out of concealment, and the click of a dozen weapons greeted his appearance.

The expression of the faces surrounding him made him aware at once of the outlandish sight he presented. His clothing was in rags, his hair and beard long, dirty, and matted, his outstretched hands dirt-seamed and the nails begrimed and broken, and his bare arms and legs were crisscrossed with the pale scars of old injuries and the red welts of fresh ones. He was a tall man, and loss of weight now made him appear even taller, and gaunt as a specter. Compared to the trim group before him, he was indeed an apparition.

"I greet you in peace. Welcome to Bellaterra," he said, startled momentarily by the sound of his own voice spoken aloud to other men.

"The rest, where?" demanded the leader of the men in black.

"Buried," Will replied, indicating with a nod of his head the mounds beside them. "I'm the only one left."

"And in hiding, why? Spying on us, why?"

"To see if you were the pirates, returned."

"And if pirates we are, what then do you do?"

"If you were pirates, I would have fled. But since

you're not, I welcome you and offer you hospitality. In return, I ask to leave with you."

The leader, a lean, wiry man with big hands and a brush of white hair set like a cap on his narrow head, fixed him with eyes as pale and expressionless as two pebbles, evaluating, alert, suspicious. At length he said, "A warship our vessel is. Not for passengers."

"You can't just leave me here. I've been alone on this planet for two years," Will said. He struggled to keep his voice from cracking.

"Travel with us, dangerous it is. Your skills, what?"

Will recited his abilities, exaggerating only slightly, while the unwavering pistols of the troopers held steadily on his chest. When he had finished, the leader stepped forward, close enough to touch him. He sniffed once, stepped back, and folded his arms. "An explicator and a skillman, these you are. Also very dirty. A warrior, not. The crew of *The Huntsman* warriors are," he said.

"I've never seen weapons like yours, but I can learn to use them."

"A training ship, this we are not."

"Another ship may never come, don't you understand that? The pirates landed here by sheer chance," Will said, his anxiety growing.

"About these pirates, tell."

"They landed where your ship is now and came to the settlement just as you did. The Bellaterrans were peaceful people. They had no treasure for anyone to steal, no weapons to defend themselves. I'm sure they welcomed the pirates as guests. And the pirates butchered them. That's all there is to tell." He saw no need to speak of his wife and son. They were gone, and the men in black could do nothing for them. That was all over.

The leader studied him carefully. "And you they spared, these pirates. Why?"

"I wasn't here. I came back and saw the bodies. One old man was still alive, and he died soon after."

"What did he tell?"

Will repeated Qballan's story. The leader weighed it for a time, then with a quick decisive gesture he signalled the troopers to lower their weapons and said to Will, "Here, two planetary days we spend. On the second day we leave, and you come." He stopped Will's thanks with a raised hand, and went on, "With us as a refugee you come, not a passenger, not a warrior. Your passage you will earn. But while aboard *The Huntsman*, the rules you must know and obey. Over-sergeant Kellver will instruct."

"I'll learn them, I promise," Will said earnestly.

"This, always remember. The strength of the Sternverein, in training and discipline it lies. Orders are obeyed, questions not asked. Exceptions we do not make. Come with us, and these conditions you accept. The penalties, very harsh they can be."

"I accept."

The leader signalled to a hard-faced man with a broad chest and shoulders and thick stumpy legs. He stood a head shorter than Will, but extended to about three times his breadth. "Over-sergeant Kellver, this man in our regulations you will instruct. With us he comes." Turning to his new addition, he said, "Your name, tell."

Will Gallamor was a creature of Bellaterra. He no longer existed. He was as extinct as Lon Rimmer. From out of a book came a long-forgotten name, and he gave it without hesitation. "Caliban."

"Colonel Blesser of Sternverein Security I am, commander of the pursuit craft *Huntsman*. The others soon you meet."

With that, Colonel Blesser left them, and the first regulation Over-sergeant Kellver taught the new recruit was the one concerning cleanliness. He led him to the lake, watched him scrub down and shave, personally trimmed his hair to a fingernail's length, and outfitted him in a coverall that was worn and patched but spotlessly clean.

"Now you're human again," he said. "A clean trooper is a disciplined trooper, remember that and no trouble."

"I'll remember it."

"Remember this, too, Caliban." Kellver pointed to the seven red stripes that slashed diagonally across the forearm of his tunic. "When you see a man with stripes like these, or with anything on his shoulders, like the Colonel, him you call 'sir.' Understand?"

"Yes, sir."

"Good. Now, some more rules I will teach," Kellver said. He proceeded to recite a list of regulations that seemed to cover every possible eventuality. When he had gone on for some time, he stopped and announced that these were the basics, and the more detailed ones would follow the midday meal. "Any questions?" he concluded.

"Yes, sir. What's the Sternverein?"

"The Sternverein a trading league is, with the largest fleet in the galaxy. Of all the driveships in active use, one out of eleven belongs to the white fleet of the Sternverein, it is said. Proud to be part of it, so I am," Kellver said.

"But you don't *look* like traders, sir."

Kellver gave one sharp bark of laughter and slapped the handle of his pistol. "Sternverein Security trades with these, Caliban, and we are the Security force in this sector. For our freighters, the spacelanes must be kept safe, free from pirates and raiders. This we do." He laughed once again, shaking his head, and said, "No, traders we are not. Now, no more questions. Come and eat."

The crew accepted the newcomer easily enough. After

a few unimaginative remarks about his changed appearance, they returned to their own conversations, amicably ignoring him. In an attempt to win their friendship, he pointed out some of the choice fruits and berries, even picked some and tried to distribute them, but the troopers preferred ship's rations to the fruits of Bellaterra. He did not try to press them.

He listened to them talk, and found that some of the others spoke in the same odd way that Blesser and to some extent Kellver employed, a pattern he found almost comical. But he found nothing funny about Sternverein Security or the troopers. Whatever their way of speaking, they were very serious men, in a very serious profession. Their mission was to hunt down and destroy anything that threatened the merchant fleet. This they did devotedly and efficiently, and they were well paid for it. They spoke of their work with evident pleasure.

The Huntsman lifted off precisely on schedule, entered highdrive minutes later, and Caliban was off duty for the next two watches. He went to his quarters and sprawled out on his bunk, but could not sleep. Aimlessly, for no reason but simply to occupy his time in hopes of boring himself to the point of sleep, he drew out his Lixian dagger and went through a complicated feat of manipulation. While he was in the midst of it. with the blade whirling and flashing forbiddingly, Trooper Eis entered the compartment and at once seemed transfixed by the feat. Caliban flashed his quick performer's smile of welcome, climaxed the stunt with a difficult twirl, and ended by balancing the blade on a fingertip.

"Where did you get that blade?" Eis asked at once.

"A Lixian I once knew gave it to me."

"Then you witnessed his termination. He made you kin," Eis said.

"Yes, that's right. I was to stand for all the males of his family——"

"And a woman stood for the females. This took place where no other Lixians were to be found."

"How do you know?" Caliban demanded.

"I, too, am a Lixian," Eis said proudly, drawing himself up to his full height. He was a good size for a human, deep-chested and broad-shouldered, but he would have been a dwarf among the towering Lixians.

"I've seen Lixians, Eis. I know what they look like."

The reply was cold; something close to a challenge, by its tone. "My parents were human. I was raised on Lixis, in the household of a major clan father. I am Lixian by nurture, as you are by your act of witness."

"I'm sorry, Eis. I misunderstood," Caliban said sheepishly.

"I accept your apology. Tell me of the Lixian you knew."

With plenty of time at his disposal and no inclination to sleep, Cal was prepared to tell the story of Longshank in minute detail. He had not gotten much past the beginning when Eis interrupted him. He looked very uncomfortable.

"Do you speak the High Lixian dialect?" he asked.

"No, I don't."

"Not even a few words?"

"Not even one word, Eis. Why?"

"When the subject is honor, one speaks in High Lixian. It is the custom."

Cal shrugged. "Too bad. I guess I can't tell you about Longshank."

"Apparently you can not. But then . . ." Eis frowned as if he were weighing a deep matter of conscience. He went on, a bit cautiously, "It may be that the restriction was intended as a measure to assure secrecy. If that is so, then between the two of us . . . certainly, it would not be . . ."

"I think you're right, Eis," Cal said, sensing the desired answer. "Longshank didn't use High Lixian."

"Yes, it must be," Eis said confidently. "And so you may continue in your own tongue."

Cal proceeded, and found himself taking even more pleasure in the telling than Eis was evidently taking from his role as listener. It was good to have an audience again, even an audience of one, and that one an undemonstrative Lixian permanently preoccupied with the demands of an intricate code of honor. After two years of solitude, any audience was welcome.

When the story was completed, Eis clasped Caliban's hand firmly and said, "Be encouraged, brother. The one you knew as Longshank is restored to honor. I myself was on Lixis when the woman arrived, and I saw all the necessary ceremonies performed."

"That's good news, Eis. I wondered whether Poldo would ever make it to Lixis."

"She did indeed do so." Eis slumped back on his bunk and sighed. "Longshank chose well: a woman who cleared his name and a man who can spread the story of his final honor. I will think of him in my next meditation."

Caliban hesitated, but then decided to ask, "Eis, can you tell me why you left Lixis?"

The trooper did not reply at once. He pondered, looked searchingly at the newcomer, and at last said, "You are a Lixian by virtue of your witness, and a warrior by your presence on this ship. You may be told." He rose and checked the corridor, then closed the hatchway firmly and returned to his bunk. "My family were free traders," he began. "They came to Lixis in a time of plague, and all succumbed but me. I was raised by a clan father as one of his own brood. It was a good life. I won honor early. One day humans came, and when they saw me, and heard me addressed as a Lixian, they questioned me. Their leader advised me to leave with them. When I declined, he said, 'You're human, boy. You're not one of these cat-faced, spider-legged freaks, you're a man.' The insult was beyond endurance, and I slew him. Since he was a guest, I was disgraced."

"Too bad you killed him," Cal said sympathetically.

"If I had not slain him, I would have been equally disgraced."

Cal said, "That's a hard spot to be in. I'm sorry." Eis was silent, and Cal went on, "So you left Lixis and joined Sternverein Security to regain your honor."

"Precisely. Soon we will run these pirates down and do battle, and I will have my opportunity."

Caliban nodded absently. He could think of no suitable comment. Whatever Eis might think, he did not consider himself a Lixian, and he certainly did not share the Lixian enthusiasm for honor through battle. He was hoping for a brief uneventful voyage and an early planet-fall, not for combat. His long isolation on Bellaterra had led him to conclude that honor—or anything else —purchased by blood is purchased at too dear a price. Had he been in the settlement when the pirates arrived, he would have fought, and would certainly have been killed, and quite honorably, in anyone's eyes—except perhaps the pirates'. He would be just as dead as if he had died a whimpering coward, and nothing at all would have been accomplished. It was not that he favored cowardice; but it seemed to him that other alternatives must exist, some unexplored middle ground scorned by Lixians. This was not a subject to discuss with Eis. Indeed, there were few topics on which one could converse with a Lixian. They were a dignified race, loyal to friends and kin, with a high sense of honor; but they were devoid of humor and uninterested in any talk not involving honor won or lost. Caliban reflected sourly on the prospects of sharing quarters with Eis, and hoped the third man in their compartment would be livelier company.

He met the third man at the end of the watch, when Eis went on duty. His name was Atha, he was immense in size and bulk, as strong as any other two men on board, loud of voice, and reasonably pleasant company except when he was boasting of his battle exploits. The boasting came naturally, for Atha was a Skeggjatt. He wore his near-white hair long and plaited, in the style of the Skeggjatt battle schools. His appearance was formidable, but Cal won his respect by a letter-perfect recitation of a Skeggjatt battle-chant, and from that point on, could do no wrong in Atha's eyes.

The big man looked forward to a showdown with the pirates as eagerly as did Eis, but for a different reason. He did not care about honor; he craved battle.

"I've got nothing against the pirates personally, Cal," he said cheerfully one day in the mess room. "I expect we'll find a number of my people among them. For that matter, I could as easily be a pirate as a Sternverein trooper, and they could be wearing the black uniforms. It doesn't matter."

"But aren't you fighting *for* something?" Caliban asked.

"Sure. The joy of battle. The matching of skills, the test of manhood," Atha said. There was a look of anticipation in his eyes that Caliban found more disturbing than the words.

"No, I mean something beyond all that. A cause. An ideal."

Atha looked around the table, mystified, and shook his head. He turned back to Cal. "You just don't understand. Look, Cal, I've seen you juggle seven daggers right here in the mess room, after a meal. Now, why do you do a thing like that? Idealism?"

"No, it's my skill. I'm good at it, and I want to be better."

Atha grinned broadly. "There's your answer. I'm a Skeggjatt warrior, and I feel about battle the way you feel about your skills."

A voice from the other end of the table said, "If you like fighting, Atha, you ought to join the Expedition."

"What, that rich man's hunt for ghosts?" Atha said with scorn.

"No, no, I mean the expedition against the Rinn."

Another trooper broke in, "They've tangled with the Rinn a few times in recent years. They're still recruiting, and the pay is good."

"It should be," the first one said. "The Sternverein is backing it. That's what I hear, anyway."

Atha shook his head. "Not for me. They keep saying that one day they'll commission a battle armada to wipe out the Rinn. A Skeggjatt fights face to face. I don't want any part of something as big as the Expedition."

"I hear they've seen some action already," the first trooper said.

"Not the kind I crave. I want to meet those pirates."

"You will, Skeggjatt. Blesser can smell them out halfway across the galaxy."

"The sooner the better, I say. I feel like I'm rusting." Atha dug Cal in the ribs, nearly unseating him, and said, "Do something to cheer us up, skillman, before we get so bored we start fighting with each other."

"The knife trick," someone called, and another said, "Give us a battle song."

"Let him decide," Atha bellowed. "It's his skill, and it should be his choice."

Cal thought for a moment, then announced, "I'll tell

106

you a tale that I learned from Qballan, a Qreddn reciter. I tell it in one voice." And he began to recite the fable of the sheep and the wolves as Qballan had told it.

The troopers were silent for an uncomfortably long time after he ended. They avoided his eyes, and each others' as well. Their reaction unnerved Cal. He had never before affected an audience this way, and it made him uneasy. He had to do something.

He sprang to his feet, rapped on the table to break the awkward silence and catch their attention, and said in the rapid singsong he had mastered aboard the *Triboulet*, "Well, now, look at all of us sitting here with our faces hanging down in our laps like a circle of merchants with a cargo of nice ripe *streefrit* eggs and a pair of burnt-out drivecoils, and no replacements to be had between here and the far edge of the next galaxy. That's not your style, troopers, and I who know it say so. You're off your beat, out of phase, sub-light shufflers in a drivespeed race, and what you need to get those gut coils turning once again is a skillshow . . . yes, that's right, troopers, I said a skillshow," he chanted, moving smoothly around the table to pry first one man, then another, from his mood. They listened. One smiled, a second joined him, and Cal went on, "And it just so happens that aboard this magnificent vessel, on this self-same spotless deck—in fact, within the confines of this spacious and luxurious dining hall (here several of the troopers burst out laughing), we have a skillman of galactic fame and incredible achievement, nimbler than the feather-jugglers of Grnx, faster than a Karrapad blackjack dealer (here Atha, a notoriously unskilled shuffler of cards, guffawed and delivered a bruising nudge in the ribs to his neighbor on either side), more mystifying than even The Amazing Saltimbanco, Boy Wonder of the Nine Systems and Precocious Prestidigitator of Skyx. . . ." He paused, spread his arms dramatically, and then announced, "Caliban the Conjuror, who will now perform, for the delight and edification of this select circle, a feat of legerdemain taught him by——"

His spiel was rudely interrupted by a summons over *The Huntsman's* intercom: temporary trooper Caliban to report immediately to the bridge. The little group of loungers broke up, and Cal himself was off at once, wondering what reason Blesser might have to see him. He felt a vague uneasiness, a kind of pre-established guilt, although he was unable to think of any cause, favorable or unfavorable, for the order. He had done a bit of storytelling, performed a few tricks for the crew, won a comfortable sum at cards (but won it honestly), and heard neither praise nor blame for his behavior aboard ship. He had not seen the Colonel since leaving Bellaterra. Given his choice, he would have left their acquaintance unrenewed. But he had no choice. And "temporary trooper Caliban" had an ominous sound.

Immediately upon his arrival at the bridge, before he could say a word, Blesser pointed to him and said, "You have certain voice skills, so you claim. True?"

"Yes, sir."

"These skills, tell. Can you imitate the voice of a woman and a child?"

"It's been a long time since I tried, but I think I can do it, sir."

"Good. At the end of the next watch, our speed we will reduce. A distress message you will transmit for the pirates to hear." He turned and beckoned to another officer. "This trooper you will instruct and prepare." The order given, he turned his attention elsewhere.

Over-lieutenant Zoss, the communications officer, led Cal to the transmission unit and expanded on Blesser's terse order. Zoss looked like a younger version of the Colonel, but was a bit less formal.

"The pirates don't know we're this close, trooper," he said, "and they've never seen our ship, so they'll probably follow their usual method and cruise at sub-lightspeed, monitoring for distress signals. We're going to give them one, and hope they'll attack." The prospect drew a fierce smile from Zoss.

Cal swallowed, convinced now that the Sternverein Security troopers were all mad, officers and enlisted men alike. Not satisfied to pursue pirates, they had to lure them into attacking. He had no love for the pirates, to be sure, but this seemed to be an excess of zeal. "Will they attack a pursuit ship, sir?" he asked.

"Not knowingly," Zoss said, and laughed unpleasantly. "But *The Huntsman* will show up on their scanners as a freighter. All our combat modifications are internal. They'll line up to board a helpless freighter with all the men injured or dead and only a few women and children left, and instead they'll find us waiting for them. Now, here's the message you're to transmit . . . ."

Cal rehearsed the message, and after a few tries his voices were perfect. The watch ended, they dropped to sub-lightspeed, and his heart-wrenching plea for assistance was broadcast in all directions. Zoss had him record twelve different calls, and he set them to go in sequence at irregular intervals. He threw the last switch, turned to Cal, and said, "Now we wait. You stay here, in case you have to respond."

After two uneventful watches he was allowed to return to his quarters to sleep. He reported back to the bridge for the next watch. Blesser, too, had just rested and eaten and was now checking the instruments and reports. When he had satisfied himself concerning the ship's readiness, he sat down, took a mug of *scoof*, and beckoned to Cal to join him.

"For alertness, drink. A long wait it may be," he said.

"Thank you, sir."

"This skill of yours with the voice, very good it is. Much time you must have been in learning it. Tell."

Cal told of his days with the Twelve Systems Repertory Company, and went on to speak of his early days with Prospero and The Original Galactic Circus. Talking relieved the tension that had been building in him, and he went on at length about his training, the people he had met and places he had visited. Blesser appeared to take an interest in his story, and interrupted him from time to time with questions. His manner was almost friendly, and Cal felt his apprehension diminish as they talked. Perhaps Blesser and his troopers were not so bad after all, he told himself. After all, they were protecting the decent inhabitants of the galaxy from pirates and raiders, improving trade, civilizing, increasing contact between civilizations . . . and then he happened to mention Prospero's dream of recovering the weapons of Old Earth. It was a slip of the tongue; he had sworn secrecy long ago and would have honored his vow, but the words came out before his remembered promise could check them, and Blesser pounced on them at once.

"This old magician of yours, a fool he is," the Colonel said angrily. "In all the centuries since exodus, no one else has sought the Old Earth weapons, this he believes? Scientists of the Sternverein, since its foundation, methods they have been testing to enable us to carry fusion projectiles and laser devices on shipboard. But no success have they had. A shield must be found so the drivecoils insulated may be; otherwise all explodes. Someday a shield will be found, this I believe. Then the pirates and all enemies we will destroy."

"I *thought* Prospero was on the wrong track, sir. It just didn't make sense that the men of Old Earth would come out here without their weapons."

"Not by choice did they without weapons come. Some tried. On reaching drivespeed, they brighter than a star

110

in nova flared up. The exact reason no one knows, except that a drivecoil reaction it is. But our scientists the solution will find." Blesser was silent, a brooding look on his narrow face, then he said in a voice of absolute confidence that restored all of Cal's fears, "Disorderly and undisciplined this galaxy is, trooper, and in it many dangerous races are. With the great weapons of Old Earth, the Sternverein peace and order and safety for all would bring. Under our rule, all would prosper. A good place it would be. First the galaxy, then all the universe we would pacify."

"Yes, sir. But maybe some races . . . ," Cal began tentatively.

"Yes? Tell."

"Maybe some races would rather be left alone to take their chances."

"Dangerous races they would be. With them we would begin."

Cal nodded. In the face of such words he could only remain mute. Blesser, given those elusive weapons of Old Earth, would have descended on Bellaterra, found the natives dangerous, and destroyed them. The pirates had done it first, crudely and brutally, acting without design, but the end result in either case was identical. The pirates killed innocent strangers in the name of sport or plunder; Sternverein troopers would kill them in the name of peace and order. Either way, the innocent people died, and then the killers hunted one another down. Cal faced the fact that Blesser and his troops were indeed mad, and their madness was a contagion in the galaxy.

Cal had another tense uneventful watch in which to ponder his conclusions, and then the pirate ship appeared in the scanners and every alarm on *The Huntsman* went off at once. The men took up shipboard battle formation and waited for contact.

111

The black ship drew closer, and after a bit of maneuvering, settled to a parallel course a few hundred meters away. Two suited figures emerged, then a third. The trio joined themselves by a line and crossed the emptiness to a gaping airlock of *The Huntsman*. Ordinarily, an open airlock was a certain sign that nothing survived aboard a driveship; but *The Huntsman* had been redesigned, under Blesser's direction, with a double outer lock. The pirates boarded, made their way through an inner port, and sent back promising reports of an apparently unoccupied and well-laden freighter. The distress messages caused an uneasy moment until one of the boarding party explained that they must be recordings, programmed to transmit until the ship no longer functioned. Meanwhile, Zoss was monitoring and recording all communication between the pirates.

As soon as they passed the second port, Blesser gave the signal. Zoss jammed all communication and secured the inner port. In seconds the pressure was up, and the startled pirates confronted a rank of armed men. Their helmets were roughly removed, and they were led to a compartment where Blesser awaited them. He was unceremonious.

"For piracy, to death you are sentenced. Tell us what we want to know and your death, easy and fast it will be. Otherwise, slow and painful." he said.

The spokesman for the boarding party weighed Blesser's words, gave a contemptuous laugh, and said, "We have an offer for you, Blesser. Stop crowding us, and we'll let you and your men live. Chase us all you want, but don't crowd us. We don't like it."

Blesser nodded to Kellver. The husky Over-sergeant stepped before the three captives, his long-barreled pistol at the ready, and said, "All right, you've made your boast. Now, how will you die? Fast or slow?"

The three remained silent. One glanced about nervously, but the others were unmoved. Kellver took his place before the one who had addressed Blesser and said, "Well?" The man grinned lazily and spat. He and the others laughed. Kellver studied the spittle crawling down his tunic, looked over the three prisoners, and then with a sudden flick of his wrist laid open a gash on the spokesman's forehead with the barrel of his pistol. "You're as stupid as the rest of them," he said wearily, and ordered the troopers, "Get them below. The Colonel wants the information before the end of the watch."

Cal returned with Blesser and Zoss to the bridge, where he was put to studying the voice of the boarding party leader. He found it unpleasant to think of a human, even a pirate, being tortured to death while he sat up here learning to mimic his voice in hopes of luring others to the same fate, and tried to fortify himself by thinking of Bellaterra after the pirates' departure. It did not help as much as he had expected it to.

Before the turn of the watch, Kellver reported to the Colonel. On his way out, the Over-sergeant stopped beside Cal. "This is the bunch that destroyed your people, trooper. I'd have given you a chance at them, but we were in a hurry. When we get the others, a chance for revenge I'll save you," he said.

"That's all right, sir. You don't have to."

"I do, trooper. A right and a duty, vengeance is," the husky Over-sergeant said solemnly.

Zoss burst in on their conversation with a message for Cal to deliver. He asked first, "The voice of the leader of these three—have you got it?"

"Pretty well, sir. If you keep the interference at a fairly high level, I should be able to pass."

"I'll do that. His name was Chandy, and he was the second-in-command of *The Hunter*."

Cal looked up sharply at what he took to be a slip of the tongue. "*Hunter*, sir? Do you mean——"

"No mistake, trooper. Their ship is called *The Hunter*," Zoss said. "Captain's name is Ascher. You will speak to no one else. Ready?"

Cal scanned the message, nodded, and Zoss opened the channel. "Ascher, do you hear me? Are you receiving me? Come in, Ascher," Cal said in the harsh voice of the dead raider.

"What's wrong, Chandy? Do you need help?" a voice crackled across the space between the ships. "I've got another party ready."

"No need, Ascher. Everything's under control. There was an automatic reseal set on the airlock, and the mechanism must have caused the interference."

"Can you get back?"

"I've got a better idea, Ascher. This ship is the best haul I've ever seen. She's *The Pandora*, a cargo ship bound out from Stepmann with supplies for a new colony."

"What's your idea?" came the distant voice.

"Let's get *The Pandora* to the nearest planet and strip her at our leisure. From the looks of her, she can move as fast as *The Hunter*."

"Got to think about that," came Ascher's voice. After a pause, he said cautiously, "I don't know this sector well, Chandy. It could be risky. I think we ought to take what we can and let her drift."

"Ascher, she might have the weapons we've been hoping for. We could fit her out as a battle cruiser. We'd have our own fleet."

The voice from the black ship sounded thoughtful this time. "With two ships, we could finish Blesser and his blackcoats once and for all."

"Right. Give me the coordinates of the nearest habitable planet. I'll set a course and meet you there as soon as I can."

"Don't rush me, Chandy. I've got to think."

Zoss, listening in on the exchange, turned the interference to a level that made communication marginal, and signalled to Cal, who said frantically, "Ascher, can you hear me? Send those coordinates fast, before we lose contact!"

Ascher's reply was a set of coordinates. As soon as they were received, Zoss increased the interference to the blocking point and turned the directions over to Blesser. When he returned, he thumped Cal's shoulder.

"Good work, trooper. You've earned your passage," he said.

"Thank you, sir. Do you think they believed it?"

"The coordinates look right. I think we've got them at last."

"That one I imitated, Chandy—he seemed to know the Colonel."

Zoss nodded. "They all do. The Colonel's been hunting down pirates for as long as anyone remembers. Get yourself some rest now, Caliban. We'll be touching down in about seventeen hours, and after that we'll be busy."

"Fighting, sir?"

Zoss beamed and rubbed his hands. "With any luck at all, we're in for a good scrap at last."

Cal tried to smile. "Just what I wanted, sir."

He went to his compartment and threw himself down on his bunk, exhausted from the prolonged strain and the anticipation of worse to come. Atha came bursting in just as he was on the verge of sleep. The big Skeggjatt was in high spirits, humming and chuckling to himself as he checked over his issue and his own personal armory, calling out to passing shipmates who answered

115

with battle-boasts of their own. Everyone aboard seemed to be looking forward to an encounter with the pirates, and Cal feigned sleep to avoid a conversation that would only make him miserable. They were all mad, every one of the troopers and the pirates as well, and he saw no way he might win them back to sanity. With luck, he might manage to save himself, but they were beyond help.

The Huntsman was a busy ship in those final hours before planetfall. Cal made himself as unobtrusive as possible, but Kellver came upon him and led him off to the issue room.

"Lucky to have you aboard, we are. You can be our anthem-maker, and give us a battle song," the Over-sergeant said as they hurried along the passageway.

"I guess that means no fighting for me, then," Cal said, trying to conceal his relief. The relief was immediately deflated by Kellver's remark.

"We'll see that you're in the thick of it, we will. Your fighting privileges and honor-rights, we could not deny them to you."

Things were getting serious. "You know, sir, I never did get a chance to fire a weapon," Cal said.

"That you will do now. Also try out blades. Do you know swordsmanship?"

"I know it somewhat," Cal replied. He had learned a rather flamboyant style from Vallandis: flashy, often impressive moves, but all for the show. His combats all ended with a clean and graceful lunge trapped between elbow and ribs, followed by a death scene, the whole repeated as often as the audience demanded. No one was put to death on the stage these days except in the cycle-dramas of Av, and the Twelve Systems Repertory Company had stayed far from the Avic domain for this very reason. Their devotion to the theatre did not exceed their commitment to longevity.

They began with the long-barreled pistols. Kellver watched in pained silence as his newest trooper sprayed round after round everywhere in the firing range except into the target, then said with forced heartiness, "The hand gun is not your weapon, this is plain. I thought that all along, so I did. You have the moves of a swordsman." He turned to the arms rack, plucked out a pair of long, light, basket-hilted sabres, and tossed one to Cal, who caught it gracefully and went to the guard position. "You look more like a warrior with a sword in your hand. Let's see how you use it," Kellver said, relieved, taking a cut at Cal's head.

Cal parried and retreated, and Kellver pressed his attack. "Stop defending, trooper. Attack!" he cried. "I'm not your shipmate, I'm a pirate. I raided your planet and killed your people, remember? Will you run from me?" Cal moved in, and Kellver said fiercely, "Ah, that's it! That's the way, now. Slash, slash, thrust. Quicker with your recovery. Change your patterns and keep me guessing. Good."

After a workout that left them both winded, Kellver pronounced Cal a fit swordsman and led him to a corner of the issue room where a row of black jerkins hung. The Over-sergeant looked through them, selected one, and tossed it to Cal, who nearly collapsed under the sudden weight, much to Kellver's amusement. "These are battle-jackets, trooper, No hand weapons can penetrate them. You may collect bruises or broken ribs, but you won't get any steel in you."

"What about the head and arms?"

"For the head, you get a helmet. Arms and legs, they're your lookout, so they are."

Cal hefted the thick jerkin. It was a staggering weight to bear into battle, but he would gladly have carried twice as much to increase his chances of returning alive. His only objection was to the effect all this extra weight would have on his speed. He did not mention the fact to Kellver, but he was planning to base his personal tactics on fleetness of foot. His swordsmanship might be passable, even praiseworthy, for an actor and reciter; but he knew that the clumsiest of the pirates would be his master in close combat. The mere fact of their survival made that a certainty. So he accepted his sword and battle-jacket gratefully, set his helmet securely on his head and adjusted the neck shield for maximum coverage, but put his trust in his feet.

The planet had no name. Centuries before, it had been rejected for colonization as "environmentally undesirable," a term which might signify a wide variety of surface conditions, all of them unpleasant, though not necessarily fatal. On this particular planet, the term stood for two things: a planetary day 761.6 galactic days in duration, and eternal rain.

Rain fell from an iron-gray sky, through sodden air, to inundate this nameless waste of stone and mud and water. The uplands were smooth-scoured to naked glistening rock by an unceasing fall that varied from light drizzle to buffeting downpour. The hillsides were corrugated into sharp rock ridges and broad channels of foaming runoff, the lowlands buried beneath an impenetrable mist from which bloated yellow vegetation protruded in random clusters, and the roar and rush of white water rose in unintermitting muffled thunder.

Landing was difficult and dangerous, and the long march on the pirates' base was a grueling ordeal. Before the men had covered a single kilometer, their battle-jackets were soaked through and the troopers stumbled under the additional weight. Even Atha panted from exertion. Blesser called for a halt and conferred with his officers. The word came down through Kellver that battle-jackets were to be removed and cached on this spot.

They pressed on directly to the pirates' camp, a barren plateau rising from an irregular clearing. The mist lay heavy and obscuring on the open ground. At one point, a spur of vegetation reached almost to the base of the plateau. The ascent was steepest here, difficult but not impossible. On the far side of the plateau the rock face sloped gently up from the clearing and could be gained by a running man, but the lack of cover made it a poor route for the initial assault. Blesser surveyed the ground personally and then withdrew to plan the attack.

Cal waited with Eis, Atha, and two other troopers. They did not talk much. Eis, two bandoliers of Lixian finger knives crossed over his chest, sat with his back to a tree, in light meditation. Atha stood with one hand on the hilt of his sword, the other on his pistol butt, lips moving soundlessly as he recited an ancient Skegg-jatt battle-charm. The two other troopers sat sheltered beneath overhanging branches, chewing *zaff* leaves. Despite the taciturnity of the group, Cal felt a closeness with them that he had never felt among the skillmen or actors he had traveled with, or even among the peaceful folk of Bellaterra. The show people were total individualists, proud of their own skills and respectful of others', but isolated and distant from those among whom they spent their entire lives. Even the Bellaterrans, for all their belief in the unity of life, lived it for the most part in separation from their neighbors. He remembered words of his father's—the first time he had thought of him in many years—and felt ashamed of the ready acceptance he had once given them. "Teamwork is fine for Quiplid tumblers and weaklings," Kynon had once said, "but the real man, the skillman, works alone. He wins or loses through his own efforts." To a bedazzled boy, those were fine bold words. But here, with a little band of men facing death together, they rang hollow.

Cal disliked the Sternverein and its ways, rejected the galaxy-wide enthusiasm for revenge, and had no great desire to spill any man's blood, nor to have his own spilled. And yet he felt a kinship now that he had never felt before. These men were closer to him than friends and family. They were going into battle, and it was likely not all would return from it; perhaps not one of them would survive; but Cal no longer entertained thoughts of flight. What fortified him was not consideration of honor or reputation, but the trust he shared with these men. He despised their cause, abhorred their principles, and believed them all to be mad. But he knew they would put their lives in danger for him, and he had no choice but to do the same for them.

The more he reflected on this, the more it troubled him. Was it possible that men could only feel the true bond of friendship and trust in the face of violent death? Could this, he wondered, be the reason why nations had been annihilated, continents rendered lifeless, the arts and learning of generations swept away, in the notorious Bloody Centuries before the great exodus? Was this the reason why man, with a galaxy open to him, still squandered life on pursuit and flight, conquest and confrontation and the pitting of life against life, as if all the universe were no more than a vast arena? If, indeed, man could only realize his best in the pursuit of the worst, then all was madness, and there was no hope at all, ever, anywhere. With this conclusion, Cal sighed, squatted down under a broad leaf, and leaned back against the thick stalk of vegetation that rose into the mist overhead. He longed for the old life in which thoughts like this did not occur, and any problems could be postponed to far tomorrows.

Kellver soon joined them with four men and passed the orders for the attack. The ten of them were to work through the vegetation and climb the steep face of the plateau to strike at what was presumably the least guarded point. At the sound of firing, Blesser would lead the main force of the troopers across the clearing and up the shallow face in a direct assault. The issue would be decided here on the plateau. The victors would grant no mercy, and the losers could expect none.

Kellver assigned each man a place in order of ascent, taking the first spot himself. Cal he set between Eis and Atha, and told him, before they set off, "You're a trooper now, Caliban, and your life depends on being a good one. When this battle's over, you'll be a skillman again, and we'll want a victory song from you, truly we will. Fight well." Cal found his words unexpectedly encouraging, even moving.

They crept through the sodden growth in a steady ankle-deep current, and made their slow way up the rock wall, gripping through a veil of water at elusive slick handholds. Off to his right, from beneath a blanket of mist, a steady rushing roar came to Cal's ears. The sound, and the unseen torrent from which it issued, made him even more cautious. He fell behind, and was the last to reach the top.

The others were hunched in twos and threes behind low rounded outcroppings. Cal slithered across the open ground and reached Eis, who gestured for silence and pointed ahead, into the mist.

Visibility was slightly better at this height. Cal strained and squinted and made out vague figures— more than twenty, fewer than thirty. He was troubled by the uncertainty of how many more lurked invisible in the mist. The pirates were believed, on the strength of Chandy's information, to have thirty-four men left, which made their number exactly equal to the troopers'.

But Chandy might have lied, Cal thought, and set a trap for Blesser and his men even as he died in agony at their hands. It was clearly possible; given the circumstances, it was more than likely. Cal swallowed hard and gripped his sword.

He jumped at the sound of speech, and grinned shamefacedly at Eis when he realized that he was hearing the pirates' voices, carried far on the moist air. The words were not distinct, but the tone was plainly irritable. When his heartbeat had returned to normal, he cupped his hands behind his ears and caught the name "Chandy" and a word he could not at once distinguish until it was repeated twice more: *"Pandora."*

He listened further, and picked out enough to gather that these men were waiting here not merely for a trophy but for a means of escape. A momentary break in the mist explained their predicament. In the center of the plateau, canted over precariously and close to toppling, stood the black ship. It was no longer capable of liftoff. This nameless, forsaken planet had never merited construction of a landing ring, and thus any landing called for skills long forgotten by most spacefarers. Cal recalled the difficulty with which *The Huntsman* had set down and gave a retrospective sigh of relief. To be here was in itself unpleasant. To be marooned here . . . He shook his head and shuddered. It was too awful to contemplate. And the pirates were sure to feel the same way, and fight all the harder.

The mist closed in once more. The sky darkened and the rain increased. Kellver passed the word to form for attack. Five gunners readied their weapons and slipped forward. The others drew their blades. At Kellver's shout, they rose and advanced, the gunners in a tight line, walking slowly and steadily, laying their fire into narrow overlapping sectors. Behind them, in the interstices, the swordsmen followed. The ten made as much noise as they could, and sounded like a small, angry army.

The pirates were surprised, but they did not panic. After a few shouts and some momentary confusion, they seemed to disappear into the bare rock. The gunners maintained marching fire until the first return bursts came, then went flat to the ground and proceeded at a crawl, covering one another in turn. Cal squirmed ahead and tumbled into a broad basin. A figure sprawled in wait for him against the opposite bank. Cal scrabbled for a footing in the waist-deep water, raised his blade to defend against the blow to come, and only then noticed that the man did not move. The water was red and one of the pirate's eyes was a black hole from which the blood still oozed. Cal turned away quickly. Avoiding the body, he pulled himself over the rim and moved forward.

A sudden uproar burst from the mist ahead: shooting, cries of pain and anger, the clashing of steel and the splash of heavy booted feet and falling bodies. The main force had made contact. Still no order to charge came from Kellver, and soon Cal saw why. With Blesser and twenty-four men at their backs, the pirates had no retreat from their first attackers. They quickly turned back against the smaller force, who now lay in wait for them.

A shape loomed before Cal. He sprang up, winced at the size of the figure rushing straight for him with his blade aloft, growing bigger and more formidable with each headlong stride. He braced himself for a side slash. The pirate was upon him before his arm was fully cocked. He did not bother to use his uplifted sword, but simply roared a battle cry and crashed full-tilt into Cal, knocking him over backwards. Cal's sword flew out of his hand, clattered against a rock, and sank into a shallow pool. Disarmed, he rolled to one side and scrambled to his feet. The pirate did not press his advantage. His mind was on escape, not combat, and once Cal was out of the way the pirate kept going.

Cal sank to one knee, gasping, trying to regain the breath knocked out of him by the impact. He saw something moving in the direction the big pirate had gone, and rose, ready to run. At the sight of Atha he gave a sigh of relief and waved to catch his attention.

"Hurt? Where's your sword?" Atha asked.

"I'm all right. Big pirate knocked me down. Went your way."

"He didn't get far. Here, take his sword. Come on, let's move up before it's all over," Atha said, leading the way.

Three figures burst from a swirl of mist before them and froze at the sight of Atha, who rose like an upthrust rock, sword in one hand, empty pistol in the other. He charged, and Cal followed, going for the smallest of the three fugitives.

At the first exchange, Cal knew he was outmatched. The pirate, a smaller man and lighter of frame, had the features and coloring of a Malellan. What was worse for Cal, he had all the legendary Malellan speed and agility, and swordsmanship to match. He countered Cal's first attack and beat him back easily. As Cal took up a defensive stance, the Malellan lowered his sword, shook his head, and gave a short, derisive, sniff of laughter. Then he came at Cal like a bladed whirlwind. He leapt, almost dancing, from rock to rock, while he drove Cal into knee-deep puddles and laughed at his awkward floundering. He seemed to weave a cage of steel around Cal, forcing him back step by step, steadily and inexorably as if he had been on tracks under the pirate's direction. A second time the Malellan broke off the attack, allowing Cal to rest, panting. Then, with a fierce grin, he lunged. Cal sprang back and found himself in empty air.

124

He glanced off the steep mountainside about five meters down, hit again, and slid and bounced along the slick rock face, tumbling and rolling helplessly toward an ever-louder roar. He tore his fingers against the stone in frantic efforts to arrest his fall, but nothing was there to grip. He rolled off the final ledge into cold misty air and plunged at last, battered and only half-conscious, into a churning fury of water at the foot of the hill that dropped from one side of the plateau.

The shock revived him. He had learned to swim well on Bellaterra, but no swimmer could survive long in the wild turbulence of a torrent fed by the runoff of a rain that had never ceased to fall. He managed to stay afloat until through sheer luck he was swept aside into a branch of the main stream. The current was as powerful, but the turbulence here was less and the channel narrow at intervals. He was carried far downstream before he was able to clutch at an overhanging rock and pull himself out of the water. The ground was scarcely drier, but he fell upon it, gasping, and gave thanks for his deliverance from sword and flood.

He lay there for a time, regaining strength, then started back to the plateau. It was a long way, and the going was difficult. He had to stay near the river to keep his bearings, but the banks were steep and slippery, with poor footing, and he was often close to falling. He could only guess at his exact point of entry. The roaring of the mighty river drowned out any sounds of battle that might otherwise have drifted down to him.

In that nearly featureless mist-enshrouded setting he wandered without hope until he staggered and fell from hunger and exhaustion. Drenched and shivering, aching in bone and muscle and every joint from his long ordeal, he longed to sleep where he lay. But he forced himself on. He had to regain the plateau. Only from the plateau could he hope to find his way to *The Huntsman*.

The search was nightmarish. Weak and pained by hunger, he tried eating the leaves of one of the yellow bushes that clung to the lowland marsh, and after a single swallow was racked by spasms of vomiting and knife-like pains in his chest and stomach. He was long in recovering his strength, and he made no further tests of the planet's food stock. Starvation was preferable to death by poisoning. His sodden clothing and boots chafed him painfully. He shivered, coughed, and sniffled up river in misery, almost unaware of his surroundings until at last a parting of the mist revealed a high rock wall rising before him. He gathered all his remaining strength and began the long climb to the top. Halfway up, he was able to work around to the open ground where the grade was less steep, and soon he knew he had reached his goal. He saw the first corpse.

The pirate had a scrip of moldy food dangling from his belt. Cal tore it loose and plucked it open, stuffing the food into his mouth in handfuls until the wallet was empty. He moved on, up the shallow slope, and found more bodies. Two things occurred to him—to secure a weapon and start a count.

On the top of the plateau he saw the aftermath of the main engagement, and the sight turned his legs limp beneath him. The rain was lighter now, and he could see clearly. Troopers and pirates lay in a red lagoon that covered the hilltop. Men—shot, slashed, run through, disemboweled and dismembered—were strewn about like a madman's broken toys. Even in death, their hands gripped weapons and their faces were drawn into ferocious masks. The rain beat down, carried off their blood, mixed with it and flowed down the hillside to fall at last into the torrent far below.

The count went ever higher. Cal found the bodies of his friends near the place where he had gone over. Eis lay beside two pirates. Both of his bandoliers were empty. His hand still gripped the dagger buried in the chest of his larger opponent. Cal stooped to pry the dagger loose and take it and the pouch from around Eis' neck. He would see that they got to Lixis somehow. Nearby, Atha sprawled on his face, dead from a thrust under the shoulder. The Malellan who had forced Cal off the cliff lay on either side of Atha, cleft in two at the waist. Cal threw down the long sabre he had taken and picked up the Malellan's slim Iboki blade.

He found Kellver and the others all dead, and swept the forward part of the plateau for the main force. They had fared no better. As he stood over Blesser's body he heard a sound nearby and sprang to guard at once.

"Help me, trooper," a weak voice called.

"Zoss?"

"Here. Hurry."

The Over-lieutenant lay back against a low hummock of stone. His right arm was gone below the elbow and he held a tourniquet just above the ragged stump.

"What can I do?" Cal asked.

"Take the pouch off my belt and open it. Now hold this," Zoss said, nodding to indicate the tourniquet. He fumbled in the pouch and drew out a power ampule. "Cut off the sleeve so I can inject myself," he said. He sat back, eyes shut, while the injection took effect, then ordered Cal, "Help me back to the ship. I can make it now."

The Huntsman was closer than Cal had expected. He brought Zoss back and under his direction cleaned and dressed the wound and administered a sedative. His hands shook so badly he had to re-tie the bandage three times. His head was swimming, and he felt close to passing out. When Zoss closed his eyes, Cal stripped off his drenched rags, gathered all the covers he could find, and collapsed, shivering, on the nearest empty bunk.

He awoke and found Zoss propped up in his bunk,

speaking into a small machine. Zoss snapped the apparatus off at sight of Cal and greeted him cheerfully. "You've been out for three watches. Feel better now?" Cal nodded, and Zoss went on, "I've been making a report of the action. Since we're the only survivors, you're now second-in-command. I've made you a brevet Sub-lieutenant, Caliban."

"Thanks. How do you feel?"

"Better. Promotion or not, you'll have to do most of the work, you know."

"I'll start by getting us some food," Cal said, and headed for the galley.

With a clean dry uniform on his back and a meal in his belly, he felt in a better mood than he had known since Bellaterra, in the days before the pirates. Zoss, too, seemed in improved spirits, and now that Cal was an officer he treated him in a friendlier manner.

"I can handle navigation and communications," Zoss assured Cal. "It's all a matter of knowing which switch to throw. You'll have to run everything else."

"As long as we don't have any mechanical problems, I'll do fine. I can keep us fed and tend your arm."

"We've got a long trip ahead. We may both wish we had a lot more to keep us occupied."

"I've got one thing I want to do before we lift off," Cal said. "Bury our men."

"How? Where? That plateau is solid rock."

"I know, but we can't just leave them like that, Zoss. I couldn't bear to think of them rotting away out there under the rain."

"Well, you can't bury them, not on this planet. All you can do is drop them over into the river."

"That's not much better than leaving them on the plateau, is it?" Cal said dubiously.

"It's a lot worse. I don't know about your customs and

beliefs, but I know those men didn't expect burial. You can do better for them."

"How?"

"You have word-skill. Make up a tale, or a song. Something like that. It will give them honor, and they would have wanted that more than burial." Zoss paused, then added, "It ought to keep you busy, too."

All the long way back to the Sternverein base planet, Cal worked on "The Song Of The Seventy," and when at last they landed, he was bursting to perform it for a larger audience than Zoss. The Sternverein officials showed little interest in his efforts. They offered him admittance to the academy with the opportunity of permanent Sub-lieutenancy upon completion of the course. He declined. They awarded him a double portion of the bounty on the pirates. He haggled for more, and wrung from them passage on the next freighter to the Twelve Systems, where he hoped to find Vallandis and resume his old life. When at last he was able to perform "The Song Of The Seventy," the only comment offered was a complaint about his inaccuracy. There had, after all, been only sixty-eight men in that battle on the nameless planet.

He decided not to argue the point. All he wanted to do was get away.

IV.

Bard and Fugitive

THE WHITE SHIP set him down on Basraan, and that was the last he wanted to see of the Sternverein. He found the spaceport city little changed. It was as run-down and shabby as it had been on the night he jumped the *Triboulet* and took up with Vallandis and his company. Still, he considered it a beautiful sight.

His first stop was at a clothier's, where he bartered his Sternverein coveralls and a small stack of cashcubes for a truly splendid outfit, as gaudy and flamboyant as ever a master skillman had worn. With a confident stride, he went next to the best lodging house in Basraan City, took a room with private bath and a prospect of the sea, and signed himself "Will Gallamor."

"Is the Twelve Systems Repertory Company in town?" he asked the clerk.

"No, sir. We get two or three good skillshows a year, but I don't recall that one."

"They used to do *Ricardo, The Usurper of London.* I saw them do it here on Basraan once, in this city."

"You did? Must have been a long time ago, Mr. . . ." The clerk took a quick glance at the name before him and continued, "Mr. Gallamor. *Ricardo* hasn't played here since I was your age."

Will studied him, and knew that this man's youth was well behind him. And so, in a sense, was his own, but not quite so obviously. Time was getting confused again. He asked the year.

"Planetary or GSC, Mr. Gallamor?"

"GSC."

"Just a moment, I'll check." The clerk disappeared for a time and returned to announce brightly, "It's 2619, sir."

"2619?" Will repeated faintly.

"That's correct, Mr. Gallamor. If you want exact date and month, I can have it computed, but since——"

"No, no, the year is enough. 2619."

"I gather you've been a long time at drivespeed," the clerk said. Will responded with a distracted nod, and he proceeded, "I've seen a lot of people surprised to learn the year when they come off a long drivespeed trip. That's why I wouldn't set foot on one of those driveships. I'm not afraid of pirates and slavers, but I like to know just how old I am."

"How old are you?" Will asked, assuming that it was expected of him.

"Forty-seven years, GSC. Just over a hundred and eight, planetary."

Will examined the man and found him a sorry specimen, a poor slope-shouldered groundworm who could scarcely get both hands around his sagging belly and was out of breath after opening a door. There was something infinitely depressing about the sallow, puffy-eyed face with its yellowed smile and its dismal fringe of hair. But there was something paradoxically encouraging in the sight, as well, and Will felt his mood brighten. At fifty-one, GSC, he looked to be scarcely half this fellow's age, and felt even less than that. Drivespeed had its advantages, after all.

He spent the next few days making inquiries. From what he could gather, Vallandis and his company had not been to Basraan since the visit on which he joined them. Will thought back to their last parting on Bellaterra and recalled the words he had taken so lightly then: if space doesn't get us, time will. Farewells between starfarers were more significant than he had suspected.

He stayed on Basraan for a time, not because he wanted especially to be there but because he did not want especially to be anywhere else. He gambled now and then, and had the practical good sense to invest one lucky night's winnings in a magnificent centuries-old linlovar with a tone that could melt a listener's soul. After some serious practice, he began to visit the grogshops and pleasure houses, and found that his songs and stories brought him as good a living as his gambling, and one that was safer and more dependable. He remained on Basraan for three short planetary years, by which time he was quite bored with this life. It was too settled. When the Imperial Galactic Theatre Company visited the planet, he paid them a business call. They had heard of Vallandis' group, but not of Will Gallamor, actor and playwright. They had a repertory of four plays, two of which showed signs of diminishing audience appeal. They were definitely interested in a brand-new tragedy based on the life of the Old Earth tyrant Moran. Will became a member of the company, and departed Basraan with them. It felt good to be in space again, among skillmen, going to a performance of his own—practically his own—work.

He kept to himself during the long trip aboard the players' ship, a dumpy but dependable old hulk named *Merryandrew*, and probed the deep corners of his memory for *The Downfall of Moran*. If Val and the others had been lost, they would have no further need of it, and he saw no sense in letting a good play vanish with them, particularly when it could do him needed service. Where memory failed him, he improvised, creating

132

entire scenes of his own. He had come to enjoy working with words and language. Even the unruly gibberish that served as *lingua franca* in space, the debased end product of the long decay that had begun in the last centuries of Old Earth, had its own beauty and grace if one approached it properly. He recalled that on Bellaterra he had doubted his power to create; but his songs had been popular on Basraan, and his new *Moran* was an improvement on the original. He felt that his true gift was becoming apparent at last, and delivered his play with pride.

The Downfall of Moran was as successful this time around as it had been earlier. It played long engagements on three planets, and became the mainstay of the Imperial Galactic Theatre Company's repertory. Things went smoothly enough until one night when Seskian, the manager and chief actor, fell suddenly ill and Will went on as Moran. He was in good form, having resumed his training for minor roles, and his final duel won thunderous applause. When Seskian returned to the title role, attendance fell sharply. The crowd wanted Will Gallamor, and it was Will who gave the final performances.

Seskian, ordinarily a proud and temperamental man, seemed chastened by the experience. He took his setback with a grace that surprised Will. Following the last show, Seskian took the company to dinner and spoke solemnly and at some length on such topics as sacrificing one's own interests for the good of the company, stepping aside for the greater talent, and recognizing one's own strengths and weaknesses. He had never been known to speak so before.

Once in space, his deference toward Will increased. He installed the playwright in his own cabin to allow him privacy in which to create, and appealed to him to provide his fellow actors with more work of the caliber of *Moran* so that they too might display their talents to best advantage. Between Seskian's flattery and his own feeling of guilt, Will was driven to heroic effort. When *Merryandrew* touched the landing ring on Stepmann VII, the company were rehearsing two brand-new tragedies from the hand—and memory—of Will Gallamor.

The new plays were great successes, and after an extended run, Seskian once more entertained his company, this time more extravagantly than ever before in the memory of the oldest player. He lavished praise and gratitude on everyone, but most of all on Will. He could not do enough for his playwright and new chief actor. He ordered the choicest delicacies, and decanter after decanter of the heady green-gold wine of Stepmann VII, for Will's sole consumption. When Will at last went under, it was Seskian himself, with the assistance of the burly innkeeper, who carried him up to a quiet room, settled a pillow beneath his head, hung his linlovar carefully over the bed, and tiptoed out after a last whispered word of gratitude.

Will awoke at sunset. He was rested and his head was clear, but he felt a consuming thirst. A bucket stood on the bedside table. He raised it, drank deeply, and then put it down and plunged his face and head into the cold water. Then he drank again.

He stretched, rubbed his neck, and became aware of the growling in his stomach. With his thirst attended to, his hunger now demanded relief. He went to the door, found it locked, and began to pound and kick it, meanwhile bellowing imprecations in his best Moran voice.

The innkeeper, Fiscon, opened the door and stood beaming down on him, a great mound of smiles and apologies. "We locked the door to be sure you'd have no disturbance, Mr. Gallamor, and I'm glad to see you slept well," he greeted Will.

Mollified, Will said, "I slept excellent well, thank you,

and now I'm starved and would eat. Have the others eaten?"

"Oh, yes, sir, eaten and gone, long ago."

"Gone?" Will repeated in a small voice.

"Yes, sir. They lifted off just after you decided to turn in, sir," Fiscon said, smiling comfortably at his own delicacy. "Seeing as it was your farewell party and you had, in a way of speaking, made your farewell, they saw no cause to prolong their stay. The older gentleman explained that they had pressing engagements elsewhere in the Systems, and it was only because of your leaving the company that they stayed so long, feeling it wouldn't be right to let an honored colleague depart without proper ceremony, as he put it, sir."

"I don't suppose he said where they were going, did he?"

"No, sir, that he did not, not a word about it. Would you like your dinner now, Mr. Gallamor?"

"Yes, I would. Are you sure that's *all* he said?" Will asked.

"Well, now I recall, sir, he was particular careful about your linlovar—a beautiful instrument, sir, and I'm a good judge of them, having seen many in my time. He carried it up with his own hands, sir, and hung it over your bed careful as a mother with a baby. He said when he left that you'd be depending on the linlovar for your livelihood from now on, and we mustn't let anything happen to it."

Will gritted his teeth, smiled, and nodded.

"There was one other thing, Mr. Gallamor, sir. The older gentleman said you had been kind enough to invite your friends to this dinner, and you'd be ready to settle up as soon as you had a good night's sleep."

"He told you that, did he?"

"He did indeed, sir," the innkeeper said. His smile remained as benevolent as ever, but he flexed his arms in a rather menacing way. His forearms were about the thickness of Will's thighs. Will drew out his pouch of cashcubes and tossed them to the big man.

"Take what's due, and a fair gratuity for yourself," he said grandly. "Is this your best room?"

"It is, Mr. Gallamor, sir, and though I can see you're a man accustomed to far greater finery, I promise you you'll find no cleaner quarters nor no finer service anywhere in the Twelve Systems. Shall I have your dinner sent up, sir, or will you honor us below?"

Will honored the innkeeper below. After dinner, when he received his money pouch, fearfully lightened, he negotiated terms for an extended stay. He had told himself, as he dined and pondered, that he would be philosophical about all this. He needed a rest, time to polish his stock of songs and stories, unhurried hours to practice the linlovar. His true skill lay in shaping songs, not in acting. Seskian, all unknowing, had done him a service. That was the sensible way to look at it; not to rant and curse, but to make the best of a situation.

The philosophical view sustained him for a time, and when it began to pall, Fiscon's daughter, a randy wench named Bes, offered a new anodyne. It was her father's precautionary custom to lock her in her room every evening. Not that he mistrusted Mr. Gallamor, sir, he was quick to explain, but living near a spaceport as they did, with all sorts of strangers passing through, a truly affectionate father could do no less. Will understood perfectly, and publicly commended the man's prudence. He could afford to be open-minded. On his third day at the inn, Bes had presented him with a duplicate key.

In time, both philosophy and Bes lost their appeal, and Will turned more and more to Stepmann wine to help make his days endurable. His last cashcubes went, and he was removed to a dingy little closet behind the kitchen. Every evening he sang and played the linlovar for a handful of surly customers, and in return was given his room and board, an occasional decanter of wine, and a varying portion of abuse from Fiscon, Bes, or both.

Awakened one rainy morning by the clatter of cooking utensils and the raucous voices of cross slaveys, he went for a long walk, and made a cold assessment of his situation. It was appalling. He was falling to pieces, doing to himself exactly what Seskian had hoped he would do. At his present rate of descent, he would soon be thrown out of the inn, most likely with his linlovar impounded by the thieving Fiscon to offset a list of fictitious expenses incurred in maintaining him. If he settled down to win redemption through sobriety and hard work, he might one day find himself husband to Bes and master of the inn, a prospect scarcely more appealing than the first. He was no groundworm, he was a skillman and a spacefarer, and a shabby inn on Stepmann VII was not where he chose to end his days. At twenty-five or twenty-seven—or sixty or seventy, whatever he was—he was not ready for this. He had to get back into space. The destination was unimportant; what mattered was being on the way.

He took a firm grip on himself, and began scouting the spaceport in his free hours. Stepmann was a medium-sized port, fairly busy, and a driveship could be expected about once in three galactic weeks. Will knew that the odds against his leaving were high. He lacked the cash to travel as a passenger, and the training to sign on as a crewman. He had to win himself a berth among a troupe of skillmen, or buy his passage among travelers with his skills. He knew it could be a long wait, but now he had something worth the waiting.

Driveships came and left, and Will remained at the inn. His standing with Fiscon had improved somewhat once he returned to concentration on his songs and skills, but his determination to move on was undiminished. At last, one evening, his heart leapt at the sight of a familiar face. His release was in sight.

He stopped at the table where his old acquaintance and another man sat, and said, "A song for the travelers? I can sing of heroes and fair ladies, brave deeds and true love. If that's not to your taste, I'll sing a laughing song, or a song to make you weep like a child. Name your choice, gentlemen."

One of the men, a swarthy, frowning fellow with a patch over one eye, waved him off; but the other bid him stay, saying, "Wait, skillman. That's a fine instrument you have. May I examine it?"

"Of course you may," Will said, unslinging the linlovar and handing it over. "This was made on Karrapadin, sixteen generations ago, by Kerikam-kam-Civor-vor-Sixla. So I was told, and I believe it. Look at that carving."

The other man took it in one hand, inspected it closely, and laid it face upward on the table. "You were told truth. This is a rare old instrument." He splayed his right hand into position on the strings and looked at Will.

"Go on, pick it up and play. Do you remember *The Dragon Song?* Hard chords for the left hand in that one, Tib," Will said.

The other stared hard at him for a moment, then burst out, "Lon Rimmer! What in the blazing rings are you doing on this sorry chunk of rock?"

"Oh . . . just resting up. A little time off between engagements. Nothing permanent," Will said casually.

"How long have you been here?"

Will decided to abandon all pretense. He reached forward and gripped the Karrapad's arm firmly. "Too long, Tib. Can you get me off? I don't care where you're headed, so long as you get me away from Stepmann."

"We've got a long trip ahead of us, Grypus," Tib said to his companion. "It would be wise to have a third man along, even if he does nothing more than play the lin-lovar when we're bored."

"You don't need anyone to play the linlovar for you, Tib. You always——" Will broke off sharply as Tib raised his left hand, a tangled, claw-like knot of twisted fingers. After a painful pause he asked, "What happened?"

"Bad accident, Lon. The same accident that cost Grypus his eye. We'll tell you about it when we're underway." To Grypus, he said, "All right with you, partner?"

The man with the eyepatch nodded. "We might need a third man before we're through," he said.

"We're leaving an hour before sunrise," Tib said. "The scoutship on the farthest ring."

"I'll be there," Will assured him.

"Good. Now, let's hear *The Dragon Song*. And be careful of those chords."

Two hours before sunrise, as Fiscon snored away and Bes slept contentedly, Will picked open the lock on the cashbox concealed beneath the hearth. He had planned only to reimburse himself, at a fair rate, for his labors. But when he saw a bulging sack of cashcubes, and re-called the abusive remarks of Fiscon and the shrewish tirades of his daughter, and when he recalled the sneer-ing contempt he had swallowed from the spacetrash that comprised Fiscon's clientele, he decided that everything here could scarcely cover one-tenth of their debt to him. Words from a long-ago life came back to him, and he smiled a dry smile at the memory: if it's not nailed down, it must be mine. He slipped the sack into his tunic, and left in its place the key that Bes had given him. It occurred to him, for the first time, that the key was very much worn, although it was not particularly old. It had seen frequent use, no doubt.

But there was no time to think on this. He had to make his break, and leave Stepmann VII for good.

Their destination was Verdandi, in the Skeggjatt system. It was a long haul, but the ship could have made it without a stop. She was a Third Stage scout, designed to carry a four-man crew, with full equipment and supplies, on a trans-galactic mission. And yet she had touched down on Stepmann VII, and once they were in drivespeed range, Tib and Grypus took out charts of an erratic, zig-zagging course that would triple their time en route and bring them to planetfall eleven times, with the last charted stop still half a galaxy away from Verdandi. This made no sense at all. Will suppressed his curiosity for as long as he could, then put the question bluntly to his old instructor. Tib conferred with his partner, and after much whispered discussion, they summoned Will to a meeting on the bridge.

"We'll tell you everything," Tib said. "But first, we want your word as a skillman that you'll never repeat anything you hear. Agreed?"

"You have my word, Tib."

"Good. Satisfied, Gryp?" the Karrapad asked his partner, who nodded once and then remained silent. Tib seated himself, poured out three mugs of hot *scoof*, and when the others had taken theirs, began his account.

"When the *Triboulet* stopped on Farr III, I decided to quit the circus. It was getting harder and harder to pry my wages out of Prospero, and anyway, I was sick of space. A group of retired skillmen had opened a sort of academy there, and they offered me a place instructing on the linlovar. That suited me, and I took it. Gryp started there just after I did, and we became friends.

"It was a good life, Lon. I married, had two daughters. Probably sounds boring to a young fellow like you, but I was happy. Then, about, oh, I don't know, a year or so ago, slavers landed. We learned of the raid and managed to get between them and their ship. Those Daltrescans are cowardly scum, won't fight unless they have

140

sure twenty-to-one odds, but this time they had no choice. It was a grand battle. We wiped them out, but we lost twelve men, and Gryp and I . . . well, you can see for yourself.

"They called us heroes, and gave us all the sympathy we could ask for, but you can imagine how much that means to a skillman who's lost an eye, or a hand. We wanted to be fixed up, and the only ones who can do it are the Skeggjatts—best surgeons in the galaxy, that's what everyone says—and they're a long way off and ask a lot for their services. So it looked as though we were out of luck.

"A little after that, when Gryp and I were still feeling sorry for ourselves, a Sternverein trader made an emergency stop on Farr III. We got to talking with one of the crewmen, and he let slip that they had a box of green diamonds on board. Now, you know how rare they are—never been found anywhere but on Old Earth. Well, to make it short, Gryp and I decided that we needed those diamonds more than the Sternverein did, so we took them. Got away in the Daltrescan ship, traded it for this one, and now we're on our way to Verdandi for a new eye and a new hand."

Tib exchanged a conspiratorial grin with his partner, and they lifted their mugs and drank to their benefactors with mocking solemnity. Will waited for a time, and when they volunteered no more, he said, "I suppose the Sternverein Security troopers are tracking you by now."

"Shouldn't be surprised," Gryp said coolly.

"They're a conscientious bunch. I'll give them that," Tib added.

"They're relentless, Tib—worse than Lixians! They'll follow you across the galaxy, and when they find you, they'll kill you on the spot!" Will cried.

"So we've heard," Tib said. "But it's too late to give the diamonds back, and besides, we still want to go to

141

Verdandi." He rose and laid a hand on Will's shoulder. "We're not worrying. We've got faith in *you*."

"Me?"

"You, old friend. You're going to take this ship on a crazy course, starhopping all over the galaxy until the blackjackets don't know what to think. Meanwhile, Gryp and I will make our quiet way to Verdandi, disguised as Poeite explicators on pilgrimage. Remember Drufe?" Tib adopted a solemn expression, made the circular sign over his heart, and intoned, "Hear now the revelations of the prophet Poe, and contemplate their significance as I shall explicate it."

Will shook his head and gestured wildly. This was getting out of control. Better Stepmann VII forever, better servitude to Fiscon and marriage to Bes, than pursuit by the white ships of Sternverein Security. "Tib, sooner or later they'll catch me, and when they do, they'll make me talk. I've seen them operate. I couldn't hold out, skillman's honor or not," he said.

"We don't expect miracles," the Karrapad said gently. "All we need is two galactic months head start, and we have almost that much now. We'll make up a story they'll believe. It won't have to be far from the truth, either." He concentrated for a moment, then brightened and began, "You're stuck on Stepmann VII, desperate to get back into space, when you meet a crazy old spacerat you once knew. He gives you a lift, and one day, without warning, he and his partner up and disappear, leaving you with the ship."

Gryp came up and placed his hand on Will's other shoulder. "There you are, a young skillman with a drive-ship all your own. You're not going to sit still, are you? Of course not! You're going to go starhopping, learning new material and spreading your reputation," he said. He was very convincing.

142

"Even a blackjacket would believe that," Tib assured him. "I believe it myself, just looking at you. You've got an honest face, old friend. You could tell the blackjackets this ship fell out of your linlovar and they'd believe you."

"And don't forget, you keep the ship," Gryp pointed out.

Will felt his determination wavering. "That's true. I hadn't thought of that."

"It's a nice deal," Tib declared. "The blackjackets—if they ever catch up to you, which isn't certain—can't do a thing. They have nothing on *you*, they want *us*. We'll get to Verdandi, you'll get a nice little ship of your own, and nobody will be hurt. Is it a deal?"

Will hesitated for just a moment, then nodded and held out his hand.

The partners left him on the second planetfall, and Will proceeded on the itinerary they had laid out for him. There was no sign of pursuit until he reached the seedy industrial complex on the remote world known as Trigg-Embroe. He was received there with enthusiasm, and signed for a full planetary month at the spaceport inn. The crowds were big and responsive, and he gave them his best. He juggled daggers and flaming brands. He enacted scenes from *The Downfall of Moran* and his other works. He played the linlovar, sang, chanted, and told stories that made his audience shudder, or cheer, or laugh, as he wished. He felt like a true skillman again, and although he worked hard, he found that he was enjoying himself. When he was asked to extend his stay for an additional month, he agreed readily.

One morning he returned to his room at the inn just before dawn, yawning and ready for sleep. He had scarcely closed the door behind him when a soft, urgent knock came. He opened the door and a pretty young serving girl slipped inside. Motioning him to silence, she closed the door and drew him apart all in an attitude of great urgency.

"What's wrong, Grissa? You're welcome here anytime, you know that, but I wasn't expecting you until tonight. Why all——"

"Someone's asking about you, Will," she broke in.

He smiled, gestured spaciously, and said, "Of course people ask about me, darling. It's only natural. I'm . . ." At a sudden suspicion, his smile faded and he took her by the arms. "Who's asking, Grissa? What do they want?"

"A couple of men in black, off a big white ship that touched down not an hour ago."

Wide-awake on the instant, Will swallowed with some difficulty. "What did you tell them?"

"I didn't like the looks of them, Will, so I told them you were staying in town and wouldn't be back until tonight, for your show. Was that the right thing to say?" she asked anxiously.

He hugged her tight, kissed her lovingly, and said, "Grissie, love, you couldn't have done better. Help me get my things together."

"Will, what have you done?"

"Nothing at all, but I've seen Sternverein Security troopers in action. If they're asking after you, you run," he said, tossing his scant belongings on the bed. "Come on, hurry."

"But if you've done nothing, why run?"

"Because I want to stay alive to keep on doing nothing. I like it better than being dead."

Often in his solitary voyaging Will had anticipated this moment and considered various ways in which he might confront it. Since he was, strictly speaking, innocent of

144

any wrongdoing—helping an old friend regain the use of his hand could hardly be labeled an evil deed—continued flight seemed less and less advisable. After much thought, he had decided to confront the troopers directly at their first encounter, and demand an explanation of their pursuit. He pictured himself as cool and defiant. His bold glance would drive the blackjackets off whimpering. He would dismiss their feeble suspicions with a scornful laugh and concoct a tale to send them scurrying off to the far rim of the galaxy. All this he had settled long before landing on Trigg-Embroe.

Now, with the troopers hot on his trail, all resolution gave way to an overwhelming urge to interpose great gulfs of space between himself and the white ship. It was easy to be brave out there, alone, with no adversary in sight, but things were different now. He remembered Blesser's curt sentence of death, pictured Chandy's broken corpse floating forever between the stars, and saw once again that rain-soaked, blood-sodden final battleground. He had no more desire to confront Stern-verein troopers, now or ever. While he could run, he would run.

"Grissa, do you know the old mechanic from the spaceport?" he asked suddenly.

"What do you want with *him*?"

"I want a set of his coveralls and his tool caddy. Can you get them?"

With Grissa's help, Will was on his way to the spaceport by sunrise, deeply grateful for his grueling lessons aboard *The Empress of Space*. His hair was whitened, his face as wrinkled as the skin of the old mechanic whose greasy coverall he wore. In the tool caddy slung over his shoulder were all his belongings except the plentiful stock of cashcubes he had pressed on Grissa.

145

His ship was encircled by six troopers. Their pistols were on him as he shuffled up to the Under-sergeant in charge, saluted him lazily, and said, "I'm here to disable the fugitive's ship. Is this here the one?"

The Under-sergeant loomed before him, blocking his way. "Who sent for you?"

"Port director called me. Woke me out of a nice sound sleep, as a matter of fact, though I don't suppose you blackjackets care a spit about that," Will said, glaring at the troopers with a sour expression in his rheumy eyes. "He told me to get on over here and take out the drive coils on the ship you're guarding."

"Is that all the equipment you need?"

"I can do it with my fingernail, if you'll stop asking dumb questions and let me through."

"Show your credentials," the Under-sergeant ordered.

"Credentials! Ain't a man on this spaceport who don't know me. Know me and *respect* me, blackjacket, you hear that?" Will howled in a high, cracking voice. "I'm doing a big favor for you, and if you start playing a lot of foolish games about credentials, you can do the job yourself."

"Take it easy, take it easy. I just have to be careful, that's all."

"Why? Who you after, anyway? I seen the fellow who came in this ship, and he seems decent enough. Don't look like the kind of person you'd be after."

"Stick to driveships, old timer, and don't try to judge people. Will Gallamor is a thief and a murderer," the Under-sergeant said. "He killed two busted-up old spacerats for some diamonds they stole from the Stern-verein, and then he took their ship. What's wrong with you?"

Will had paled at this news. He rallied his spirits and explained, "I had a drink with him, that's what's wrong.

146

Ain't every day you find out you got drunk with a thief and a murderer."

The Under-sergeant laughed most unpleasantly. "Don't worry, old timer, we have him cornered. He won't leave Trigg-Embroe. We'll have him buried before sundown."

"I better get to work, then. Wouldn't want to miss that," Will said, easing past the Under-sergeant and starting in a slow, flat-footed old man's shuffle toward the open port of the scoutship. It was the hardest sixty meters he had ever walked. At every step, he wanted to drop the tool caddy and run.

Three minutes after he had set foot inside the ship, he was aloft.

In space Will had time to think and plenty to think about. His thoughts were not encouraging. All his bold resolve had failed him at the crucial moment. His carefully-reasoned plans, had he followed them, would have put him in the hands of remorseless executioners. Sheer luck plus his own skills had gotten him off Trigg-Embroe, and while his faith in his skills was undiminished, he had no illusions about his luck. A man who does an innocent favor for an old friend and finds himself accused of theft and murder can hardly be said to lead a charmed life, he reasoned. The future looked grim. Even worse, it looked brief.

The thought of Tib's betrayal of a fellow skillman brought his spirits lower, and awakened him to the need to alter his course. Tib might well have alerted the troopers to the programmed itinerary.

He rerouted the ship to Xhanchos, a little-known planet far from the main spacelanes. Xhanchos had a one-ring installation, which meant that no second ship could easily land while he was on the surface. That guaranteed at least a warning, and the isolation of the place assured him of a welcome. A skillman's visit would be a rare event indeed for such a remote station. That offered some encouragement. He needed it badly.

The worst problem was loneliness. He could not think his way out of that, however hard he tried. If only there had been some way to smuggle Grissa aboard. She was a sweet, obliging girl, pretty as a man could ask, and she thought enough of him to risk crossing the black-jackets. She would have come along gladly. He could have taught her some of the speeches of Lady Moran, and worked out dual acts for them to perform together. He could have made songs for her to sing to tired, lonely spacerats on the dismal outpost planets where the cast-offs drifted to forget and be forgotten. It could have been good, he reflected wistfully, and best of all, they would have been together. But there had been no way. Now they were apart, and the inevitable betrayal of time had already begun. He was aloft in the eerie dimensionless zone of highdrive, she was planetbound, and their lives moved at different rates of speed. Their parting was farther in her past than in his: she was closer to forgetting than he; nothing could ever be the same for them.

Space had much to offer a man, but it demanded much in return, and the price was inescapable. Will thought of this sadly at first, then bitterly, and at last objectively. He was, after all, a skillman, and he turned to his talents for consolation. His miserable plight held the possibility of a song. He worked on this song and many others on the long ride to Xhanchos.

Landfall was no different at first from any other. The ship homed in on the landing ring, adjusted position, and began its downward drift. It locked into place with a bump so gentle it could scarcely be felt, and the whine of the coils died abruptly.

The first jolt was only a shade more perceptible than the touchdown, but the grating shriek that followed it, and the sidelong lurch that came after, were signs of disaster. Will sprang out of the port and hit the sand at a run, expecting any second to feel the weight of a driveship crash down on him. Safely out of range, he looked back. His ship was still erect, but visibly tilted from the perpendicular. He moved closer, and saw the sand all around the landing ring. The protective field had broken down—long ago, to judge from the depth of the sand.

A sudden horror gripped him, and he turned and raced for the nearby building. Halfway there, he knew his worst fear had been realized. The port was abandoned, the buildings empty, the ring untended. He was marooned on Xhanchos. It was Bellaterra all over again, but this time harsh, hot, dry, and forbidding.

That night, in the empty station, Will weighed his choices. The next morning he changed into a loose work outfit, packed all the food and water he could carry, sealed the ship, and set off in the direction his feet happened to be pointing.

He soon learned that one did not travel on Xhanchos during the hours of light. The days on this open desert were like nothing he had ever experienced. Before the sun was a hand's breadth above the horizon, the entire landscape was an oven of stifling dry windless heat. It literally crushed Will to the ground. He set up a hasty shelter, stripped off his clothing, and lay supine in a leaden sleep until the first stirring of the breeze at dusk.

The rising night wind stimulated his spirits and his energy, and he was soon on his way, moving steadily and purposefully onward over sands bleached white by the seven moons of Xhanchos that passed overhead in an irregular ever-changing line. The brisk wind covered his tracks, but at intervals, he marked his trail with sounding devices taken from the station. He traveled for eight nights, and on the ninth, at dawn, he had his first glimpse of the mountains. Two more nights of walking brought him to an oasis, where he replenished his water supply and rested. He had time to spare, and knew he would need his full strength to survive.

After five days, he left the oasis and directed his steps toward the mountain range that stretched across the horizon. It girt the planet like a great studded belt, and the closer he drew, the more formidable it appeared. Sheer unbroken rock jutted from the sand as if upthrust by some brutal subterranean force. Nature itself seemed to have palisaded this desert with an impassable wall. Will looked up with mixed feelings at the looming smooth planes of gray. Was he walled in, or walled out?

He marked the rock face to identify his starting point, and set out to his right. After two nights of walking past an unbroken surface, his hopes were low, but at last he came to a narrow passage.

He started through at daybreak. The going was difficult, and progress cost him much effort and a good bit of skin. He struggled on, exhausted, through the long day and into the night, stopping only when the darkness became too intense to allow him to continue. He resumed his slow journey at first light. Late in the day, as he squeezed around a sharp corner, he saw a slender shaft of brilliance far ahead. He began to run, heedless now of the close scraping walls, and soon burst into the open on the far side of the mountains.

There before him, as far as the eye could see, lay gold-white sand under a merciless vacant sky. He gave a single low cry, fell to his knees, and sprawled headlong. The days that followed were never clear in his memory. He was in the desert, his food and water were low, and one day they were gone. Then he awoke in a cool dark place and saw men in gray robes. They spoke a high chirping language he had never heard before, and paid little attention to him. He slept much of the time, and his impressions were confused. His head, arms, and legs felt raw and burned, and his mouth was always dry, even though the men in gray gave him all the water he wanted.

One day a man inspected him closely and two other men came to take him away. They threw a ragged outfit—not his own—at him, and indicated by gestures that he was to dress and follow them. He stepped outside, and the sudden glare of the setting sun nearly blinded him. One of the men showed him how to make a cover for his head and eyes with a scrap of cloth. Protected thus, he was led to a string of *haxopods,* great desert lopers twice the size of any he had ever seen before, and bid to mount.

He traveled through that night and the next in the company of the gray riders. They made no effort to speak to him, but they were not unkind. He was fed the same food, given the same portion of water, and allowed to sleep under the common shelter during the day.

At the end of the second night's ride they arrived at a compound in the desert, built near a low construction of stone. In the faint pre-dawn light, Will could distinguish pyramidal shapes in the far distance. Nearer, on the sand, lay row upon row of huge bluestone blocks, cut and dressed. He remembered stories he had heard, vague and half-legendary, of a desert planet ruled by a race of builders . . . slave labor . . . giant pyramids. He glanced at the gray rider beside him. The man grinned and offered his water-case. Will took it gladly, His throat was dry.

151

The gray riders sold him to a pair of lean, flat-faced men, and departed at once into the desert. The pyramid builders paid for him not with the silvery cashcubes used everywhere in the galaxy, but in coins of gold. When he saw those coins and heard their heavy clink into the gray rider's hand, Will felt more abandoned and hopeless than he had ever felt before.

V.

Slave and Anthem-Maker

WILL WAS ASSIGNED to the work crew in Hut 3, Azak Sector. Like all crews, his numbered fourteen. They worked together, ate together, and at night, chained each to his narrow pallet, slept in rows in the same hut. In the eyes of their Xhanchilion masters, the men of a work crew were joined for life.

With rare exceptions, such as Will himself, the crews were obtained in lots from slave traders. Some crews were all of a single breed, while others, acquired piecemeal or purchased at some busy galactic center like Barbary, represented a sampling of the humanoid races. The crews in Huts 2 and 4 of Azak Sector, which stood on either side of Will's hut, were composed entirely of Quespodons, a squat muscular race noted for their exceptional strength. The Quespodons were not richly endowed with intellect, nor were they considered a handsome people. Their chunky bodies and small round heads were hairless, their skin mottled in intricate patterns, each as unique as a fingerprint. Quespodons seldom spoke, even among themselves, preferring to listen. They followed instructions faithfully, provided the instructions were simple and carefully explained. They made useful slaves. Some had been advanced to the post of Overseer, where they proved as harsh as their Xhanchilion masters.

Will's own crew varied widely in origin, in size, and

153

in temperament. At nearly two meters, he was not a small man, but he found himself to be one of the smaller men in this group. The biggest, and noisiest members were a trio of Skeggjatts, plainly space pirates who had fallen afoul of their leader and been sold off. They wore their beards long, plaited their hair in the style of the battle-schools, and boasted loudly of their deeds. But they were obviously pirates, and Will avoided them. A fourth Skeggjatt, a tough graying old warrior named Gurdur, he befriended, as well as a cheerful black Thorumbian named Merox. He decided, for safety's sake, to hold back the facts surrounding his arrival and identity. He told his crewmates that the gray riders had found him wandering in the desert half-mad from thirst and exposure (which was true), and that he could not remember who he was or how he had come there (which was not true). His story was accepted.

One day at sunrise he sat dining with Gurdur and Merox. They talked of the crew. They were able to converse freely, without fear of the guards, for while the Xhanchilion forbid all contact between crews, they allowed free association within each crew. They did not fear any group of fourteen slaves.

"We've got a good lot here. I'd hate to be in with a crew of Quespodons, I'll tell you that," Gurdur said, shaking his grizzled head in distaste.

Merox laughed. "You wouldn't find much to talk about."

"No. And you'd always be reminding them of their own names. They keep forgetting," Will added. He and Merox laughed at the old joke, but Gurdur looked on sourly, like a nettled parent. Will asked the cause of his displeasure.

"You shouldn't be laughing. We're not on a holiday."

"Won't do us any good to cry," Merox objected.

"We'll still be here. Laughing helps to take your mind off things, Gurdur."

"You're as bad as my three brothers," the old Skegg-jatt said, with a scornful jerk of his thumb in the direction of the three noisy pirates. "They spend all their time exchanging battle-boasts and tales of the old heroes. They don't fool me, I'll tell you that."

"They don't fool anybody, Gurdur, but why begrudge them what little pleasure a man can find here? Do you want us to be like Lixians, and never laugh at anything?" Will asked.

"We'd do well to learn from the Lixians. You don't see any here, do you? A Lixian would kill himself rather than endure such dishonor."

"I don't see much sense in that," Merox said. When no one spoke, he went on, "I never liked Lixians, anyway. They look sneaky."

Gurdur drew them in closer and lowered his voice "What I mean is this. We shouldn't laugh or boast or do anything at all to take our minds off escape. That's the important thing."

"Sure, but it's impossible," Will said.

"Just listen to me. We've got a good crew." Gurdur enumerated the others on his fingers as he recited their names. "Merox and I and Stap, the big mute, all have experience in the arena. My Skeggjatt brothers may be spacetrash, but they can fight. That's three more. Gariv was with the Expedition: he can organize men and lead them. You and Tamal have both been out on the desert. I don't know much about the other five, but I know they don't like it here."

Merox said, "I've spoken to the two Agyari. They don't want to die here."

"Would they rather die in the desert?" Will asked.

"I think they might."

"Well, I wouldn't. I don't want to spend the rest of my life hauling stone for these flat-faced barbarians, but if the alternative is death from thirst and exposure——"

"The alternative is freedom," Gurdur broke in.

Will shook his head decisively. "I've been out there, Gurdur, and it's awful. There's nothing out there. We could take food and water and men with us, but there's nowhere to go." He held back the information about his ship; he had to know more before making this ultimate commitment to his crewmates.

"Maybe not. I can't say any more, but you think about it. Maybe the desert isn't our only choice," Gurdur said, rising and leaving them.

That night Will thought about it. The locks and fetters were beneath his attention; he could pick them with a sliver of bluestone. But they were not the means of his imprisonment, they were the outward signs, more useful in fostering a properly slavish attitude than for security. The slaves could be left unchained, the hut doors thrown wide and the guards and warders sent into retirement, and the work camp would still be a prison from which escape was physically impossible. The desert encircled them like a boiling sea. On two sides it stretched unbroken around the planet, on a third it was intercepted by the sheer mountain wall, and on the fourth side, just over the horizon, lay Xhancholii, the city of the pyramid builders, where a fugitive could expect a severe reception. Although escape was impossible, the irrevocable penalty for attempting it, as written on the Wall of Laws, was death in the pulverizer. The process was slow, thorough, and agonizing.

Secured by nature and their own harsh penalties, the Xhanchilion had long ago dismissed the very idea of the slaves' escape. Their term for the slaves was "those without hope," and reason seemed to favor this designation. A few tough, experienced warriors might smash their way out of the camp, but then they faced the desert. Given the supplies, the determination, guidance, and good luck, they might make it to an oasis, where they could hold out. But the gray riders would always be near, waiting for the chance to recapture them. And the sun would be overhead by day, the winds would blow by night, eventually one man would break, then another, and soon all would be over.

Unless a ship was waiting.

It was clear to Will that he alone held the key to a successful escape. Without his ship to take them off the planet, all the efforts of the prisoners were futile heroics. He resolved to learn more about the escape plan, and to find out all he could about the men in his crew.

Nights of work and days of sleep passed, and Will became friendly with his crewmates. They treated him kindly, almost as a mascot, assuming that he was the youngest of their number, as well as the newest. He entertained them with stories and songs, and his tricks drew a smile even from the sober Gurdur. In turn, he learned their tales and legends, and added these and the Xhanchilion work-chants to his stock. He revealed that he was a skillman, but said nothing of his identity and his origins.

Even Gariv, the leader of the crew, a man habitually silent and aloof, began to talk more with the men. Will listened with fascination to the story of his long wanderings. He had left Skorat, left his beautiful wife and their infant son, to lead a fleet of the First Rinn Expedition. After the Battle of the Three Systems, he turned for home, but a series of mishaps had carried him halfway across the galaxy. He had traveled far, even visited Old Earth, and he sang a song about the mother planet in his deep, sad voice. Will found it beautiful and moving; he wished his linlovar was at hand.

Gariv talked for most of one morning about his voyages to Lennerman's Planet, Hovonor, and other strange worlds, and admitted that once, in all his wandering, he had been at the point of despair. A trader had taken him within one day of Skorat when their ship was captured by the slavers who had brought him here.

"That was the lowest I've ever felt. Imagine it, men—one day from home—one day! —and I'm dragged here and put in chains. I've never given up hope of returning to my kingdom, but I came close to it when that befell me," Gariv confessed.

Gurdur said solemnly, "The evil gods have done their worst to you, Gariv. It's time for the good gods to smile."

"Believe what you like, Gurdur. For me, I don't hold with evil gods or fair gods, or any other kind. We're on our own in this universe."

A few of the men grunted their assent. Some seemed offended, others frightened by the assertion. Will, curious about such matters, asked, "If you don't believe in gods, Gariv, what do you believe in? You've traveled farther and seen more than any of us. What does it all mean?"

"It means nothing, skillman. We live, we suffer, we die, and nobody and nothing cares."

The men were silent. Again, it was Will who spoke. "But why does it happen? There has to be a reason."

"Does there?"

"Of course there does! If there's no reason, why live on?"

Gariv laughed drily and shook his head, as if at a child's question. "Because the only other thing to do is die, and that's worse than living."

The others drifted away, to think on Gariv's remark. Hurriedly, without preliminaries, Will said, "Gariv, I'm going to trust you. I've got a ship out there. I need help to get it aloft, but I can take our whole work crew off this planet."

Gariv showed no reaction. "Where is this ship?" he asked.

"Beyond the mountains. I can find it, once we reach the mountains."

"How far?"

"Seventeen days from the mountains. I don't know how far from here."

Gariv nodded thoughtfully. "Why tell me?"

"The ship is no good to me alone. I'd never reach it, and if by some miracle I did, I'd never be able to repair it. I don't think you plan to spend the rest of your life on Xhanchos. When you go, take me along. I'm offering you my ship."

"You're the one who says it's impossible to escape, skillman. Maybe I agree."

Will looked him in the eye and said, "Gariv, I'm here because an old friend betrayed me. I wasn't ready to trust anyone when I first arrived. I've decided to trust you. Do what you like. I made the offer and it stands."

At midday, Will awoke from an uneasy sleep. The hut was darkened. He heard voices, tense and secretive. He raised his head slightly and looked in the direction of the sound. Across from him, at the foot of Gariv's pallet, stood the warder.

"What is this information?" the warder demanded.

"You must protect me. The others will kill me if they ever find out!" Gariv said in the high chirping Xhanchil-ion dialect, glancing about nervously.

Will had picked up enough of the language to understand the exchange. He clenched his fists helplessly at the sight of betrayal. His own certain death momentarily forgotten in the wave of revulsion that swept over him.

159

"If you don't talk, I'll throw you into the grinder myself. What is it you have to say?" the warder asked.

"An escape is planned. I have the names of the leaders."

"Give them to me at once!"

At the warder's command, Gariv nodded eagerly and reached back to fumble at a crack in the wall. The impatient warder took a cautious look at the men sprawled on either side of Gariv in numb exhaustion. Satisfied that they slept soundly, he stepped closer to the crew leader's pallet.

"Hurry!" he urged.

"I have it," Gariv said, drawing forth a scrap of rag and holding it out.

The warder reached forward. Gariv dropped the cloth and seized the outstretched wrist with both hands, jerking the warder forward. As he fell across the narrow pallet, the man on either side went for him. Gurdur's thick forearm locked around the warder's throat, while the mute Stap pinned his flailing legs and Gariv, his arms. When the warder went limp, Gariv tore the two rings of keys from his belt, pushed the body to the floor, and unlocked the chain on his ankle. Freeing Stap and Gurdur, he left them to release the others while he stood watch at the door, the warder's knife in his hand.

"We're on our way, lad," Gurdur said, flourishing the keys before Will.

"Sooner than I expected."

"The sooner the better," Gurdur said, struggling with the lock. He looked up. "Too many people knew too much. Word would have gotten out. Gariv said we have to act now."

"Let me have the keys, Gurdur," Will said. "I'll free myself and the others."

"Good. You're better at this than I am."

Will had his chains off in moments, and freed

everyone on his side with great speed. He felt hope once again. This time there had been no betrayal.

By sunset, the camp was in the hands of the slaves. They had not lost a single man; not one Xhanchilion had escaped. Two thousand men, free and unchained, gathered before the main tower of the camp to cheer their liberators and new leaders, the men of Azak Hut 3. Within the tower, these men sat in conference. Will felt out of place among warriors and tacticians, but they were his friends and he preferred to stay with them as long as he was welcome.

"We're agreed on the plan, then. The relief column arrives in four nights. We'll waylay them here and return at once to Xhancholii as the party from the camp," Gariv said in summary.

"We're gong to lose three-quarters of our men storming Xhancholii," one of the Agyari observed.

"Not that many. Maybe half, but no more," Gariv said. "We won't be up against the gray riders, we'll be fighting soft city-dwellers who haven't had to face an enemy for generations. In any case, we have no choice. There's a landing ring on the far side of Xhancholii, built especially for the slave ships. A Daltrescan transport is due to land there before the end of the third moon cycle to come. That's our transportation home."

Gurdur shook his head glumly. "There'll be trouble. Even the biggest slavers don't carry more than two hundred. We'll have a thousand men fighting for a place."

"Not all the survivors will be able to fight, Gurdur. Some of them won't be able to travel for a long time. We'll work out a fair system."

"If you say so, Gariv, I'll go along."

"Good. Let's begin," Gariv said, rising. "Set up your training groups, get the men fed, and then I'll talk to

161

them. We start training at once." As the others filed out, he turned to Will and said, "Stay, skillman. I have a special task for you. We need a battle-anthem."

"You'll have one."

"Work fast. I want you to teach it to the men after I've announced our plan. We'll be short of weapons, and a good battle-anthem will give the men courage."

Will nodded and said, "I'll make it for you." He had great confidence in his skills, and he knew the power of words well crafted and skillfully strung together. He would deliver as rousing a battle-anthem as any Gariv had ever heard. But he knew, too, the limitations of words. He would not send men into battle armed only with bold words and expect a victory. Even his best work would not protect an unarmed man from a sword thrust.

Gariv caught the doubt in his expression and laughed aloud. "I can see what you're thinking, but you're wrong. Words have strength. They can make men fight harder."

"Can they make them win?"

"Yes. Sit down, and I'll tell you how I know." Will took a place at the table, and Gariv went on, "I'm a skillman, too, in a way. My skill is in battle. I'm Gariv of Skorat, Master of the City of Thak, Warlord of the High Range and the Four Rivers, Warden of the Marches, First Ranger, Protector of the Free Cities, Commodore of the First Expeditionary Force, and from this night, Commander of the Free Army of Xhanchos. Two of those titles I inherited; two were conferred; the rest I won in battle."

Will was visibly impressed, and greatly encouraged. "We knew nothing of that, Gariv."

"I saw no reason to mention titles before. They fit awkwardly on a slave. I only mention them now to convince you. In my court in Thak I had a skillman, much like you. He led us into battle, singing our war-song, and the men were inspired by his example. He was worth a legion of warriors." Gariv was thoughtful for a moment before continuing, "He made songs to celebrate my marriage and the birth of my son, and I took him on the Expedition with me to make a battle-anthem and a victory song for us. He was killed in our last engagement."

"I'm sorry to hear that. He must have been good."

"He was the best," Gariv said. He pointed to Will. "One day ago, when we were slaves, you told me of your ship. I want to do something to reward that trust."

"You already have. I'm free."

Gariv waved this remark aside impatiently. "That's no reward, it's your right. At present, I can only give you a name and a promise. Since you've forgotten your old name—or chosen to forget it—answer to the name of my anthem-maker, Alladale. You resemble him somewhat. Ride into battle with me, like your namesake, and when we've settled our business on Xhanchos, come to Skorat and join my court."

Will considered the offer. Life on a warrior planet, making songs on other men's orders to celebrate other men's deeds, was not much to his liking. Still, with Will Gallamor, thief, murderer, and fugitive from Sternverein justice, forever buried in the wastes of the Xhanchilion desert, he had to be someone. Alladale was as good a name as any. He had nowhere else to go, and it cost nothing to be agreeable. No situation was permanent in this galaxy, anyway.

The only truly unpleasant aspect of the offer was the necessity of riding into battle with Gariv, who was sure to be in the vanguard. Everything would be so simple—and safe—if only Gariv and the rest of their work crew had decided to accept the offer of the driveship and leave revenge to the others, he thought ruefully.

163

But what can one expect from Skeggjatts and Skorat warlords? Still, one could try.

"I deserve no reward unless you intend to make use of my ship, Gariv," he said.

"You must forget the ship."

"But why not use it? With Tamal to guide us, and *haxopods* to carry our supplies, we could be aloft before the battle begins."

"No chance of that, Alladale. I'm a warlord of Skorat. My duty is clear. If I can lead men into battle, I must."

Will—now Alladale—chewed his lip and nodded. "And you want me to ride right up front with you."

"How can you sing of my deeds unless you've seen them?"

"Of course. Yes, you're right." Alladale, maker of battle-anthems, tried not to think of the approaching battle for Xhancholii. He began to wish that Gariv had not been so lavish with his rewards. A simple "Thanks" would have done nicely. "I was only thinking of my swordsmanship. It's not very good. I might be in the way," he said lamely.

Gariv looked at him, puzzled. "You'll be in no one's way. It sounds to me as though you have no stomach for revenge on the creatures who enslaved you. Is that right?"

It was a time to be blunt. "Once, long ago on another world, my wife and son were killed by pirates. I wasn't there to see it, but I was with the men who caught up with them. When I could have had revenge I didn't want it, Gariv, I swear to you I didn't. I wanted my wife and son back, and since I couldn't have that, nothing else mattered. All I wanted from the Xhanchilion was my freedom, and now I have it."

Gariv stared at him for a time, then said, "Alladale, you're a very strange man."

"What about you? You've told me about your beautiful

wife, and your son, and your kingdom, and now we can go back there in my ship, but you choose to fight your way through Xhancholii."

"We're different, Alladale. I'm a warlord, you're a skillman."

"We're both men."

Gariv sighed and shook his head. "There are humans on Kepler who have lived underground for centuries. Their definition of a man is 'a reasoning creature who dwells in tunnels.' Do you understand, Alladale? To me, a man is first of all a warrior. To you, he is a shaper of words. And yet we're all men."

"I think I do understand."

"The men want revenge and a ship to take them home. That means a battle, and I'm the best one to lead them. And so, being what I am, I *must* lead them. If you wish to go, you may. I'll have mounts and supplies made ready."

Alladale rose and stood before Gariv. "They need me, too, I guess. I don't want revenge, but I can't run away when my friends are going into battle." He paused awkwardly, then forced a smile and said, "The only thing I really wanted from that ship was my linlovar, anyway. It was a good one."

Gariv pointed to the doorway behind him. "Look in the other room, if that's what you want. We found a few strange instruments here, and the owners won't be playing them anymore. Don't waste time. I want that battle-anthem soon."

On the seventh night following, the spearhead of the Free Army approached the Sunrise Gate, the main gate of Xhancholii. They were a picked force of two hundred and ten, riding double on big desert *haxopods*. Two hundred and nine of the men were veteran warriors eager for battle, their appetites keen for vengeance and plunder. The two-hundred-and-tenth was an uneasy anthem-maker, newly named Alladale, who rode in the first rank, at his chief's right hand, in the tradition of the Skorat bards.

Alladale's thoughts were not on revenge and looting. He was preoccupied with the mutability of life as exemplified by his own experiences. All he really wanted to be was a good skillman, and yet he repeatedly found himself sidetracked. To have remained an actor, or become a reciter and language-maker, would not have been so bad, but this warrior business was awful. Better than slavery, to be sure, but that was not much of a choice. He rode on in silence, wondering what it was that kept thrusting him into these situations where the air was thick with heady talk of valor and honor, while the other side always seemed bigger and better-armed. More to the point, he wondered how he was going to come out of the seige of Xhancholii alive and intact.

His surroundings kept him from becoming as gloomy as he might otherwise have become. The desert at night was a still world of dazzling cold beauty, all the more beautiful now, seen through the eyes of a free man. The seven moons wheeled overhead in their ever-changing patterns, bathing the pale sands in shifting light as they swung in their irregular progress from horizon to horizon. At the midpoint of the night, the sixth and largest moon, Ctab, sank behind the walls of Xhancholii, directly ahead of the hard-riding column, and threw the city into dramatic silhouette. It was a striking sight. The walls were high and forbidding, studded with squat turrets and guard towers, but the spires that rose within those walls soared gracefully to breathtaking heights and glittered in the light of the fast-falling moon.

Ctab dropped below the horizon, and in the deeper darkness the sounds of the column's passage through the silent desert seemed louder and clearer. Alladale listened, fascinated, to the medley of common noises. The broad padded feet of their mounts made a muffled rumbling on the sand, and the snorting and blowing of the great beasts burst staccato on the cool still air; swords and harness and mail gave off the creak of leather and the ring and clatter of metal on metal; men exchanged mumbled words, the incantations, ritual boasts, and battle-prayers with which they prepared themselves to face the enemy.

Sudden exhiliration stirred in Alladale, an inexplicable sensation of fellowship. These strangers are my brothers, he thought. And even in the moment of thinking so, the shadow of a deeper awareness darkened his exultancy. They were my brothers in the camp, on the pyramid, but I only feel the kinship when we band together in battle, just as I felt it among the Sternverein troopers. . . . What kind of creatures are we? he asked himself. But he pressed his inquiry no further. He had had enough of philosophy. It troubled him, and still gave no answers. He struck a chord on the linlovar he had found in camp—a simple thirteen-stringed model, little more than a practice instrument, and badly out of tune, but sufficient for his purposes—and softly sang the final stanza of his battle song.

"Nevermore will you see us as slaves.
Now, risen in wrath from our chains,
We will crash on your walls like a wave;
And for all of the friends you have slain,
For the years, and the shame, and the pain,
We will make of your palace a grave."

The men in the long column to his rear picked up the song, and he listened to the chorus of deep voices with satisfaction. It was a good song. Not my best, he thought, but not bad, considering the speed of composi-

167

tion and the fact that very little of it is borrowed. Now, if only Gariv would stop trying to make a Skorat bard out of me, and let me do my own work my own way. . . . He sighed and watched the walls of Xhancholii rise ahead of them.

Soon Gariv spoke to Qat Maril, the Agyari who rode on his left, and then he turned to the anthem-maker. "Silence from here on. Pass the word."

Alladale passed the message to the men behind, and rode on. A breeze came to them from the city, bearing the scent of the gardens and terraced orchards. He inhaled deeply, and recognized the scent of the sweet blue-skinned fruit of the oasis.

When they entered the long shadow of the walls, Gariv gave the signal for the seven foremost riders to pull ahead of the others. Like Alladale, these seven rode single. They were to overcome the guard at the gate, and admit the rest to the city. Alladale had been accorded the honor of riding with them as the eighth man.

The two guardians opened the gate for the mounted party without question. Alladale saw a quick flash, heard the hiss of blades, and the men were down. Two riders on one side and three on the other jumped to the narrow steps that led to the guard tower and burst in at either end, securing the doors behind them. Stap, Gariv, and Alladale remained on guard below.

As they waited, a patrol of six riders approached the gate from within the city. They halted in a semicircle before the invaders, almost within touching distance, their outriders enclosing the flanks.

"Night patrol three," the leader announced, and pointed to the tower. "What's going on up there?"

"Our leader is in conference with the guard commander," Gariv replied.

"Who are you? Where are you from?"

"From Azak. We've just been relieved."

The patrol leader peered with evident suspicion into Gariv's hooded face. His *haxopod* snorted and moved uneasily. The uproar in the tower had ceased, but the remainder of the mounted force had nearly reached the gate, and the rumbling of their mounts was loud. "You're ahead of time. You were expected in two nights," the leader said.

"We hurried."

"How many . . . ? There are too many! You're not——"

Gariv moved at once, drawing his sword and rising in his stirrups to hack down the two men in his reach with a quick right-and-left slash, then goading his mount forward to close with the patrol leader. Stap was busy on the other side. Alladale found a rider bearing down on him, broad crescent-shaped sword raised aloft. He ducked under the sweeping cut and lashed out in a wild backhanded blow with his linlovar. It connected on the rider's skull with a discordant *plang*, and he went sprawling. The incoming force rode over him where he lay.

They flowed into the city, branching out according to a precise plan. The remainder of the Free Army, traveling on foot, would reach the walls just before sunrise. The five major gates of Xhancholii had to be taken and held until their arrival.

Gariv's force held the gates. The Xhanchilion, sensing the danger, threw their best troops against them, and the losses on both sides were great, but when the main body of the Free Army crossed the final stretch of sand before the walls, they found the gates gaping to admit them.

They poured in like a murderous tide, sweeping the defenders before them, and a brutal, merciless, two-day battle began in earnest. The last of the invaders to enter closed the gates firmly behind them. This was to be a battle without survivors on the losing side. The Xhanchilion forces outnumbered the invaders nearly three to one, and were better armed; but the advantage of weapons was lost as the slaves threw aside their makeshift arms, snatched blades from the dead, and finally broke through to the armory. The numerical advantage of the defenders had no tactical effect. Their best forces had been lost in the first furious battle for the gates. The rest were garrison troops, poorly trained, disorganized, and ill-prepared to face determined opposition. The advantage of surprise was on the side of the Free Army, and it proved to outweigh all others. When the last moon rose on the second night of battle, Xhancholii was theirs.

After striking that single frantic blow with the linlovar, Alladale did not raise his hand to attack or defend. He rode unarmed by Gariv's side in a growing numbness compounded of fatigue and a surfeit of horror. Invaders and defenders fell by scores all around him, but he was untouched.

From the Sunrise Gate, the invaders rode across the city to strike at the other gates from within. Gariv, with a force of thirty men, moved on the armory, which he seized and held until the main force arrived. Then, with a larger force, Gariv proceeded against the palace. The seige lasted through that day and the following night. The palace guards fought with trapped ferocity, and the Free Army forces were beaten back six times after having penetrated to the inner court in their first attack. At last Gariv rallied the men for one headlong assault on the Xhanchilion's strongest point; with that broken, he told his battered, bleeding, exhausted warriors, the palace was theirs. They charged, struck; the defenders wavered, gave ground, and finally broke. The palace had fallen to the Free Army.

The floors of polished stone were slick with blood, and the high corridors echoed with the sounds of battle and its aftermath. Some of the Free Army began looting on the spot, stripping the jewels from fallen courtiers, thrusting precious objects into their tunics or belts. What they could not carry, they destroyed. Gariv ordered a halt to this at once. He bid the men rest and refresh themselves in shifts, and prepare for the final decisive encounter. The battle was not yet over, and the time to enjoy the rewards of victory had not yet come.

The sun was high on the second day of battle when Gariv led his assembled forces against the Blue Temple, the last stronghold of the Xhanchilion. At sunset, the last defender lay dead in the high sanctum. The long narrow staircase was strewn with bodies, and blood ran to the streets below.

Some of the men dropped to the ground and slept where they fell, while others went off to seek plunder. Alladale, too exhausted for sleep, wandered through streets lurid in the glow of looters' fires, and he witnessed sights far surpassing the horrors he had seen in battle. Xhanchilion women were raped, mutilated, and then killed by laughing conquerors. Infants and small children were flung alive into fires, or impaled on swords and javelins and brandished aloft as trophies. Alladale came upon a group of Quespodons, one of whom was dismembering a child, plucking it apart as one would pluck a flower, while the others watched, amused. The aged were shown no more mercy than the young. An Agyari who noticed one old woman furtively swallow some object slit her belly and groped through her innards for the treasure. He drew out a bright ring, and the others around him, seeing his luck, took to doing the same to all the Xhanchilion they found, dead, wounded, or whole and begging for mercy.

Though he felt scarcely able to stand erect, Alladale

broke into a shambling run back to the temple where he had last seen Gariv. On his way he saw more evidence of the Free Army's revels. Down one street was a trail of severed hands. He followed it to a Skeggjatt who reeled from corpse to corpse and stopped to hack off every right hand. His own right arm ended in a stump, over which a blood-soaked rag was bound. When the Skeggjatt knelt to hack at the hand of a wounded ancient, Alladale's stomach gave a lurch and emptied. He leaned against a wall, drenched in his own cold sweat, trembling, spitting out the sour aftertaste of his vomit, and asked himself what had become of the friends and brothers who had ridden into battle with him.

He walked the rest of the way unseeing. There was no point in hurrying. Nothing could help, no one could stop this holocaust until the accumulated hatred had spent itself and the victors lay sprawled, exhausted and sated, on the bloody ground of Xhancholii. The slaves had suffered much at the hands of their masters, it was true, but the vengeance extracted was far in excess of any crimes the Xhanchilion had committed. Even the pirates who had annihilated the little settlement on Bellaterra had not gone this far.

The slaves had risen to seize their freedom, and their freedom was being celebrated by this butchery. Alladale confronted the dismal truth that long suffering need not ennoble a man, nor freedom regenerate him. Slave or master, we are what we are, he thought, and all we can change is our scope for expressing it. He wanted to think this out, weigh it carefully, ponder it from many viewpoints and find a flaw. He wanted to prove himself wrong. But he was too tired, and his mind was confused, and he feared that after all his efforts he would find that it was true.

He came upon Gariv seated outside the Blue Temple. The leader of the Free Army was a grisly sight: caked

172

blood covered his lower legs and forearms; a flap of skin hung from his ribs where he had ripped a javelin free; a long ribbon of blood still oozed down his neck and over his chest from the stroke that had carried away half his ear. But he was alive, his wounds were not serious, and his forces had won. The expression on his face was a boast of victory.

"I knew you were alive. I didn't see your body inside," he greeted Alladale.

"I've been walking."

Gariv wrinkled his nose in disgust. "You stink. Do you find the sight of battle so sickening?"

"It's the victory that sickened me."

For a long moment Gariv looked at him blankly, then he growled, "Speak plainly. No skillman's word-play with me."

Alladale sank to a half-sitting position against a pillar facing Gariv. "I walked through the city, and the things I saw made me sick. That's plain enough, isn't it?"

"What did you expect our men to do, embrace their former masters? Sing them one of your songs?" Gariv asked contemptuously. "Stop weeping over the enemy and get to work on a victory song."

"I'll make no song to celebrate this victory."

"As long as you're my bard, you'll make what songs I command, and make them promptly."

"Then find yourself another bard," Alladale said wearily. He leaned back and closed his eyes.

Gariv gave vent to an oath and a burst of bitter laughter. "This sensitive remorse is a custom among you bards. More than once I nearly ran your namesake through because of it. You'll put together words that send a man roaring into battle, but if he sheds a drop of blood, you weep and call him a butcher."

"Anyone who kills women and babies and old men *is* a butcher, Gariv."

"I don't recall those fine distinctions in your battle-anthem. You made no distinctions at all.

'For all of the friends you have slain,
For the years, and the shame, and the pain,
We will make of your palace a grave,' "

Gariv recited. "If you didn't mean it, you shouldn't have said it."

"I didn't think I had to instruct warriors not to kill the babies," Alladale said coldly.

"The babies would have grown up to hate us and plot against us. The old ones grew fat while we labored and died out in the desert. We owe them nothing."

Alladale sat upright and pointed at Gariv. "And what happens when everyone's had his fill of vengeance and they've all been killed? Who'll clear the streets, and bury the dead? Who'll gather food for us? We have to live here in Xhancholii until the slavers come, you know. Why did you let the men run wild, when we'll need——"

"Three hundred Xhanchilion are locked in the upper rooms of the temple. I've posted a carefully-selected Skorat guard. Does that satisfy you?"

Alladale looked at him, nodded, mumbled a reply, and settled back against the pillar to sleep.

The memory of their bloodletting seemed to subdue the anger of the conquerors. The survivors who emerged from hiding in succeeding days, and the three hundred spared by Gariv, were unmolested. The dead were placed in a mass grave beyond the shadow of the city walls. The streets were cleared of debris and scrubbed of blood. Inns reopened, then a few shops, and soon, despite the appalling losses on both sides, normal life resumed in Xhancholii.

All told, about two thousand Xhanchilion surived, most of them women and children. Free Army survivors numbered nearly a thousand. Fraternization was at first inconceivable, but as the days passed, and the length of their wait for the Daltrescan ship became more oppressively obvious to the victors, their attitude softened. The Xhanchilion women offered no resistance. The traditions of their people demanded submissiveness of the female, and with their own males gone, they accepted the men who had conquered them as unquestioned new masters.

The leaders of the Free Army found other consorts. Among the survivors picked by Gariv were six women of the Gafaal, an ancient race related to the Thresk, brought to Xhanchos ages before to serve as courtesans to the nobility. They were strikingly beautiful, tall and long-limbed, with soft smooth emerald-green skin and hair of deep blood red. Sprouting from their back on either side of the spine, just below the neck, they had a single tentacle, slim and supple. The tentacles were not developed for use, as was the case with the Thresk, but served primarily for decoration, woven into elaborate patterns in the women's long hair. Gariv had bestowed a Gafaal courtesan on each of his five best warriors, and taken Santrahaar, the loveliest of the six, for himself.

Also among Gariv's three hundred was the daughter of a Gafaal courtesan and a high Xhanchilion templar. She had been left among the other prisoners, to be put to different work. She was small of frame, her skin a paler green, and her hair the jet-black of her father's people. When Alladale first saw her, she was huddled in a corner of the upper room, wide-eyed with terror, clutching a linlovar tightly to her breast. His heart went out to her at once. She was quite lovely, and the thought of what might become of her moved him to act quickly. He snapped a curt command to the Skorat guard, drew himself up like a true conqueror, and strode through the

175

shrinking Xhanchilion to the woman's side. Gently, he eased the linlovar from her grasp, tucked it into playing position, and struck the opening chords of a slow, sad, Bellaterran lament. He smiled to reassure her, and returned the instrument. "I'm a skillman, not a warrior. I've killed no one. Come with me. You'll be safe," he said, in halting but adequate Xhanchilion. She took his hand, and they left together.

Her name was Loriise. As he learned more about her, Alladale marveled at the accuracy of his instincts. She played the linlovar well, knew hundreds of exquisite old Xhanchilion temple-songs, and best of all, was a gentle, affectionate woman who believed that he was the greatest skillman in the galaxy. Even if she did not believe it, she said it, and he heard her with pleasure. She might not possess the dazzling sensuous beauty of the pure-blooded Gafaal, but she did not have their tentacles, either, and Alladale was relieved to find this. It would have disconcerted him to have a woman's arms tightly around his neck and then to feel a soft caressing touch on the cheek. No, thank you, he thought. Loriise was also far more appealing than the heavy-browed, long-jawed, slab-faced Xhanchilion. And, he decided, her taste was impeccable. He could not help loving her.

They lived in one of the guard towers on the wall, in roomy, well-provisioned remoteness from the palace where Gariv had established his headquarters. The location suited them well: Alladale thought it wise to keep out of Gariv's sight for a time, Loriise felt apprehensive in the proximity of the conquerors, and they enjoyed being together unmolested by outsiders.

They spent all their time together at the beginning, and later, when Alladale was drawn into the intrigues of the factions that had sprung up among the victors, he found that the prospect of returning to Loriise was all that made the life of these times endurable. Here on Xhanchos, this planet of sand and slavery and brutal warfare, he had recaptured a happiness he thought forever lost on Bellaterra. Often they would ride out into the desert, and she would listen to him talk of his travels, and the places and people he had seen. She told him more and more of the history and legends and pyramid lore of her people, and as he learned, he wondered. Familiar words, melodies, and motifs disturbed him, because their familiarity was impossible. The Xhanchilion might have absorbed random fragments of song and story from the thousands of slaves who had passed through their camps, but some of the melodies he questioned were ancient songs from cultures long vanished, and here on Xhanchos, sung in Loriise's high trill, they sounded inexplicably right for the first time in his memory, almost as if they were being sung properly at last.

Often, at sunrise, they went out to the pyramids. Alladale found the silence and the isolation necessary after a few nights spent in Xhancholii, where rivalries were hardening and one could scarcely greet an acquaintance without being drawn into a plot. He was anxious to take Loriise away before everything went wrong.

One night, as they lay on the terrace of a pyramid, looking up at the intricate circlings of the seven moons, Alladale asked, "How old is Xhancholii, Loriise?"

"It was built in the fourth preceding *mluxo*," she replied.

The term meant nothing to him, but since he had asked the question idly, he was not at first inclined to pursue it. The city was bigger than any he had ever seen, its buildings, walls, and avenues constructed on a heroic scale, but it was not much different in other respects from typical civilized cities of an almost nonmechanical culture. Nevertheless, it somehow gave an impression of great age. He yawned and asked, "How long is a *mluxo*? Is it a long time?"

"To you, it would seem very long, but to me and to my father's people, not so long. Each of the pyramids represents the passage of one *mluxo* and contains its history."

Alladale nodded, only half-attentive. On their way to Xhancholii, the Free Army had passed three pyramids. Now, on the far side of the city, from his perch on the pyramid nearest the walls, he could count nine more receding toward the horizon. Between the sixth and seventh, and again between the second and third, were low ragged mounds that might have been the remains of two more. As he studied them, Loriise spoke again.

"How do you calculate time, Alladale?"

"As a rule, I don't even try. It just confuses me."

"But everyone does! Tell me, please."

Alladale explained the Galactic Standard Calendar as best he could, omitting the fact that drivespeed travel made it meaningless simply because he would then have to explain drivespeed. Loriise marveled at his account. "Why do you do it in such a complicated way?" she asked when he was done. "On Xhanchos, time is very simple. From sunset to sunset is one *imlux*. A thousand of these is one *hranxlux*, and a thousand of them is one *mluxo*, the time of a pyramid."

"Yes, I see. It does sound like a long time," Alladale said. He made a few rough calculations in his head. Someone in the camp had once said that the Xhanchilion day was thirty-eight GSC hours in duration, so a *mluxo* was thirty-eight million hours. It did seem a long time. He propped himself on one elbow and furrowed calculations with his finger in the shallow layer of blown sand. Loriise watched the unfamiliar symbols with a quickening interest that matched his own. He reached a figure,

178

shook his head, effaced it with a vigorous swipe of his hand, and started over. When he had arrived at the same figure five times in succession, he rose shakily, lifted Loriise to her feet, and looked at the walls of Xhanchos in awe.

"That city is more than seventeen thousand years old," he said in a soft voice.

"It is very old," Loriise agreed.

"And the pyramids, the ones out there . . . eleven of them . . . forty-seven, forty-eight thousand years more."

"There are many more pyramids beyond these," Loriise said matter-of-factly. "More than you see now are buried under the desert."

He pressed his temples tightly, fearing, for a moment, that his mind would jar out of place; he felt like a man who innocently opens a door in his home and finds himself looking out at the nothingness beyond the borders of the universe. The timespan represented by the visible pyramids was staggering; if even more lay buried, it became awesome. And the thought of the time that must have elapsed before the first pyramid was raised . . . He closed his eyes and shook his head.

"Are you all right, my love?" she asked anxiously. "Has something upset you?"

"The sheer age of this civilization . . . unimaginable!" He turned to her. "Loriise, can you understand? Your city was ten thousand years old when the first cities appeared on Old Earth, where my forefathers came from."

"Old Earth is a very young world."

"Yes, and most of the others are even younger. And I've helped to destroy what might be the oldest surviving race in the galaxy."

She laid her hand on his arm and smiled up at him.

"The people of Xhanchos cannot be destroyed. As long as the universe exists, we will exist."

"You've been conquered, all but a handful of you wiped out. Now the Xhanchilion women are breeding with Skeggjatts, Quespodons, Thorumbians, a dozen different races. Your people will disappear."

"The Xhanchilion blood is strong. Other conquerors have come to Xhanchos, but no trace of them remains. The blood will overcome, in time. The child I carry, your child, will resemble my father's people more than yours."

"It will?"

"Yes, just as I resemble my father more than my mother. Does this matter to you?"

He shook his head. "If they all resemble you, I'll be happy, Loriise. I love you very much."

As they rode back to the city, under the brightening sky, Alladale recollected old legends he had picked up from drunken spacerats and half-mad stardrifters in the byways of the galaxy. Bits and pieces, fragments, little more than hints, but they made more sense to him now, those tales of an old race, the First Travelers, who crossed the galaxy when the stars were young, so long ago that no relics of their existence remained, not even a memory, only whispers and imaginings. They vanished into oblivion long before the first pyramid rose on Xhanchos; but perhaps, in the oldest of the ancient structures out there, some trace of the First Travelers lay buried.

"What's in the pyramids? Why do you build them?" he asked as they approached the city.

"We build them because we must," Loriise responded.

"But why must you?" he pressed.

"As each *mluxo* draws to an end, all the records of

the era are gathered, to be sealed within. The king and his family prepare themselves for eternity."

That had an ominous sound. "Why?" he asked.

"They are put to death gloriously, with great ceremony, and placed in the pyramid. Their faithful adherents are spared the anguish of living on without them. Then the pyramid is sealed, and the past is forgotten. Some songs and tales are passed on, and some legends live, but nothing more. A new *mluxo* begins, with a new king."

"Loriise, would you think there was something wrong with me, or that I was being unkind to your beliefs, if I sought the first of the pyramids and tried to look within?"

"No. You do as you must. But why do you care?"

He gestured helplessly, seeking words for a half-sensed notion. "There's so much missing, so much we've lost. We really don't know where we came from, or who was here before. We know nothing. I'm hoping the pyramids will tell. I'm going to ask Gariv to let me take some men out and look."

At sundown that day, Alladale presented himself at the palace. After a long initial absence, he had gradually resumed a minor role in court circles, but he found the life painfully constricting and artificial, and was an irregular attendant. The intrigues repelled him even more than the ceremonies, and so he was impatient when Ninos, a smooth, well-dressed Skorat, drew him aside immediately upon his entrance and led him along a dim gallery.

"We see little of our anthem-maker these days," Ninos said. "You appear to have a liking for Xhanchos."

"I've stayed longer in worse places," Alladale replied.

"True enough, for all of us. And we're glad you like

the planet." The Skorat threw his arm around the bard's shoulder. "You're a man we admire, anthem-maker. We saw your deeds in battle, and were impressed. You fought bravely."

Alladale shrugged. That was a plain lie, lacking even the saving grace of subtlety. Here was a man looking for a favor, he realized, and knew that all he needed was patience, and details would unfold. "I'm a skillman, not a warrior, Ninos. I fought poorly."

The Skorat stepped back, halted, and looked him in the eye. "You have friends who think you fought well, and would fight well again if the cause were just."

"Against the slavers? I suppose I would, yes."

"Slavers? Where have you been, anthem-maker? The slavers' ship isn't coming. I'm talking about——"

"Not coming?" Alladale broke in. "Are we here on Xhanchos forever?"

"Perhaps. And if we are, it's our business to create a Xhanchos worth living on. Do you agree?"

Alladale's thoughts went instantly to his ship, standing alone in the desert, waiting. Only he and Gariv knew of it. When he became aware of the Skorat's inquiring eyes, he quickly said, "Yes. Yes, I suppose I do. Yes, I agree."

"We thought as much. Several important men—at the moment, I'm not at liberty to mention names—several leaders, as I say, believe that we should seize this opportunity to make a fresh beginning. They hope to establish a commonwealth based on equality and justice for all."

"That sounds good to me, Ninos. How does Gariv intend to go about it?"

Ninos looked away, frowning slightly. "Unfortunately, my friend, the leaders are not unanimous in their views. Before they can proceed further, certain obstructive elements . . . they will avoid bloodshed if at all possible, you understand, but . . . some things must be done."

The words were similar to words he had once heard from Gariv. He even looks like Gariv, Alladale thought. But then, all Skorats resembled one another rather closely. Must have been a lot of inbreeding on that planet. Skorat heredity, however, was not the point at issue. "Are you asking me to kill Gariv?" he asked Ninos bluntly.

Ninos looked horrified. "Of course not. I myself am not even a party to this group, Alladale, I merely repeat a rumor I have heard. You must understand the situation. For Gariv's own sake, I had hoped you might speak to him, sound him out, perhaps try to enlighten him. Certainly, I do not suggest that you raise a violent hand against our liberator and our leader."

"I see. I'll talk to him, Ninos. I like the idea of a commonwealth, and I'll try to persuade Gariv to consider it. But I won't conspire against him."

"The fair gods be with you, anthem-maker," Ninos said fervently, clasping his hand in a firm grip.

It took some time to penetrate to Gariv's presence. He had surrounded himself with a personal guard of Skorats and Skeggjatts, and few other breeds were to be seen around the palace. At the same time, throughout the city, the old ties among work crews had dissolved, and men were gathering with their own race and tribe. Ancient rivalries, forgotten in the camp, were mentioned once again. Fights were becoming common. This all struck Alladale as an inauspicious preliminary to a commonwealth.

Gariv received him in the throne room, where three armed Skeggjatts stood out of earshot. Beside him, on a smaller throne, sat Santrahaar. Beauty seemed almost to emanate from her, as light from a flame. Alladale gulped at the sight of her inviting smile and tried to turn his eyes away. She was wearing—not wearing, really, so much as slowly emerging from—a most revealing gown that glittered silver against the green of her skin. Her hair hung to her waist, and her tentacles were wreathed with a rope of precious stones into a high crown.

"What brings you here, bard, besides a wish to gape at your queen? I thought you'd wandered off to the desert to weep for the Xhanchilion. You're as bad as that crazy medico, Anders," Gariv greeted him.

"I want a favor, Gariv."

"I'm sure you do. What is it?"

"I'd like to organize a work force to go out and dig for the first pyramid."

Gariv leaned forward and stared at him incredulously. Then he roared, "Haven't you had enough work out there? You've lost your mind, or else you're playing a poor joke. Why did we rise up, but to escape the bondage that forced us to work in that murderous desert!"

"This is work that will benefit *us*, Gariv. Those pyramids may go back two hundred thousand years —think of what we might find in them!"

"Dust and sand is all you'd find."

"Maybe. But we might find knowledge that was lost before our races were born. Gariv, let me take a hundred Quespodons, volunteers——"

"Quespodons? Are you suddenly a comrade of those blotchy half-wits?" Gariv broke in.

"I'm no more their comrade than I ever was, and no less. I want them because they're strong and they're good workers."

Gariv laughed. "Yes, good workers. I'm glad you're acute enough to perceive that, Alladale. There may be some hope for you."

"Do you agree, then?"

"No. I have other work for you, more important than

184

digging holes in the desert." He summoned Alladale closer with a gesture, and lowering his voice, went on, "The Daltrescan ship isn't coming. That means we may be here for the rest of our lives. It's time I started putting things in order."

"I've heard rumors of a commonwealth———"

"So have I. Equality and justice for all, that's what they promise. I'll end that talk soon enough," Gariv said, frowning. "Men who conquer are the only ones fit to lead. The rest are born for the harness. No Quespodon or Thorumbian or Trulban will ever call himself the equal of Gariv, Monarch of Xhanchos."

Alladale winced inwardly at the new addition to Gariv's roster of titles. Hopes for a commonwealth seemed small, but he made one last try. "They all fought well for their freedom, Gariv. Should it be taken from them so quickly?"

"Have you forgotten how they acted when the city fell? Their kind need a master, and they shall have one. There's a place for you among the rulers, Alladale, if you can stiffen your spine and learn to do what must be done. I can use your skill with words. Proclamations must be issued, laws drafted. When things are all in place, we'll want a myth to guide and inspire us. I'll build a proper order on Xhanchos, where everyone serves in his proper place. That's the only kind of justice worth having."

Gariv dismissed his bard with orders to return at sunrise, prepared to settle in the palace. Alladale hurried through the halls, anguished at the prospect of so much to decide and so little time to think. Whichever side he chose, more blood would flow. Friends and comrades would die. The old fellowship of the desert and the camp were gone forever. The Free Army had become a mob.

He passed an alcove and heard his name spoken softly.

With a start, he turned and saw a husky, pale-haired young man of Gilead summoning him. He looked around, saw that he was not followed, and slipped into the shadowed alcove, where two large Quespodons were also in attendance.

"What do you want?" he asked.

"We would make use of thy skills, bard," the man of Gilead said. "Our brothers have left the smooth path and become slaves to the abomination. Their ways have become dissolute and evil."

"They certainly have," Alladale agreed readily. "What can I do about it, though?"

"*The Book Of The Voyage* tells us, 'Sweet sounds shall purify their hearts and raise their thoughts.' And again, 'The hand that touches the strings shall point the way to the smooth path.' Leave thy servitude to busyness, and put thy skills to use as Rudstrom ordains."

"Are you all Rudstromites?" Alladale asked.

"Truly we are," said the man of Gilead. "As yet we are few in number, but we will increase. We will lead all our brothers to the smooth way. Already, signs are fulfilled. The Chapter of Maledictions tells us, 'Accursed be the planet where rise the works of pride, and woe befall the builders of high walls!' and again, 'Woe befall the makers of stone dwellings!'" The pale-haired youth raised his hand and intoned, "Behold, the hour approacheth when every man must choose."

Alladale did not have the heart to point out that any woe that had befallen the Xhanchilion had been a long time in coming. He returned the gesture of benediction and said simply, "I must think on it." Then he slipped from the alcove and made his way back to Loriise. They had much to discuss, and very little time. Xhancholii was going to be a lively place before long.

For a woman trained to submissiveness, Loriise was remarkably quick in sizing up a situation and reaching a decision. Before the night had reached its midpoint, they were past the second pyramid, veering off toward the mountains. Each rode a *haxopod*, and a caravan of six galloped behind them, carrying food and water. Their strength would pull the ship into liftoff position; failing that, they would take the fugitives to safety among the tribes. Whatever happened now, there was no turning back.

Loriise was silent and withdrawn all during the long journey. Her pregnancy was visible now, but she did not spare herself. They rode furiously for seventeen nights, then began the ascent of the mountains.

Progress was slow. The unceasing wind had long ago scoured all trail marks from the barren upland rock, and Loriise, who knew the way only from ancient songs and legends, soon fell back on guesswork. The way led steadily upward, and the air became thin and cold. Their progress slowed to a stumbling, almost comatose walk, and still they ascended.

The *haxopods* held up well until they reached the highest regions. The smaller mounts, stripped of their saddles, were able to survive in the scanty air; but two of the big pack animals collapsed in convulsions, bringing up bloody foam from their double lungs and lashing out wildly with their long spade-footed legs. Alladale put the beasts out of their agony, and they pressed on, dragging most of their supplies behind them, hauling the surviving *haxopods* over the bleak ledges.

At the very top, humans and beasts stumbled in a nightmarish caravan across the harsh barren plateau. A strong wind buffeted them, penetrating even the heavy riding robes to chill them to the bone. Their hearts pounded erratically, their heads ached and spun, and the solid ground seemed to swim beneath their unsteady feet. Their faces were raw from the steady wind and every breath felt like a draught of cold fire drawn into lungs scraped raw by strain. They lost all track of time and direction. Often, Alladale came awake from an awful dream of eternal wandering in this bitter, darkening emptiness and for all his exhaustion he could not force himself to sleep again.

They traveled now in the brief times of dawn and dusk. The nights they spent huddled in one another's arms, away from the wind, in crevices or behind outcroppings. By day, they sprawled under crude shelters.

One dawn, Alladale noticed that the horizon was much closer. He dropped the reins of the *haxopod* he was tugging behind him and broke into a run, heedless of the ache in his lungs at each breath, and there, at the edge of the plateau, he saw the trail, narrow and rocky, but unmistakably leading down. He threw himself on the ground and looked out to where the desert began again, and far off, indistinct but undeniably there, awaiting them, was the oasis.

They rested for three days. The ship was not far away for a mounted party, and Alladale was concerned for Loriise's health. He fixed a shelter for them by the water, and gathered a supply of sweet blue-skinned fruit for them to eat. Still she seemed preoccupied. When he asked how she felt, she merely replied, "I am well."

"How soon is the child coming?" he asked. "I don't like the idea of your giving birth alone, out there in space."

"I will not give birth in space," she replied. Seeing his concern, she added, "The working of our bodily processes is not the same as it is for other races." She would say no more.

When they reached the landing ring, Alladale's work

began. He harnessed the *haxopods* to pull the ship forward, hairbreadth by hairbreadth, while he rushed furiously back and forth to clear away drifted sand, maintain ring position, and check the alignment gauges in the cabin. After four exhausting nights of unceasing effort, the ship was ready for liftoff. He satisfied himself on the alignments, then went to the shelter he had fixed in the abandoned station to inform Loriise.

"You will leave alone. I must stay," she said.

"You can't stay here, Loriise. You'll die in this desert! Come with me."

"No, I cannot. My child must be born on Xhanchos, and I can never leave. I have food and water enough to reach the tribes."

"Do you plan to stay with them forever?" he demanded, recalling her descriptions of the tribesmen's bleak lives.

"You will return to Xhanchos one day, when the fighting is over, and we will live once again in Xhancholii," she said. She took his hand and looked up at him lovingly. "If I had told you I cannot leave Xhanchos, you would have stayed in the city for my sake, and been slain. I had to get you away. The conquerors will destroy themselves, Alladale. They always do. The other women know this, and they are simply awaiting the day of their liberation from the despoilers of their city. I could not feel that way."

He drew her close. "Loriise, I love you. You're not a prisoner, or a trophy, you never were, you're my wife. We'll go to the tribes together."

She pulled away, shaking her head. "No. They would not accept an Otherworlder. Too much has been done to them. You must leave Xhanchos, Alladale. There is no other way."

He thought of the old enemy, time, that would divide

them despite any vows they made. "If I go, it will be a long time before I return. Our child may be older than either of us is now, before I come back. You may not live to see it."

She said what she had said before. "The working of our bodily processes is not the same as it is for other races. We grow old slowly and we live long. Leave now, but come back to me, Alladale. I will not change. Come back to me and our child."

He left at sunrise.

VI. Bard and Fugitive Once More

TRULBA SEEMED AS GOOD a destination as any. It was distant, but not so far that a solitary, memory-oppressed voyage would be unendurable. Alladale recalled rumors about a dynastic struggle on the planet, and the accession of a new ruling family. Such events usually meant opportunity for a bard and anthem-maker. New regimes were always short of legitimizing myths and legends, and a song of celebration seemed somehow to lighten the burden of a freshly-won crown. Gariv had mentioned something along these very lines, he reflected, and it was likely to be the same everywhere. A stay on Trulba, then—a year or two, no more, or he would lose the advantage of novelty—and he'd be on his way back to a peaceful Xhanchos, to regain his wife and child and settle down for good.

Things were not so bad, after all. He would miss Loriise, to be sure, but this time he could anticipate a reunion. She was not dead, or separated from him by the capriciousness of time . . . and he frowned, then, thinking of possible future complications that might arise from her slowness to age, but he soon put such things from his mind. No point in wasting this day worrying about those to come. Perhaps there was something in the air or water of Xhanchos, or in those delicious blue-skinned fruits, that retarded aging. It was possible. In any event, there was always drivespeed. So far, it had

191

treated him well. Here he was, seventy or eighty GSC years old, perhaps more, perhaps as much as a hundred, and yet scarcely more than a youth in terms of true lapsed time.

He reconsidered this opinion once he had a chance to look at himself. The beard he had sprouted in crossing the desert had a number of white strands. Not more than half-a-dozen, and premature, of course; but they were there, visible, too many of them. It's the strain, he told himself. The heat, thirst, diet, all that hard work, the battle . . . it can happen overnight. Everyone knew that. Gariv and Gurdur, after all, used to call him "lad" and "youngster." Nevertheless, he shaved very closely.

The passage of time was as gloomy a subject as his solitude. To occupy his mind, he drew up a strict regimen of practice on the linlovar and a review and reordering of all the songs, legends, and stories he had learned and created since leaving Bellaterra. He remembered some old log books that Tib had tucked away, unused, early in their travels, and he hunted them down and began to transcribe all the pieces as they came to mind, even the lines and half-lines that floated in his memory as tantalizing isolated fragments. When he grew tired of remembering, as he now and then did, he went back over what he had copied, smoothing and polishing the lines to his greater satisfaction. In this way, the voyage passed painlessly. When he landed on Trulba, he had three thick log books of works under his arm.

The Trulbans were direct descendants of Old Earth pioneers from the earliest phase of the exodus. They were a chunky people, smaller and broader than Alladale, fair-haired and blue-eyed, with a limited range of emotions and facial expressions. The women were rather too brawny for his taste (his thoughts returned to Loriise, slim as a wand, just a shade under his own height), and the men much given to public flexing and chest expanding and loud oaths sworn by their strength of arm and hand-might. They actually did nothing, but their boasts were terrifying.

Like any good bard, Alladale established himself at a popular inn where he could be seen and heard and could learn the local traditions and customs. Trulban history was a spotty affair. Since all the inhabitants were descendants of the original settlers, succession was often a matter of violent dispute, with the victor revising the past to legitimize his own claims and annihilate others'. Nine dynastic wars in six centuries had hopelessly buried the facts.

Alladale quickly learned that his own information was outdated. The most recent struggle, which resulted in the overthrow of the S'snpuaris, had taken place about fourteen planetary years before—about a decade, GSC. The present ruler, Krankl, was the sixth of the Sdrat'sa Bizan kings. He had been in power for three full planetary years, a record tenure for this planet. Krankl was a squat, soft, paunchy man with long, lank hair and scarcely any chin. He had close-set, slitted eyes which he kept turning suspiciously on his eldest son and heir apparent, Fegg. Krankl trailed a list of titles twice as long as Gariv's, and Alladale was certain that he had not earned a single one. Most of them were not the sort that one could earn, honorifics like "First Light of the Universe," or "Unwavering Beacon of Enlightenment." Others, like "Mighty Arm Wielding the Sword of Domination," appeared distinctly out of character for Krankl.

Some of the people of the crown city had conferred other titles on him, the least hateful of which was "Krankl the Remorseless." It soon became obvious to Alladale that this, and his other unofficial titles, Krankl had richly earned. He had doubled the number of prisons in the kingdom, and filled every one. He had designed new torture chambers with the best equipment, and made frequent inspection tours in person. At his command, sixteen spectacular new methods of execution were devised or reintroduced, the number of capital crimes was increased fourfold, arrest quotas were established, and trials were abolished. Krankl announced his intention of eliminating all subversives and enemies of the throne in order to make Trulba safe for his loyal subjects. One elderly gentleman, listening to the proclamation, remarked that Krankl was more likely to eliminate his subjects and make Trulba safe for the wind. The man was executed, as was the high minister who presented Krankl with figures to prove that at the present rate of executions, the population would be halved in two planetary years.

This news convinced Alladale to revise his plans, but he did not act quickly enough. On the day he was ready to leave the inn, four palace guards arrived to escort him to Krankl. The monarch, having learned of the presence of a renowned bard in the crown city, commanded him to attend his court. Refusals were not possible on Trulba, nor was there much apparent point in trying to explain that he was not the original Alladale. Trulba seemed less and less to be the sort of place where a reasonable explanation would be accepted in a reasonable spirit. Alladale Anthem-maker went with the escort.

The grand palace was in keeping with the rest of the city: a low building of stone, elaborately decorated in the very worst taste imaginable, spotlessly clean, and in poor repair. As they approached, Alladale noticed long, oddly-shaped pennants flapping in the mild morning breeze. He questioned his four escorts, but they gave no sign of hearing his words. Passing through the gate, he glanced up for a close look at the pennant directly overhead. He stopped in his tracks and fought down a seismic churning of his insides. The pennants were human hides.

The two guards marching behind thrust him forward, and he moved on, perspiring freely, his mind racing in panic. He had to get off Trulba as soon as possible, no question about that. Stock up the ship, return to Xhanchos, hide out for a few years at the oasis. It would be hot, uncomfortable, painful at times, but anything was better than this. Anything. Even the Xhanchilion did not flay people. They might work them to death, or throw them into the pulverizer, but they were not unnecessarily cruel about such things.

Once in the palace, Alladale was carefully searched, then turned over to a courtier for instruction in court protocol, which consisted chiefly of obsequious gestures and elaborate forms of address. To his relief, Alladale learned that an Otherworlder might call Krankl "Your Galactic Supremacy" and skip the litany of titles required from his native subjects. The courtier who acted as his mentor, a young man with a pronounced facial tic, informed him that the penalty for omitting a single title was death by boiling alive—unless Krankl was in the mood to impose a more severe punishment.

Led at last into the throne room, Alladale did his best to make a strong impression. His skillman's regalia made him the most colorful figure in the roomful of drab-clad Trulbans, and he carried himself straight and erect as he walked to the foot of Krankl's throne and made a graceful, sweeping bow from the waist. He held the position for the prescribed time, then repeated the bow in a less profound form to the three unattractive young women seated on a lower dais to Krankl's left, and again a third time to the evil-faced little Fegg who crouched at the foot of the dais on Krankl's right.

"Enough! No need to bow to that miching little *kekket*," Krankl snapped, shying a half-empty goblet at his son. Fegg ducked the missile, and two courtiers sprang to catch it before it touched the floor. They collided, and the goblet rang upon the stones. The throne room at once became very still. Krankl turned and glared at them in silence, while they trembled, and then he smiled a ghastly smile and said, "I am inclined to be lenient. Since you have failed in my service through clumsiness, I will provide you an excuse for all future clumsiness. Each of you will have a foot struck off. I will allow you to select the foot you are to lose." With a gesture, he summoned the guards to carry out the command, then turned his attention to Alladale. "So, the famed Alladale Anthem-maker comes to Trulba. Tell me, bard, do you consider yourself worthy to perform in the presence of Krankl, Embodiment of All Harmony and Sweet Singer of the Stars?"

That was an unfamiliar title, probably created on the spot. Alladale protected himself with a bow and some courteous blather. "The decision is for Your Galactic Supremacy to make, the command yours to give. I await your pleasure."

Krankl cast a pompous look around the throne room, and said, "We will hear a song. A brief song, bard. We do not choose to be bored."

After more bowing, Alladale struck a soft chord on the linlovar and began to sing the song of Old Earth he had heard from Gariv. It was a revision, of his own devising, shorter and more poignant, suggestive rather than assertive. He finished, and not a sound could be heard. All eyes were on Krankl, awaiting his cue for reaction. The Embodiment of All Harmony and Sweet Singer of the Stars lowered his head, raised a hand to his brow, blinked in an exaggerated manner, and wiped a corner of one eye with a delicate gesture of his little finger. At once, sniffles and whimpers arose from the courtiers.

The three princesses sat slack-jawed on their triple throne, staring at Alladale. The youngest one began to sob loudly. Krankl turned to the others and growled, "Weep, or be flogged, do you hear? Weep, all of you!" he roared, and the throne room was filled with ululation and moan. When he had had his fill of this Krankl silenced the uproar with a gesture and summoned Alladale to the foot of his throne.

"You have moved the heart of Krankl, Fountain of Compassion for All Life, bard. Tell me, can you do as well with a battle-song?"

"My words can inspire an aging Quiplid to do battle with a score of Skeggjatts, Your Galactic Supremacy," Alladale said, bowing low. "And defeat them."

"And story songs? Ancestral tales?"

"I excel in all these, Your Galactic Supremacy."

"Then hear your reward, Alladale Anthem-maker," Krankl announced. "Henceforth, you are bard to this throne. I permit you to devote your life and skills to the celebration of my reign, and to the achievements of those illustrious ancestors whose magnificence has reached its culmination in me."

Alladale was stunned. This was a form of slavery worse than that of Xhanchos, a bondage of soul and skills as well as of the body. "But I . . . I am unworthy of such a . . . an honor, Your Galactic Supremacy," he stammered. "I never imagined . . . it never occurred to me . . ."

"Of course you are unworthy, bard, but I am disposed to overlook your unworthiness. I will admit you to my presence at intervals, to allow you to glean inspiration. Please me, and you will be well rewarded."

When Alladale was dismissed, he asked his twitching courtier if Krankl had had a previous bard, and learned that he was the fourth to be so honored. Reluctantly, he inquired as to the fate of his predecessors. He was told that they could be found among the crowd of beggars at the lower gate. They were the ones with no hands.

Two tense but uneventful days passed. Alladale was installed in a small private apartment in the castle, given robes to wear at court, a seal to signify his bardic rank, a vast array of Trulban instruments to study, and a private bodyguard. He saw no one, heard no news, and began to wonder if he had been forgotten. Six times in those first few days he tried to slip away to the spaceport, but the bodyguard was persistent. He could not lose them. So he bided his time, experimenting with the instruments and producing some bizarre effects.

On his third day as bard to the throne of Trulba, he was summoned to court and informed that he was to instruct Krankl's youngest daughter, the Princess of All Worlds and Most Beautiful of Creatures, in the linlovar. The lessons were to begin that very day, after the midday meal.

Alladale presented himself at the royal apartment, his stomach unsettled (as it had been since the day of his appointment) but nevertheless relieved that no more drastic whim of Krankl's had been visited upon him. A pair of formidable crones ushered him inside, and took their watchful places as he and the princess, whose name was Fruda, took seats facing one another, each holding a linlovar.

Fruda was a pleasant, tractable girl, not terribly pleasing to the eye—or the ear—but earnest and eager for praise. She spoke seldom, and when she did, her words revealed a mind very like a thick, sweet pudding. She was much given to smiling for no apparent reason. At the end of the first lesson, Alladale had taught her a few simple chords and led her through an easy melody, and when he gave polite praise to her quickness and talent, she asked him to return that evening and instruct her further. She was her father's favorite. He could scarcely refuse.

Upon his return, they took their places as before, flanked by dour ancients, Fruda smiling more frequently and mischievously than ever. In a short time, the chaperones began to nod. Soon they were snoring. Fruda tossed aside her linlovar and threw her arms wide. "Come, Prince of the Rosy Dawn, and claim your reward!" she cried breathlessly, and closed her eyes. Alladale sighed, put down his linlovar, and claimed his reward with as much enthusiasm as he could muster. His training as an actor carried him through.

As the chaperones sank deeper and deeper into slumber, Fruda's enthusiasm grew, and she babbled wild romantic extravagances. Worst of all was her insistance that her Prince sweep her off her feet and carry her off to her bedchamber. It would have been far easier for her to tuck him under one arm and saunter down the long hallway, Alladale reflected as he reeled under the burden of the simpering princess. Fruda, interpreting his exhausted gasping as the hot breath of passion, whispered, "I am yours, Conqueror from the stars! Possess me, destroy me, my Prince!" and melted enormously in his straining arms. The discovery that the royal family of Trulba trafficked in titles even in their assignations, though it depressed Alladale, did not really surprise him. He expected no better from them.

At the next afternoon's lesson, his back and arms ached so badly he could scarcely hold his linlovar, and was forced to concentrate on lyrics. A feeling of guilt added to his suffering, and he tried to salve his conscience. Surely he had not been unfaithful to Loriise in any meaningful sense. He had not enjoyed himself, that was certain, and unfaithfulness presumed pleasure on one's part. He managed to reduce his feelings of guilt to mere uneasiness, which he could handle. He was accustomed to it.

The chaperones were wide awake, watchful as hungry *snargraxes*, but Fruda's smiles promised another strenuous evening. Desperate, Alladale slipped out of the palace immediately after the lesson, concealing himself in a long brown cloak, and made his way to the spaceport. He had devised a story that would get him past any guards, and once aboard, he would be off . . . . On arriving, he stopped and stared at a terrifying vacancy. His ship was gone. He walked completely around the spaceport, checked the number of the landing ring a dozen times, and at last made discreet inquiry as to the whereabouts of the recent arrival. He learned that it was indeed gone, left that very morning on a diplomatic mission to one of the inner systems. He was stranded once again. He returned to the palace like a man ascending the scaffold.

That night, when Fruda's romantic yearnings had been satisfied and she lay smiling in the arms of her aching Conqueror from the Stars, Alladale sought some straight answers. At first he was rewarded with sighs and pouts, but he persisted. "I'm a lonely, desperate man, my little moonbeam, and on all this planet I have no one to trust in but you. Is the rumor true? Has my ship been taken?"

"But my prince needs no driveship," she said, looking up at him coyly. "He is a member of the court of Krankl now and for all time. Would he leave his helpless slave of love and flee to another world?"

"No powers could tear me from your side, my snowflake. But if anyone should try . . ."

"Yes? What would you do?"

His voice was steely. "I would cut my way through

a warrior host and carry you away to the farthest stars. If I had a driveship."

"Once a man enters the service of the crown, he has no further need of possessions. All he has becomes the property of my father, to use as he sees fit."

"Of course," Alladale said, and held his tongue from further comment. He was in trouble enough. He could sense high impenetrable walls rising on all sides.

At their parting in the morning, Fruda gave him welcome news. She was quite matter-of-fact about it, dropping all titles and trappings.

"We can't meet for a time, bard. I'll let you know when I want you again," she said, still smiling.

"Is something wrong?" Alladale asked.

"My father has completed his negotiations with the free traders. They depart this day. He will want you to attend him at all hours, and you must be available." She giggled and pulled the bedclothes over her face. "If he were to summon you . . . and found you *here* . . ."

Terrifying possibilities dawned on Alladale. He had never imagined the crude and loutish Krankl in the role of protective father. Indeed, his assumption from the first summons to Fruda's quarters had been that Krankl had chosen this method to upgrade the royal bloodline in an indirect manner. Now, the thought of Krankl's revenge on the Otherworlder who had led his youngest daughter astray turned his spine to a column of ice.

He was accustomed to traveling light. With his skillman's regalia on his back, a pouch of cashcubes at his belt, log books under one arm and linlovar slung over his shoulder, he had all the worldly goods he needed. The court robes, seal, and instruments in his palace apartment were well-earned, but all in poor taste and much too bulky to carry off; all but the tiny oscillating instrument called the *rillif*, which he carried in his pocket. Still, the more he could offer the free traders, the better his chances of buying passage off Trulba.

On Fruda's finger glittered a ring inset with a single large green diamond—fair payment, he thought, for a stolen driveship, a command performance, and other services of a personal nature. Murmuring a sweet farewell, he took Fruda's ample hand in his, stroked it, kissed it, squeezed it tightly, and then, with a wave, quickly departed.

As things turned out, his supply of cashcubes sufficed to buy his passage. The free traders, having basked in the presence of Krankl, First Light of the Universe, for ten planetary days, were quite sympathetic. He was convinced that they would have taken him along free, but he felt better paying his way.

The ring was an interesting souvenir. It was comforting, too, to find that his old skills had not forsaken him. The touch was as light as ever, and as sure. Kynon himself, in his best days, could have done no better.

The free traders were bound for Skorat to negotiate a trading covenant with one of the warlords. They agreed to conduct Alladale here and no further, and he accepted the offer willingly. Skorat was not high on his list of desirable planets, but it was not Trulba. That was good enough.

The Trulban experience had ended all enthusiasm for court life and the company of kings, or so Alladale thought. But after one long planetary month of wandering from one smelly inn to another to perform for rude, sweaty *trettle* herdsmen, he was ready for a change. He was, after all, a master skillman, bard to kings. And he also had some information that would be of great interest to Nikkolope, Queen of Thak, and could mean a considerable reward for the one who delivered it. He directed his wanderings toward Thak.

202

His approach was straightforward. With his clothing cleaned, refurbished, and thoroughly aired out, he appeared at the royal palace, gave his name, and requested an audience with the queen. The guard's response was immediate. He took him to the guard captain, who personally escorted the bard to a small chamber deep within the palace, and there left him in the care of two guards. When Alladale tried to make polite conversation with the guards, one of them called him a foul, filthy, water-drinking son of a five-legged *trettle* and vowed to smash his jaw if he dared to speak again.

That got him thinking. He had seen enough of the galaxy by now to believe in coincidence, even absurd coincidence, but he felt that it was being overdone in his particular case. It seemed scarcely possible that Alladale had decamped from Skorat under circumstances such as he had just experienced on Trulba. Were all royal bards habitual fugitives? Was some malevolent galactic force out to destroy him because of an obscure taboo he had violated, all unknowing, on a distant world? That seemed as likely as anything else. Why does it always go wrong? he asked himself plaintively. He wanted little enough: an audience for his skills (a small one would do, provided that they were appreciative); a chance to learn, and create, and live a normal life. Not *too* normal, but free from battles, pursuits, enslavement, and the mad whims of royalty. Things were not working out that way. He sat and waited, brooding, and managed to generate a considerable amount of sympathy for himself by the time his visitors arrived.

Suddenly, dramatically, the door swung wide and Alladale caught his breath and rose to his feet at the sight of the most magnificent woman he had ever seen. Instinctively, he bowed low before her. He knew and loved beauty, and willingly gave it the tribute it deserved. But to call this woman merely beautiful was to call the sea moist, or speak of the mild warmth at the heart of a dwarf star; she was beautiful beyond measure and description. Her splendor filled the little chamber like sweet song.

"I, Nikkolope, Queen of the city of Thak, demand to know by what right you come to my palace and ask audience under a stolen name," she said. Her voice was at once so exquisite and yet so deadly cold that he pictured a superbly chased blade flashing in swift descent.

"The name was conferred upon me by a man who called himself Gariv of Skorat, Master of the city of Thak and husband to one Nikkolope, Your Majesty," he replied with a bow and a flourish.

"Where is this Gariv?" demanded the man who had accompanied her. He was an impressive specimen, tall and muscular, handsome in a surly, threatening way, and had he entered the room alone his entrance would have been an event in itself. But by the side of Nikkolope, no one could attract attention. Until he spoke, Alladale had been unaware of his presence.

"Wait, Sounitan," the queen said. Then, to Alladale, "Describe the man who claimed to be Gariv of Skorat."

"A big man in his middle years . . . taller than I, and a formidable warrior . . . thick dark hair and beard, a lot of white in it . . . long scar across his chest——"

"Describe the scar," Nikkolope said.

"It started just below the right shoulder and ran to the lower left ribs. It was jagged, as we picture lightning, Your Majesty."

She turned to her escort. "Gariv received such a scar when he fought for my hand."

"We must know more than this."

"We shall," she said, and returned her attention to Alladale. "Who was this anthem-maker whose name was given to you? Why did Gariv give you the name?"

Alladale recited the story he had carefully worked out on his way to Thak: after a long illness that destroyed his memory, he found himself a slave in Gariv's work crew on Xhanchos. When Gariv heard of his skills, he befriended him. For his courage in the slave uprising, Gariv gave him the name of his fallen bard and commanded him to make a battle-anthem for the seige of Xhancholii.

"And what has become of this Gariv? Did he fall in battle?" Nikkolope asked.

"No, Your Majesty. He led the Free Army to victory over great odds. But I fear he's fallen now."

"An assassin?"

"Perhaps. I left Xhancholii at a time when the victors were divided among themselves. Some wanted to form a commonwealth, some a holy nation. Many wanted no government at all. Gariv and a few close supporters intended to establish a military state. The surviving Xhanchilion were waiting for their conquerors to destroy one another."

"I'm sure the surviving Xhanchilion were women."

"Most of them, Your Majesty. Several women of the Gafaal were spared to act as servants to the leaders of the Free Army."

Nikkolope gave an icy laugh. "I'm sure the most beautiful of them served Gariv in his bed. Is that not so?"

"It's true he chose the most beautiful one as his servant, Your Majesty," Alladale said uneasily.

"He always did. But you say he is now dead?"

"I believe he is, Your Majesty. When I left Xhancholii, the situation——"

"I want no beliefs, no opinions, imposter," Nikkolope said impatiently. "I want a statement. You have come to inform me of Gariv's death, have you not?"

Alladale hesitated for a moment before answering. He

knew what Nikkolope wanted to hear, and could see no reason to tell her otherwise. Gariv could not have survived the plots that were sure to be laid against him; even if he escaped his enemies, he would never leave Xhanchos. In effect, he was doubly dead. "Yes, Your Majesty. Gariv lies dead on Xhanchos," Alladale said.

"Then I must choose a consort and remarry. Thak has been too long without a king," Nikkolope said coolly. Alladale had his doubts about that. With a woman like this on the throne, a king was superfluous. Nikkolope was no pining, languishing space widow, she was a ruler whose word was law. "As for you, anthem-maker," she began, then paused and studied him for a bit, and at last said, "attend my court tonight and entertain us. If you merit the name of Alladale, you may retain it until I decide to execute you."

"Execute me, Your Majesty?" he asked.

"You have brought news of the death of a king. For this, the penalty is death. It will be swift and honorable, bard, I promise you that. In the meantime, enjoy your life and show us your skills. If you please us, I will spare your life until the wedding and coronation are complete, and allow you to commemorate them."

Alladale gestured uncertainly. "It will be difficult to enjoy life and display my best skills when I know I must die, Your Majesty," he said, in as offhand a manner as he could manage.

"You speak like an Otherworlder," Sounitan said.

"I *am* an Otherworlder."

"All men die, bard. The brave and the fortunate fall in battle; the weak and the cowardly die trembling behind their doors; the unlucky are executed. But all die. On Skorat, a man does not fear death. He lives his life to the full, every minute of it, even to the last. A woman does likewise. Learn this lesson," Nikkolope said. She swept out of the little chamber, Sounitan trailing behind her, and Alladale was given his liberty within the confines of the castle.

That night he won the acclaim of the court. Even the moody Sounitan rapped the arm of his chair to show his approval of a Skeggjatt battle-charm, and the eyes of the oldest warriors shone when Alladale sang the war-anthem of the Free Army. At the end of the evening, when he finished a long, moving story, told in five voices, about a father who mistakenly slays his own son in battle, Nikkolope rose and announced that henceforth this bard was to be known to all as Alladale Anthem-maker, and his life was to be spared for one planetary year following the royal wedding. All those in attendance cheered such magnanimity. Alladale, though not over-whelmed, was encouraged by the extension and said so in a witty verse. Still in an expansive mood, the queen summoned her armorer, who fetched a beautifully-made court sword which she presented to Alladale. He raised it high for all to see, and extemporised a song of thanks in an old Skeggjatt meter:

> "Breath against the sea wind,
> Rain against the salt wave,
> Spark beside the hot flame,
> Stars beside my fair queen:
> Such, the fate of all swords
> When they meet my bright blade,
> Gift of Queen Nikkolope
> To her anthem-maker."

Everyone approved. Nikkolope listened, and when he was done, she once again raised her hand to signify an announcement. The court fell silent, and she said, "Alladale Anthem-maker has won his life. Let all men hear my words and honor them."

He thanked her effusively, and when she had withdrawn, he lifted a pitcher of dark, pungent wine and drank to the long life and ever-increasing happiness of the kindest and loveliest woman in the galaxy. He sincerely meant it.

Often in the next few days Alladale was summoned to the palace to repeat before various groups of court officials and nobles his testimony of Gariv's demise. Somehow, in the time since his first meeting with Nikkolope, conjecture had congealed into history, and Gariv was now unquestionably dead. When he was not so occupied, Alladale was left to himself, and he spent his time filling the blank pages of his log books, reworking old pieces, and experimenting with the linlovar.

Quite by accident, he had found that the small oscillating instrument brought from Trulba could be attached to the linlovar in a number of ways to produce unusual effects. Some of them were most unsettling. One evening, reclining in a dark corner of the throne room, unnoticed by anyone, he had begun to finger the strings idly at a time when the *rillif* was affixed inside the sound box. He soon grew aware of a subtle change in the mood of the room. It felt close, dark, hostile. Directly before him, in the line of the clearest notes, two friends had fallen to bitter quarreling. When he stopped playing, they seemed to come out of a trance; they laughed and looked about them, embarrassed. He tried the same chords on others and found that they, too, gave vent to sudden anger and near-violence while they remained in the path of his music.

He experimented no further that evening, and mentioned his discovery to no one. On other occasions he tried it with results that were often unpredictable and sometimes dangerous. More than once, trying it out in a tavern, he had to duck a flying stool or dodge struggling bodies. Yet he had only to stop playing, and the seizure vanished. Experimenting further, he found that by varying the placement of the *rillif* inside the sound box, he could induce different emotions—fear, disgust, hilarity—nearly all possible states of feeling, except for love. Try as he might, he could find no way of using the *rillif* to stimulate the gentler emotions.

That disappointed him. He had found that men, on the whole, could stir up hard and bitter feelings easily enough without need of bardic aid; it was love, pity, and forgiveness that were in short supply, and the man who could rouse those sentiments could justly claim to be the greatest skillman of all. He knew he could sometimes achieve success in this area by his skills alone, and he was proud of that; but it would be nice to have a dependable trick at one's command in emergencies. He sighed and filed his discoveries away for consideration at some future time.

As a royal bard, Alladale was free to travel about Skorat with impunity. Rival kings might try to bribe him into leaving Nikkolope's court, but no man would dare to lay hands on a maker of songs. He was regarded as something akin to a holy man. Since Skorat was a violent martial culture, this was perhaps the greatest benefit the title of bard conferred. Though it was culturally unified, with a common language, code of ethics, and mythic history, the planet was in a continual state of political chaos. The nineteen royal cities were usually at war over something or other—stolen women, disputed pasture land, hunting rights, woodlands, even points of grammar—and the hundreds of tiny principalities joined them in a kaleidoscopic sequence of shifting alliances. But the visit of a bard was the occasion of an immediate truce. Sworn enemies would sit side by side on the same bench and drink from the same goblet while they listened to his songs and stories of a hundred worlds.

He traveled widely for three galactic months, and was well received by every major ruler on Skorat. Men and women who had heard the first Alladale in the days before the Expedition had taken him away pronounced the new one to be his superior. Their sons and daughters needed no verification from their elders; they knew this bard was the best the planet had ever heard.

When the summons came to return to Thak for the royal wedding, Alladale's log books were nearly filled and the praise of many thousands rang sweetly in his memory. He could not deny that life on Skorat was good, and Nikkolope was as considerate as she was beautiful, and that a bard could spend his days here with a surer chance at happiness than he would have on any other planet known to him. That was all true, and yet he felt restless. He missed Loriise more than he had thought he would, and longed to see and hold their child, and he missed his independence, with all its dangers and uncertainties. Nikkolope's tether was long and gentle, but it was a tether nonetheless, that could easily be tightened. Experience had taught him that a queen or a king can break their royal word at a whim, and their victims have small recourse. Had he known of a way to leave Skorat, he would have been gone in an instant. But there was no way. So he sang, and practiced, and made new songs, and kept his eyes open, and his journey to Thak was soon over.

Like all long-awaited ceremonies, the wedding of Nikkolope and Sounitan seemed at some point to bound from the distant and manageable future to a frenetic tomorrow. The castle was filled with servants rushing in all directions, wringing their hands, colliding, crying out, issuing shrill orders and ignoring the orders being meanwhile shrilled at them, and expending great amounts of energy to accomplish little beyond undoing the work of others. Exhausted from travel and wanting no part of this hubbub, Alladale went directly to his chamber, where a surprise awaited him. Laid out on his pallet was a brand-new outfit to replace his now rather seedy skillman's livery. It was very gaudy and quite splendid: tight-fitting trousers, striped in the royal colors of Thak; a short jacket of crimson, the color of celebration; high boots made from the soft leather of the underbelly of a young *haxopod*; even a new woven strap for his linlovar. Apparently, word of his successful progress across Skorat had reached Nikkolope, and she was showing her approval. Just in time, too, he thought, fingering the threadbare elbows and frayed cuffs of his present tunic, wrinkling his nose at the acrid aroma of *haxopod* that clung to it. He was tempted to try on his new outfit, but fatigue overcame him. He dropped on his pallet and went to sleep at once.

Despite all the preliminary confusion, the ceremonies got off to a smooth start on the following day. In the morning, in fulfilment of an ancient custom, Nikkolope went abroad to choose threescore townspeople to attend the wedding dinner as representatives of her subjects. At midday, the festivities began. All the nobles of Skorat were in attendance; a planetary truce had been declared, and unable to combat one another physically, they competed in the splendor of their attire and the extravagance of their gifts.

The food was superb. Alladale, circulating among the noble guests, many of whom he knew, was forced to satisfy himself with a quick bite and a swallow between songs, but even these morsels were delicious. Course followed course, each more elaborate than the one preceding, served with speed and grace by serving girls of surpassing beauty. All went well until halfway through the dinner—the second meat course, to be precise—when a man at a table close to Alladale, one of the guests chosen from among the common people, rose to his feet and announced that he had news of great interest for the queen. Alladale smiled, as did most of

211

those at table, but he stopped smiling when he saw the man. It was Gariv.

He knew that there had to be an explanation. The man must be an imposter, madman, a drunken fool. Perhaps one of the nobles was indulging in a heavy-handed prank. But the man looked very much like Gariv. And if he was indeed the lord of Thak returned from the dead, Alladale was going to have a lot of explaining to do, either to him, or to Nikkolope, or to both. He had little taste for that.

"The true king of Skorat lives! Gariv has returned from the dead to claim his throne, his kingdom, and his queen!" the man roared out, arms raised high.

Alladale was near an archway that led to a seldom-used rear exit from the castle. He made up his mind on the spot—better to be sorry you've run than sorry you haven't. He eased to the archway as Nikkolope replied to the guest's outburst, and once he reached it, he ducked through. He stopped at his chamber to gather his possessions—a matter of seconds—and then left the castle and headed for the rocky hills beyond the city.

He traveled on foot, walking hard, and by sundown he had reached the hills. Once out of sight of the city, he kept to the high rocks, seeking a temporary hiding place out of the cool night wind where he could plan his next move. And there, concealed in a natural amphitheatre of stone, was a scoutship. It stood unguarded, unsealed, as if awaiting his arrival.

His first impulse was to lift off at once. Whoever had landed here had taken a considerable chance and gone to great pains to avoid notice. They were probably up to no good, and it would serve them right to be stranded. Besides, Alladale told himself, someone owes me a driveship. Perhaps this was the very craft Gariv had used to come back to Skorat and ruin everything. If that were the case, then in sheer justice . . . .

212

He took his place at the controls, reached for the coil initiator, and drew back his hand. He could not go through with it. Kynon might have mocked his softness, but Alladale could no longer live by his father's piratical axioms, not when it came to stealing another man's driveship. He had felt too often the desolation and helplessness of abandonment, and was unable to inflict it on another, whatever his crimes. There were some things that even need did not excuse.

He recalled the ring he had slipped from Fruda's finger. If necessary, he could use it to buy his passage. It was worth the whole ship, twice over, but he was willing to be generous. The main idea was to get off Skorat.

Having reached this honest, upright decision, he gave in to his weariness. Seeking out a far corner of the supply hold, he settled down to sleep with a clear conscience. He did not stir until they shifted into highdrive. Then, with some slight apprehension, a bit of stiffness in his neck and shoulders, and a ravenous appetite, he brushed himself off and went to meet his unwitting hosts.

They were seated at a mess table. Both were armed and rather wild-looking young men, but the meeting could not be avoided. Alladale stopped in the entry and cleared his throat. At the sound, the two sprang to their feet and drew their weapons, and he immediately extended his empty hands in a gesture of peace.

"Gentlemen, I offer my profound apologies for bursting in on you like this. I'm very sorry if I startled you," he said. When neither replied, he went on, "Actually, I find myself in a most awkward position. I slipped aboard your craft thinking it would be empty for the duration of the festivities, and now we're in space. Quite awkward, really."

"A stowaway," said the taller of the two, a man lean as a stick, with a lined, weathered, expressionless face.

"Please, sir, you do me wrong," Alladale said, trying to look hurt by the accusation. He went on to explain how sheer accident had placed him in their company, and they relented. For all their formidable appearance, they were a good-hearted pair, willing enough to share their driveship and their food with a skillman in return for nothing more than his songs. Unfortunately, they were heading for Watson, a planet where bards, skillmen, and their like were classified as undesirables and given most ungentle treatment. But a way could always be found around future difficulties; the thing was to stay alive. Whatever awaited them on Watson, the driveship *Renegade* was safer than Skorat.

Alladale soon came to like his hosts. The tall one, Grax, the older of the two, was taciturn, while his comrade, Del Whitby, was a good listener and an eager talker bursting with curiosity about everything. Del was a starbrat, a spaceborn orphan seeking to learn on Watson the truth about his name and parentage. He was little more than a boy, but he had lived a life of horrendous violence—a Daltrescan slaveship, five seasons in the arena on Tarquin VII, a battle-festival on Vigrid, a stint as driveship guard—and still he was able to react with almost childlike enthusiasm to Alladale's songs and stories. Grax gave the impression of having seen and done even more than his partner, but he never spoke of his past or inquired about others'. His taste for comic songs of the sort popular in low dives was an annoying trait, but all in all he was good company, as was Del, and Alladale found the journey pleasant. He tried out some new compositions on his captive audience, introduced them to beautiful myths and legends, and prided himself on giving generous return for a short driveship voyage.

Both Del and Grax had, or believed they had, Old Earth blood in them, and so anything Alladale could tell them about the mother world was received with reverence. The first piece he sang for them was a version of Gariv's song, as he had sung it for Krankl. It moved them visibly. When he had come to know them a bit better, he tried an Old Earth song of his own on them.

"Who will pity a sad old woman
Now that her strong young sons have fled?
    Once she lived in a fine green palace
    Roofed with azure and ringed by stars;
    Suitors sprang when she crooked her finger,
    Sang her praise on the linlovar,
But no one thinks of the poor old woman
Now that her sons have journeyed far.
    Once she walked in a fair green mantle,
    Crowned with a circlet glittering blue.
    On her feet were slippers of seafoam.
    Around her hair the bright birds flew.
But now she's a ragged, poor old woman
Drawing life from the life she knew.
    She mothered a million million children,
    Black as midnight, and pale as frost,
    Bright as the gold, and burnished copper,
    And all are scattered, all are lost.
The green is faded, the blue is clouded,
The seas are choked and the birds are dead.
    All alone in a crumbling castle
    The woman weeps in her lonely bed,
And no one cares for the poor old woman
Left to die in her plundered home."

Alladale sustained the final melancholy note for as long as he could, and none of them spoke for a long time after it had died away, until Del at last said, "It's an awful galaxy, isn't it? Everybody killing everybody else, and plundering, and destroying."

215

"It's the only one we've got," Grax said.

"We have others. Millions of others. We just can't get to them yet."

"Then we haven't got them, Del." Turning to the bard, Grax said, "You keep giving us sad songs, Alladale. How about a funny one?"

"Later. I can't play one now."

"Why not? You know some, don't you?" Grax persisted.

"Of course I know some. I know thousands. But I can't go from a song like that to a funny one. No bard would ever do such a thing."

"Why wouldn't he? If you know it, and someone wants to hear it, why not go ahead?"

"It doesn't work that way, Grax. It's not that simple," the bard said. Seeing their genuine perplexity, he explained, "There's a code all skillmen follow, and each kind of skillman follows it in a particular way. There are things a bard will do, and things he won't. We have our rules, our traditions . . . do you see this band?" He extended his right wrist to reveal a gold band inscribed and inlaid with blue stones. "All bards wear it. We memorize the thirty-nine meters, and the seven forms of lamentation and——"

"Why the wristband?" Del broke in.

"Just superstition, really," Alladale said uneasily.

"Tell us about it."

"There's a legendary bard, Vuran of the Golden Wristlet, from a time centuries before the first exodus. He lived in a kingdom known as Europe and consorted with magicians. The story goes that he made a pact with an evil god, traded his soul to become the greatest bard of all, and he was forced to wear a golden band on his wrist as a sign of the agreement. After many years, he fell in love and asked to be released from his bargain. As he said the words, the wristlet contracted and severed his hand." They looked at him, awed. "It's all superstition, of course. I feel silly wearing this thing, but I worked to earn it, so . . ." He shrugged and smiled self-consciously.

"Did the woman marry him?" Del asked.

"It's only a legend, Del. A story, nothing more. I should never have mentioned it. Really being a bard depends on the discipline, not——"

"How could he play, if his hand fell off?" Grax asked.

Alladale paused, sighed deeply, and closed his eyes, summoning all his patience, and said slowly, "He learned to play one-handed, Grax. And he married the woman, Del. They had four lovely children. I'm sorry to say I don't know their names."

"That's all right, Alladale," Grax assured him. "We don't have to know."

For a brief moment, when Del and Grax had shown a glimmer of interest in the ways of the bard, Alladale had felt a new kind of excitement, an urge to pass on his knowledge and skills to some willing pupil. But their interest was superficial, short-lived, and its dissipation left him frustrated. He broached the subject again before they landed, but with no better success. They did not care.

In order to move around safely on Watson, it was necessary for Alladale to adopt still another new identity. He became Scaevius, an aging freedman from Tarquin VII engaged as Del's servant and personal trainer. In less flamboyant clothing, with the beard regrown on Skorat carefully whitened and his linlovar safely cached aboard the *Renegade*, a squint in his eye and a stooping walk, he was quite convincing. He protested the need for disguise, but actually was rather pleased to play a role once more.

Watson was the information center of the galaxy. Life

on the planet was devoted to the acquisition of facts, and the chief commodity bought and sold was information. Massive buildings, each the size of a mountain, clustered around the biggest and highest structure of all, a windowless slab taller than the tallest pyramid on Xhanchos. This was Machine Central. Within its depths, long unseen by any human, stood the great machine that was the soul of Watson. The first settlers had brought it from Old Earth five centuries before; succeeding generations had enlarged and improved it to the point where it no longer needed human care. It handled its own repairs and maintenance, and kept Machine Central in a constant state of renovation and growth to accomodate its needs. In the past century alone, it had increased tenfold in size. The machine knew much of what had happened in the galaxy, and what was currently happening. It could predict, with fair accuracy, what would happen in the future. Humans were required only to feed it data and supply it with questions around which information could be organized. In every other respect, the machine was autonomous.

Since it fed on information and its appetite was insatiable, a visitor could anticipate little freedom from prying. Landing procedure involved six hours of filling out forms and a four-hour interrogation. Every room in the dormitory complex contained a listening device—Alladale, having been warned, put his companions on their guard—and every greeting from a planetary resident was immediately followed by a question. Alladale found it a stifling place, and grew very uncomfortable.

He did a considerable amount of walking on his first Watson morning, simply to keep himself from melancholy, and the sights he encountered provoked him to a different line of speculation. He saw the inhabitants of a hundred worlds on the smooth and spotless avenues of Watson, and for the first time, he was consciously aware of the incongruities that surrounded him, and filled the galaxy. Men traveled faster than light in crafts so perfectly engineered that they could be taken across the galaxy by passengers and a crew who knew nothing of the operative principles; they performed near miracles of surgery, even to the replacement of entire limbs; they constructed buildings of exotic materials, sent them soaring to dizzying heights, and filled them with machinery to perform every necessary function with perfect precision. And yet they carried swords and daggers and pistols at their belts, and used them as eagerly as did their ancestors of the dim and half-forgotten past. On some worlds men lived in stockades of logs and mud, subdued their lives to a primitive and savage code, and dressed in the skins of animals slain by their own hand. The residents of Watson dressed in blue uniforms that provided an individualized safe environment for each one; they saw everywhere men and humanoids wearing furs, cloaks of all lengths and designs, armor, gaudy uniforms, gloomy robes, tunics, togas, skirts, and trousers. They passed next to one another, and no one took a second glance. It was absurd and incomprehensible to Alladale that all these creatures could know of one another's existence and still ignore the anomalies of planetary culture without question as they did. And yet it was so.

With his curiosity aroused, he was unable to resist stopping at a Speedfact shop, one of a number of such establishments which made unclassified general information cheaply available to the non-specialist. His most pressing questions could hardly be resolved here, but he recalled a problem that had been of great importance to him long ago, and decided to make use of Watson's facilities while he had the opportunity. He sought out an Information Adviser, paid his fee, and asked, "What are books, and what became of them?" The Adviser directed him to a cubicle. He donned the earphones, and after a short wait, received an answer in a pleasant, but too impersonal female voice.

"The term *book* refers to an outmoded information retrieval system. Thin sheets of an opaque substance known as *paper* were imprinted with symbols and gathered together by a process called *binding*. The resulting object was called a *book*. Approximate dimensions of a typical book of the early twenty-first century are 22 x 15 x 3 centimeters in height, width, and thickness, respectively," the voice began. "Regarding the second part of your inquiry, specific information is unobtainable at this time. The theory of the Watson historian Harringer states that the decline in literacy of the later twentieth century, the uprising of the Free Scholars, the dissolution of the universities in 2004, and the social and intellectual unrest of the period known as the Bloody Centuries, coupled with the ready availability of visual prisms and sound tapes, rendered literacy difficult, unnecessary, and undesirable to the majority in the half-century preceding the exodus. The making of books on Old Earth seems to have come to an end in the decade following Wroblewski's worldwide dissemination of the drivecoil principle.

"Be advised of this fact," the voice concluded. "Books have been classified as historical artifacts. Any information concerning the existence or whereabouts of any object so classified must be given at once to the Antiquities Control Section of Machine Central. Failure to comply with this law will be severely punished. We thank you for your curiosity, and wish you good functioning."

"And good functioning to you, my dear," Alladale said from between clenched teeth. He was growing to hate this planet.

In the afternoon, he and Grax went to the Informart,

where information from all over the galaxy was evaluated and purchased. It had occurred to Grax that the information sought by his friend might be expensive, and he planned to sell some data to raise funds, in case they became necessary. Alladale agreed to do the same.

They entered the busy building by the main doors and joined the crowds making their way along the walls on which were posted the high-paying specific information requests. Alladale idly wondered at the incredible variety of apparently pointless information for which huge sums were offered and walked on, smiling faintly at it all, when a notice froze him in his tracks. Krankl, the Absolute Monarch of Trulba, offered an astronomical reward for the capture, alive, of the depraved seducer Alladale Anthem-maker, who had ruined the virtue of a Trulban princess, beaten her savagely, and stolen half the crown jewels of Trulba. He was wanted, very badly, on Trulba for punishment. The offer bore a fairly accurate drawing of the offender, and was signed by Krankl with his full battery of titles. Alladale felt his knees turn to water underneath him. He looked about in terror, but no one had yet identified him as the fugitive. Hunching lower, squinting more tightly, he started for the door and nearly fainted as Grax touched his arm.

"Easy, buddy. Let's get out of here, nice and fast," Grax said in a low voice.

"Did you see? On the wall . . . picture?"

"I'm up there, too."

They returned to their dormitory complex to await Del's return, and then retreated to the sanctuary of the driveship to discuss their predicament. Del's news was good. He had agreed to undertake a recovery mission in return for his desired information. A Watson ship would take him to any destination he chose once the mission was completed. The others could depart at once.

"Barbary! We can go to Barbary!" Alladale cried. "I have friends there. They'll take care of us."

"Suits me," Grax said. "I always wanted to see Barbary."

They lifted off before nightfall.

Within hours of landing, Alladale had signed to entertain in a hospitality complex near the spaceport. It was a low dive with a crude, noisy clientele, but it offered "The Masked Wizard of the Linlovar" and his taciturn assistant the safety of obscurity.

Alladale's days were always full, and when Del arrived on Barbary, he had scarcely time to greet him. Grax gladly assumed the roles of host and guide, and Alladale saw nothing of the two spacefarers until several days later, when they turned up just before his final show to say goodbye. They were off to an obscure farming planet with a few friends on some quixotic mission.

"With a ship of your own, and the galaxy to choose from, why go to a place like Mazat?" Alladale asked.

Del shrugged. "We're just stopping over for a few days. It's on the way home."

"They need us to do some work for them. It's only temporary," Grax added.

"Everything's temporary. Take care of yourselves, both of you."

"We will. You come see us when you feel like traveling," Grax said. "Sing us a funny song."

Del added, "After Mazat, we're heading for Gilead. We'll make you welcome, Alladale."

"I'll come out one day, I promise you."

After they had left, Alladale felt more alone and depressed than he had since his departure from Xhanchos. He had grown to like these two proud, cocky young men. They made him think of the son who lay buried on Bellaterra. Often during the long flight from Watson he had told himself, with absurd mixed feelings of hilarity and frustration, that he was getting too old for this sort of thing. All very well for Del and Grax to be starhopping every time the wind shifted, but for a master skillman, a man old enough to be their father—their grandfather, if anyone were simpleton enough to judge by the Galactic Standard Calendar—last time he'd checked it, he was pushing eighty . . . . No, no more of that. Physically not even half his age, he still felt the urge to find a home and stay put. Xhanchos was a long way off, but Loriise was waiting there, and their child. That was his home. He had to get back.

The melancholy mood persisted, and as a consequence, his performance that night was different from anything that habitués of the tawdry cabaret had ever heard. Cheap songs and glib improvisations were forgotten. He reached deep inside himself for long-buried lines to express feelings he could deny no longer. He sang of loss, and pain, and loneliness; of the emptiness and solitude of space, the lingering death of parting from loved ones and good friends, the mockery of time, the littleness of man and his unending search for the clean and quiet land, the good and beautiful place, the world no man had yet seen but all remembered. And he sang, too, of the courage that drove men to hurl themselves against the barriers of time and distance, to brave the pitiless uncaring infinity that enfolds them. After his first song, the crowd was still, and for the final half of his show they scarcely breathed. He left the stage in silence, and was in his room backstage when the ovation exploded with a roar that penetrated his closed door.

His shows were different after that night. The crowds grew in number and began to treat him with something approaching reverence. Nothing like his songs had ever been heard on Barbary. Visitors to the pleasure planet were not the sort to be easily moved, but Alladale moved them.

His situation improved, but the thought of Loriise gave him no respite. Praise and good payment could not take her place. He had to get home to Xhanchos. He let it be known that he was in the market for a small, fast driveship and would pay well for what he wanted. It took some time, but at last he found the ship.

That very night, after his show, he called on the three brothers who owned the complex. They were jovial until he told them of his plans to leave Barbary forthwith, at which point their gaiety gave way to loud wailing, pleading, and prophecies of ruination, poverty, and shame for themselves and all those close to them. Alladale let them rave on, then produced the green diamond he had taken from Fruda. They fell silent at once and stared open-mouthed at the stone.

"Before you all commit suicide, I'd like you to do me a favor. Put a fair price on this stone," he said.

"Are you selling it?" the first brother asked.

"Nobody on Barbary could afford it," said the second.

"He's not asking for a financial report, he's asking for our opinion. Let's give it," the third suggested.

They conferred in whispers and nods, passing the stone around like a sacred object, and at last agreed on a figure that was, coincidentally, exactly four times the amount for the driveship, and about one-tenth of the stone's true value.

"Very good. Would you consider that a fair price?" Alladale asked.

"It's fair, but who could pay it?"

"Maybe half that much."

"If we liquidated everything."

"All right, then. Give me one-quarter of your price

right now, tonight, and the stone is yours." They looked at him, then at one another, then back to him. "I couldn't make that much for you if I played to packed houses for the rest of my life." Suspicion and greed battled openly in their expressions. "Maybe I ought to explain how I got the stone," he said.

"It would help," they said in unison.

"I won it from a skillman named Will Gallamor. He had a bag of them, enough to buy Barbary and a small system to keep it company. He didn't say where he got them, and I didn't ask. About three or four nights after our game the constabulary found Gallamor's body, but they never found the rest of the stones. As soon as I learned about it, I left." He gazed into three pairs of rounded eyes and said, "I give you my word I had nothing to do with——"

"We never imagined!"

"Not in a million years!"

"A man with your talent? It's too ridiculous to mention!"

"——I only ran because I heard that Gallamor was mixed up with the Sternverein and I didn't want to have anything to do with them."

"I've seen blackjackets in action. I'd run, too, believe me," the third brother said. "Are they still after you?"

"They never were. They wanted Gallamor. I was just being cautious," Alladale said.

"Very wise. In that case, we'll take the stone. Just one condition: nobody is to know we have it." The third man looked to his partners for verification, and they nodded.

"You have my word as a skillman."

The deal was closed then and there. After one last drink with the brothers, now jovial once more, Alladale left for the spaceport.

Before he settled on Xhanchos forever, Alladale had two obligations to fulfil. One was to himself, the other to a long dead comrade.

On Mazat, he learned that Grax lay in an honored tomb, one of five Otherworlders who had fallen in the battle to rid Mazat from marauding space pirates. Del Whitby had survived, and was now King Del I of Mazat. The young king gave the bard a warm welcome and invited him to stay on Mazat for as long as he chose.

It was a tempting offer. The Mazatlans reminded Alladale of the Bellaterrans; it was easy to understand why Del had chosen to stay among them. Not too many years ago, Alladale had made a similar choice. He sincerely hoped that things would work out better for Del.

Concern for his friend, and for the future of the gentle race who had made him their king, caused Alladale much worry during his otherwise pleasant stay on Mazat. Once the people had heard him perform, they were not long in requesting, then urging, and finally all but demanding that he set his talents to commemorating the liberation of their world from the space pirates. He temporized: he had only come to Mazat for a brief visit and could not spare the time to compose a proper epic; besides, this was not his field; in recent times, he had made only short pieces, and was out of practice for a sustained effort. They persisted: he was obviously the greatest bard and anthem-maker in the galaxy, and could do anything he set his mind to; if he left it undone, a lesser bard would do it, to his shame; he owed such a tribute to his old friends, the one who lived and the one who had died. Under pressure from all sides, Alladale capitulated. Turning to his log books, he reread the long work he had composed on the *Huntsman* in memory of the fallen troopers of the Sternverein.

226

"Seventy men on a misty planet
Met in battle beneath the rain . . . ."

Thus began "The Song of the Seventy." With a few modifications, it provided a framework for "The Song of the Seven." The tight Skeggjatt alliterative convention might be ignored, simplifying things and enabling him to complete his work and be off in the shortest time possible. He worked steadily for nearly half a short planetary year.

"The Song of the Seven" was understandably popular among the Mazatlans. It was quite long, and recounted in gory detail the depredations of the space pirates and the great battle in the marketplace. The scene of lamentation over the abducted women and the desperate search of Steban were intensely moving, and the portraits of the seven defenders were among the best things of their kind Alladale had ever done. Even the descriptions of the villainous pirate leaders were masterly. What he had undertaken with reluctance he performed with pride.

Stretch, the Lixian who had survived the battle and become First Defender of Mazat, was ecstatic at the prospect of "The Song of the Seven" being heard all across the galaxy. Despite a long exile, he retained the Lixian's inbred fixation on points of honor, and the possible unpleasant consequences of such notoriety bothered him not at all. Here on Mazat, far from his home, he still lived by the stern and simple Lixian code of his early days: seek honor; serve the king; die well.

Del viewed things differently. He had aged much in the few brief years since his departure from Barbary. He had begun the serious study of Old Earth history. Now, in his third year as King of Mazat, he possessed a magnificent library of more than twenty volumes—more books than Alladale had imagined to exist in any one place—and his collection was still growing. But with increased knowledge came disillusionment. The buoyant confidence so apparent at their last meeting had given way to bitterness. In his last talk with Alladale before the bard left for the long voyage to Xhanchos, Del confessed that he had had his fill of the things that Stretch cherished as sources of honor.

"History is just one round of murders after another, Alladale. Our times are no better nor worse than any other. I've shed so much blood I can never wash my hands clean. Where's the glory in that?" he asked.

"Seven of you stood against sixty pirates. Not one of you was a Mazatlan, or had any personal stake in Mazat. I call that honorable, Del," Alladale said.

"Call it business. We were paid."

"Stretch told me how much you were paid. You didn't do it for the money."

"The amount makes no difference. We were hired to kill those pirates, and we did. That's not heroics, or honor."

"Suppose you hadn't come here, Del. What would have become of these people?"

"I've thought of that, too. It's some consolation, but . . ." Del's voice trailed off. He gestured in desperation and turned to Alladale, anguished, to ask, "Is killing the only way? Is it impossible for a people to live in this galaxy without leaving a trail of blood across the centuries behind them?"

Alladale thought of the settlement on Bellaterra, the peaceful race who had been massacred by men who laughed as they slaughtered women and children. He remembered the streets of Xhancholii after the battle. He shook his head slowly and said, "I don't know, Del. I hope it isn't. All we can do is try."

"I mean to try," the young king said. "The Mazatlans were at peace for generations—scores of generations

—before the pirates came. They literally forgot how to be violent. They had to, in order to survive. And then, because they'd forgotten violence, violent men threatened to destroy them."

"You saved them."

Del shook his head curtly. "When the battle came, and it looked as though the pirates had won, they rose up and saved us. But they want to return to peaceful ways, and I want to lead them. I want to try to make this a better galaxy for everybody in it, Alladale. I really do."

"I believe you, Del."

"Then help me. You've made an account of our battle that's mighty stirring. Too stirring for my taste—I wish you'd shown the horror, and not sung of glory and honor. But you did your work well, and the people like it. Now I'm asking you to let it be a song for Mazat alone. If you spread it through the stars, every pirate in business will head here to see if we're as good as you make us." He paused, then said, "If you like these people as much as you say you do, Alladale, give them the chance to live in peace."

"On my word as a skillman, Del, nobody will ever hear 'The Song of the Seven' from me once I leave Mazat. I don't like violence any more than you do."

"Then why praise it?"

"I'm praising the courage."

The King of Mazat looked at him curiously and smiled. "I'm sorry to ruin your illusions, Alladale, but courage had nothing to do with it. It was habit. Sheer habit."

Alladale left for Xhanchos with all debts paid. Stretch, the Lixian, had confided to him his intention to return to Lixis now that honor was restored, and had agreed to convey Eis' possessions. Free and unencumbered, his last obligation met, Alladale lifted off for home.

VII.

Lawgiver and Sage

THE EMPTINESS BETWEEN THE STARS seemed to grow greater each time out. Still, Alladale thought, given the chance to traverse the galaxy and walk on other worlds, what man could let it pass? And he found himself thinking, yes, true enough—but what man would do it all his days when he could return to a woman like Loriise? Then, as he had feared, he was plunged into deep melancholy.

Despite the elaborate framework of routine he had devised as a bulwark against idleness on his way to Xhanchos, there was always time to worry. A bitter twilight war might be dragging on in Xhancholii between the last survivors of the rival parties. Perhaps one of the factions had acted early and decisively, and now ruled the walled city. If so, had Loriise returned? Had she forgotten him, or did she still love him? Had she, perhaps, been slain by victors who judged her contaminated by contact with Alladale? And what of their child? What of *him*, if he should enter Xhancholii—would he be walking to his execution?

He found no answers, merely questions that branched into ever more complicated thickets of possibility, *if* upon *if* upon *if* as tightly intertwined as the legendary corridors of Clotho. He dwelt on them until he felt his head throb, and sought relief in ever-longer periods of complicated playing on the linlovar. But even when his arms ached and his fingertips were raw and tender, his imagination could not be stilled. When at last he settled into the ring within sight of the walls of Xhancholii, he was ready to accept any resolution of his speculations, so long as it put an end to his uncertainty. One thing he had decided: he was here to stay. He had run far enough. Xhanchos was his chosen home, and he was not running any more.

At the rising of the first moon, he slung his linlovar over his shoulder and set out across the sand for the Gate of the Ring. The night was cool and quiet, and as he neared the city he could hear faint sounds of life and activity; not war-shouts or the lamentations of defeat, but the ordinary noises of a city at peace. He hurried closer, and when a voice hailed him from the guardroom atop the gate he replied, "It's I, Alladale. I've returned!" The voice came again, with a sharper tone. He answered as before, but this time he spoke in halting Xhanchilion.

The gate opened to admit him. Three gray-clad riders greeted him, the same desert tribesmen who had sold him to the Xhanchilion when he first came to the planet. One of them smiled amicably and gestured to a *haxqpod* that stood saddled near him. Alladale mounted and rode with them to the palace. He was puzzled by the men and their greeting, but he was not worried. The condition of the city, too, puzzled him. It looked shabby, run down, as if no one were caring for it any more.

He was taken directly to the throne room. The halls and corridors down which they passed had the same dusty, neglected look, and here and there, in the poor light, he saw signs of a furious battle not too long ago.

In the throne room he learned who had won. On the throne where he had last seen Gariv sat one of the gray riders. Over his riding robe he wore a wide baldric of gaudy material, and on his head was the crown of Xhancholii. Other tribesmen stood in various parts of the big room. Alladale counted twenty. They were formidable in appearance, their skin a dull greenish brown, their eyes sheltered deep under the thick brows, their large bladelike noses downcurved, nostrils flared ferociously even in repose, mouths downdrawn and tight. They were men of the desert, not the court. Their thin hands and long bony fingers moved in swift accompaniment to their high speech. They looked fierce and predatory, and their abrupt silence and the gaze they turned upon Alladale made them seem all the more threatening. He checked his natural impulse to speak, and waited for the man on the throne to address him. An uncomfortable interval passed, and then the gray rider pointed to him and said, "You were the anthemmaker for the rebel slaves."

"I was," Alladale replied.

"Yes. And now you wonder what has become of your friends, when you see us in possession of Xhancholii, do you not?"

"No. I've come to rejoin my wife and child."

"Oh, yes, the woman. You shall rejoin her, believe that," the gray rider said. He made a remark too quickly for Alladale to understand, and the others in the room laughed in a rather unpleasant manner, then he turned his attention once again to the bard. "Your friends have destroyed one another, did you know that? First they slew the Xhanchilion, then they slew each other, and now the city is ours."

"May you long enjoy it in peace," Alladale said. "Where is Loriise? Is she well?"

The gray rider gestured to a portal across the throne room. One of the tribesmen entered, leading a woman and a child. The woman's wrists were chained, and the end of the chain was in the tribesman's hand. The child walked beside her, clutching at her robe, looking about fearfully as if expecting a blow at any moment.

232

"Here is your woman," the gray rider said contemptuously. "She came to us to bear your child. She brought us news of the fall of the Xhanchilion, and the dissension among the victors. When the last of the rebel slaves lay dying, we claimed the city."

Alladale looked closely, and saw that the woman was indeed Loriise. She was thinner, haggard, her robes ragged and dirty, and she walked with a slow step. But when she saw him, her recognition was instantaneous. She called out his name, and the tribesmen laughed aloud. At a signal from the leader, she and the child were released, and they rushed to Alladale's side.

Mistreatment had not broken her. She looked even lovelier than he had recalled, and their daughter was her mother's image. They were ragged and dirty and gaunt from hunger and hardship, but their beauty was beyond the power of the gray riders to destroy. They clung together, wordless, for a time, then Alladale said, "Forgive me for staying away so long, Loriise. Has it been bad? Are you both all right?"

"I knew you'd come, but I prayed something would prevent you. Alladale, now they'll kill us all."

"No, they won't," he said. He kissed Loriise gently, lifted the child in his arms and spoke words of reassurance to her, and then stepped before them to face the gray riders. He breathed deeply to calm himself and steady his voice. No more running, he told himself. Whatever happens, no more running. Settle this here and now. He moved a bit to one side, to a spot he knew from Gariv's days, and flexed his fingers. The gray riders looked on with amusement. They were enjoying themselves, and were in no hurry to bring matters to an end.

"Why do you treat them like this?" Alladale asked.

"Because the woman is a halfbreed and the child is a mongrel," the gray rider said. "This is our world now, and other breeds will be allowed to exist only to serve us. The Gafaal trash, the brats bred by your comrades on the Xhanchilion females, all these are now our slaves."

"And have you waited for my return just to boast of this?" Alladale asked coolly. He had shifted the linlovar around to playing position while the gray rider spoke, and now he placed one hand lightly on the strings.

"Yes, we have waited for your return. Only you could bring back Otherworlders to steal our city, and you came alone. Now the secret of our triumph is safe from all Otherworlders. The city is ours. All of Xhanchos is ours!" He leaned forward, and again pointed his finger at the bard. "And all that remains is to dispose of you."

Alladale said nothing, did not even look at the gray rider; he began to play. His fingers moved swiftly over the strings. The melody he made could not be heard, but the gray riders assembled in the throne room felt a sudden prickling of the flesh, like a cool breeze that penetrated their robes and chilled them to the bone. They squirmed uneasily, and looked at one another with apprehensive glances. One licked his lips and swallowed loudly. Another shrank back into a corner. Others could be heard breathing fast in their fright. Alladale played on, no louder, and began to speak in a soft voice. From his position in the acoustical center, he could be heard clearly in all parts of the throne room.

"I have listened to the ranting of the gray riders. Now hear the judgment of Alladale Anthem-maker, and be ever grateful for his forebearance," he said. "I have walked on a hundred worlds, and the vilest vermin on the meanest of those worlds was braver and nobler than the bravest and noblest of the gray riders, pale worms of the desert, tormentors of women and children."

One of the gray riders groped for his sword. Alladale turned toward him, and he moaned and crumpled to his knees, where he huddled, shivering and whimpering in abject terror. The others stared at him, eyes wide. The bard continued.

"You were willing servants of the Xhanchilion. You bowed, and smiled, and obeyed. You sold them free men, and if any man escaped their camp and survived the desert, you ran him down and returned him to a horrible death. You were too cowardly to fight for your masters or against them. You waited until all the warriors were dead, and then you crawled out of the desert on your vile bellies and plucked this city from the dead hands of its liberators. Admit this!" Alladale roared, striking three powerful chords that reverberated through the room and brought the tribesmen to their feet, crying, "Yes! Yes, we did this! We did all these things!"

Alladale lowered his voice once more. "You took a woman who came to you in trust, and you made her a slave. She gave you a city, and you rewarded her with chains. You took her innocent child and inflicted suffering and hardship upon her. If I chose to be just, I would exterminate you and all your race. I would grind you under my heel like insects." He played a bit louder, and the tribesmen writhed on the floor and cried aloud in a frenzy of terror. "You are unfit to exist in this galaxy. Admit this!"

"We are unfit, unworthy!" they cried. "We deserve to be destroyed! Spare us, spare us!"

Alladale shifted his fingers slightly and commenced to play a different melody. The gray riders stirred from their huddled positions. They looked up and saw a paternal smile on his face. "Like a true bard, Alladale is forgiving. He has returned to take his place as an honored guest in the city he helped to liberate. Free my wife and child. We will discuss your punishment at another time."

Six tribesmen scrambled to release the chains from Loriise's wrists and remove them from Alladale's sight.

235

New robes were brought and draped with great solicitude around her shoulders and the child's. Alladale looked on with satisfaction, but was not yet ready to dismiss the gray riders. There was severity in his voice when he spoke again.

"Hear my laws. There will be no more slavery on Xhanchos, no more talk of halfbreeds and mongrels. This will be a city of free and equal citizens———." He paused and fumbled for the word he had heard in this very palace, and went on, "———a commonwealth based on justice and equality." He knew very little about governments, but this sounded like a good kind to try. The gray riders nodded in agreement, eager to accept anything he demanded. "Remember this night," he continued. "Remember the fear that left you helpless. If any man breaks my laws, or raises his hand against me or those close to me, you will all feel that fear every moment of your life until you die."

Once subdued, and reminded of the nameless force that had overcome them, the gray riders were abject. They bowed low before Alladale and set up a pitiable outcry. "Stay among us forever, anthem-maker!" they cried. "Lead us. Let us be as your children. Accept our worship, and keep us from fear!"

"Oh, stop blubbering," he said irritably. "I've come to be your guest—your honored guest—and not your ruler. Certainly not your god. Don't be absurd. It's hard enough just being a man."

"But who will rule us?" they wailed.

"Rule yourselves," he replied. They gave him an imploring glance and wailed even louder. He raised his hands for silence. "All right, all right. Do the best you can, and when things get too difficult, I'll help you. But don't bother me with a lot of trivial problems. I have other things to do." That calmed them.

He turned to Loriise and pulled her close. "Let's go

236

to our old place, in the guard room. It will be like going home," he said. She nodded agreement, and he dispatched a cluster of gray riders to prepare their quarters at once.

The three of them left together. Alladale was surprised to find, when they reached the street, that his jacket was soaked with perspiration and his heart was pounding loudly. But he had won, defeated an army, and shed not one drop of blood. He had changed a world without losing a single life. It could be done. His only regret was that he could not tell Del of this.

As word of the events in the throne room spread, the gray riders regarded Alladale with awe. Their former slaves looked to him for protection and gave him their unqualified loyalty and gratitude. Consequently, anyone seeking advice or an impartial decision came to the guardroom and waited patiently for a few words with the anthem-maker.

In the beginning it was rather pleasant, certainly good for the ego. Alladale's opinion was sought on all matters, great and small, and when Alladale spoke, the question was settled forever. How shall a thief be punished, Anthem-maker? What shall I name my first son, mighty liberator? Which of these three suitors should my oldest daughter marry? Who will patrol the walls, maintain the ring, tend the water gates, repair the palace, train my *haxopods*, buy my wares, father of freedom? they asked him. He answered, and they always left seeming satisfied, but he soon came to feel uneasy with such power. He saw himself as a man striding along just a few paces ahead of a whirlwind; one misstep and everything would be swept up and blown away.

What the commonwealth needed was a sound framework to build on. Not a man, but laws. The laws of the Xhanchilion were brutal; the precepts of the desert people were inscrutable; neither could be adopted to this situation. Alladale searched his memory, and found the solution. From a legend of the founding of Sangglar he took "The Oath of the Equals." With a few minor deletions and the insertion of certain provisions from the *Phoenix IV* Compact, it served as a charter for the new commonwealth. For laws, he took the thirty-one admonitions of Abtai from an ancient Toxxan creation myth. In the original, they sprawled over four thousand lines; he condensed them to thirty-one short, easily memorized precepts. The code of Abtai had guided a race well for nearly six thousand years; it was worth trying.

With a statement of objectives and a code of laws, the new commonwealth needed officials. Alladale gave much thought to the method of their selection, and to the extent and tenure of their powers. Experience had convinced him that no man should have very much power over another. It destroyed them both. There would be no titles, no honors. That was how it always began. Xhanchos was not going to become another Trulba, not if Alladale could prevent it. Titles, rituals, pomp and ceremony—it was all flimsy scaffolding over the abyss of man's own littleness, and it always turned bad.

After much deliberation, Alladale hit upon a scheme that had supposedly been tried once on Old Earth. An assembly would be chosen by the people and would be accountable to them. The assembly, in turn, would appoint the necessary officials. Those who did their work well could expect to be reelected or reappointed, and those who failed would be replaced. It seemed an ingenious, yet simple solution to the problem of governing free people without sacrificing either government or freedom. He hoped he would one day be able to learn how this method had worked on the mother world.

When his design had been delivered to the people and enthusiastically received, Alladale and his family prepared to move off to the home they had been building on a terrace of the nearest pyramid, a spot with many fond memories for Loriise and Alladale. The people made one final request of him: they wanted a calendar of their own, one that all could agree on. This he refused to consider.

"Time is an absurdity," he told the little delegation. "You waste it in counting it. That's foolish."

"But it's necessary. One must know," their leader protested.

"One can't know. Even when one knows, one doesn't *really* know. Take my word for it," Alladale told them. "I could give you some horrible examples, but I can't remember the exact figures."

"But it is essential to know the time!"

"Speak for yourself," said the bard. "I don't want to document my remaining years, I want to enjoy them."

Enjoy them he did. He and Loriise settled into their home on the pyramid and left the commonwealth to itself. Their daughter, Alorii, grew more beautiful each day. She never showed the interest in the linlovar that Alladale had hoped to see, but their last child, a son named Lon, made up for that. He also looked much like his father, which pleased Alladale more than he admitted. It was good to find that the blood of the Gallamors was not so easily diluted.

One of Alladale's grand projects had been the investigation of the pyramids of Xhanchos, but he abandoned the idea after long deliberation. Much might be learned from those ancient structures, but what if he uncovered the secrets of weaponry more powerful than that of Old Earth? No good could offset that evil. The pyramids had waited long; they could wait longer, he decided. He had other explorations to make.

He had been surprised to discover all the useful knowledge he had accumulated during his wanderings, in the form of song, myth, and legend, and he decided to try to organize his materials into some form that others could employ to their benefit. His three logbooks, now swollen to bursting with interleaves and insertions, contained no blank spaces bigger than a fingernail. They were a starting point. With encouragement and help from Loriise, he was soon deeply involved.

It was slow work, for not a single song was without a full freight of associations. Some were most unpleasant, to be sure; but he found that the unpleasantness faded quickly, and what remained was the joy that not even the greatest wordsmith had ever fully captured. Fine friends and good people, brave men and fair women, love and laughter and the quiet communion of living things in sympathy, beautiful beckoning worlds of every description . . . the galaxy abounded in such things, and a good skillman could make them live forever in his words. With the passage of time, Alladale came to appreciate his profession more and more. He was proud to see his youngest son developing into a master player on the linlovar and other instruments. The boy had a good clear voice, too, and rapidly amassed a sizeable repertoire of stories.

Life was quiet and happy, and the time went quickly by. Alladale and Loriise soon found that their children were children no longer. Alorii, grown to womanhood, chose as her husband a prosperous young weaver and cloth-merchant from the city. The festivities were prolonged and elaborate, and Alladale worked hard to produce one of his greatest songs for the wedding-song of the bride.

Some nights after the wedding ceremony, Alladale and his son were seated on an upper terrace of the pyramid, a place where the bard often came to work. Alladale was instructing the boy in voice control. Lon could deliver a story in three voices rather well, but when he tried for four, everyone began to sound alike.

They worked hard. A skillman had to be absolute master of his voice, and Lon knew it. He was already calling himself Lon Gallamor—to his father's great and unconcealed satisfaction—and father and son were both determined that the name should be honored by the skills of him who bore it.

After a long work session they paused for a rest. Without preamble, Lon said, "I went aboard the driveship last night."

"You did? I haven't set foot on that since you were a little boy. How does she look?" Alladale asked.

"Perfect. The drive unit checks out, the instruments all function, and the stores are intact," the youth said quickly. "She's ready to go."

"Sounds as though you looked her over pretty closely."

"Well, it seemed to me . . . it's been standing out there all this time . . . someone ought to check it over now and then," Lon said awkwardly.

"Those things were made to last. That ship could stand out there until Alorii's children have children of their own, and still be ready to take off on short notice."

Lon looked at his father, frank and unflinching. "I don't want to wait that long."

Alladale sighed and nodded. He tried to smile. "I thought you had something like that on your mind, Lon. It's no surprise, but isn't this kind of soon after Alorii's wedding? It will be hard on your mother, losing her daughter and then her youngest son in such quick succession."

Lon dismissed that objection with a firm gesture. "Val doesn't spend all his time with the gray riders. He visits a lot. And you certainly haven't lost Alorii. Jedal is a

241

pleasant sort, but unimaginative. He's got his little shop, and his little home by the Sunrise Gate, and that's all he and Alorii want. You wouldn't get them to leave Xhancholii if you burned it down."

"Funny to hear you say that," Alladale said thoughtfully. "I've tried to picture Jedal at the helm of a driveship——"

"I bet you couldn't."

"No. I kept seeing him in his shop, displaying robes to gray riders." The father and son exchanged furtive grins at the image, and Alladale quickly added, "Mind you, Lon, I'm not making fun of Jedal. He's a good steady young man."

"But no skillman."

"Never," Alladale said firmly. "No starfarer, either."

"But I could be both. Let me go, Alladale. I'm ready."

"You're very young, Lon."

"I'm about to enter my fifth *hranxlux*. You were only about half my age when you joined Prospero. And I know more songs and stories now than you did at my age," the youth countered. "I've had a good teacher."

"A great teacher," Alladale corrected him. "That's all true, Lon, but the ship isn't mine to give. By rights, part of it goes to Alorii and Jedal, and part to Val."

The young skillman shook his head. "No problem there. I bought them out."

"Where did you get the money?"

"I've been gambling with some of the young merchants. They aren't very good."

Alladale, torn between pride and frustration, said only, "They never are, son."

"So if that's your only objection, I'll talk to Loriise. I'm sure she won't hold me here."

The youth rose and walked to the edge of the terrace, where he stood for a time looking up hungrily at the waiting stars. He turned abruptly to his father and asked, "Why didn't you ever go out again?"

"Your mother can't leave the planet, and I don't want to leave your mother," Alladale said. He thought for a time, then added, "I never wanted to. That's the truth, Lon. I guess I had my fill."

Lon shook his head slowly, appearing genuinely perplexed by the confession. "I can't understand that, Alladale. You've walked on a hundred worlds, met a thousand races, learned ten thousand songs and made as many more of your own . . . you could go anywhere in the galaxy and be received as an honored skill-man——"

"*Almost* anywhere," Alladale corrected him gently.

"All right, then, almost anywhere. You're a bard, an anthem-maker, a weaver of legends and myths . . . and yet you sit here on Xhanchos. Was it all for this?"

"I guess it was," Alladale said.

Lon was silent. Alladale looked at the pyramids diminishing in a row to the horizon, and at the walls of Xhancholii, bathed in the shifting light of four moons. He sniffed the faint scent of the city's gardens and tasted, in his memory, their succulent fruit. Life here was good, in ways that Lon would be long in understanding. Some things took a lifetime to value properly.

Alladale rose, wincing at the slight stiffness that was so much more noticeable these nights. He found himself thinking of the cramped quarters in that pitchblack chamber at the heart of a world, where he played a song to placate the Gods of Silence and Darkness . . . long ago . . . did that happen to him, or was it something he'd heard, or made up? Hard to remember, now. Time was catching up, getting even for all those years he'd stolen. Hearing was a little tricky, too, lately. Well, no matter. This old man, on the windy top of a truncated pyramid on an ancient world, still had a lot to say. He was in the good place at last, and had had his share of fun getting here. He had Loriise. He had his skills, and his work, and his memories. He had made good songs and trained a son to bring them to the galaxy. A man could do worse with his life. Most men did.

He flexed his fingers and struck a harsh, arresting chord on the linlovar. "All right, flap-fingers, let's stop the loafing," he barked at Lon. "If you're going to wear the wristlet, you've got a lot to learn. Let's get to work."